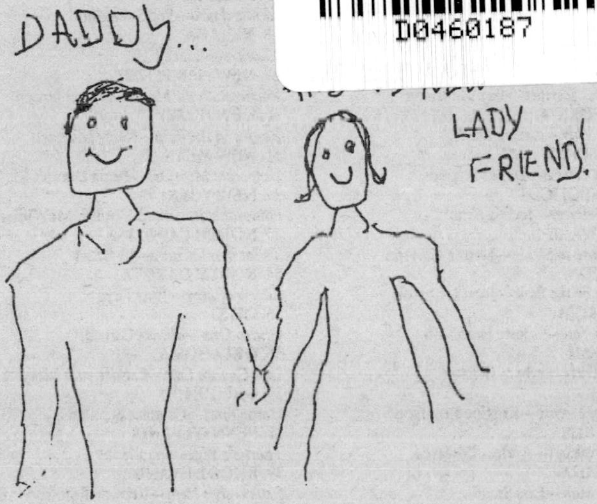
DADDY...
LADY
FRIEND!

Please address questions and book requests to: Harlequin Reader Service
U.S.: 3010 Walden Ave., P.O. Box 1325, Buffalo, NY 14269
CAN.: P.O. Box 609, Fort Erie, Ont. L2A 5X3

ALABAMA

PEG SUTHERLAND

Late Bloomer

Harlequin Books

TORONTO • NEW YORK • LONDON
AMSTERDAM • PARIS • SYDNEY • HAMBURG
STOCKHOLM • ATHENS • TOKYO • MILAN
MADRID • WARSAW • BUDAPEST • AUCKLAND

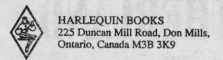

HARLEQUIN BOOKS
225 Duncan Mill Road, Don Mills,
Ontario, Canada M3B 3K9

ISBN 0-373-47151-3

LATE BLOOMER

Dear Reader,

Late Bloomer has always held a special place in my heart because it takes me back to my childhood. Although I grew up in the city, summers always found me at my grandparents' farm near the small town where I was born. One of my favorite places was my aunt Arlene's beauty shop, a shop not too different from the one owned by my heroine, Rose Finley, in *Late Bloomer*.

I hope you'll be reminded of what is so special about small towns all over the U.S. I enjoyed it so much I went home again in my recent Harlequin Superromance trilogy, THREE WEDDINGS AND A SECRET. In *Double Wedding Ring, Addy's Angels* and *Queen of the Dixie Drive-In*, I caught up on what's happened to Rose since the last page of *Late Bloomer*, and also worked on happy endings for four other couples in Sweetbranch. I hope you enjoy the visit.

Peg Sutherland

CHAPTER ONE

THE KILLING INSTINCT raged again in Ben McKenzie. His fingers itched with the compulsion. His heart thumped with it. It burned in his belly like a poison.

Through darkness punctuated only by an occasional glimpse of moonlit sky peeking between newly blooming trees, Ben sped along the Alabama highway. The cool night air didn't touch him, locked inside the smelly dankness of the unfamiliar station wagon. Locked inside his own torment.

He tried to banish the rage that craved its satisfaction in cold-blooded murder, as he had tried to do for the last eight hours. As he had struggled to do in the jungles of Southeast Asia. But each time he glanced over his shoulder at the small form slumped over her seat belt, clutching a worn red teddy bear in her sleep, murder flowed in Ben's blood again.

"Krissy." The whisper of her name soothed him at the same time that it fueled his urgency.

He applied more pressure to the gas pedal. He had to get away before they realized she wasn't coming home and started looking for him. He had to get far enough away that they couldn't find him.

She stirred. He glanced back again. She had shifted in her sleep to rest her head on the stuffed bear. Threads of dark silky hair webbed across her plump pink cheek. Ben plunged into memories of that face just three years and seven months earlier, the morning Kristen Maria McKenzie had been born. Red and puffy and twisted in infant fury, her face had been framed by tufts of downy dark hair.

Even then her face had been beautiful enough to melt the rock that had weighed on Ben's heart since Vietnam.

Now that face was soft and serene in sleep. But every time he looked at it, Ben wanted to kill. Because every time he looked at it, all he could see was the yellowing bruise under the shadow of her long dark eyelashes.

He'd seen the bruises before, since Cybil had remarried. On Krissy's arms. On her legs. And once, a small, perfectly round burn blistered the palm of her chubby little hand. But when he'd asked, she'd looked down through those long dark lashes and shrugged her small shoulders. "I falled down, Daddy."

Nothing he had said could convince her to tell him more.

Her mother had been equally evasive. Cybil's eyes had skittered away when he'd dropped Krissy off after his weekend visitation. Her hands had trembled so slightly it might have been his imagination.

"She's clumsy, Ben." The look of fear on Cybil's perfect, cool features had been so unfamiliar that Ben hadn't recognized it at first. "All children her age get bumps and bruises. Don't make a federal case out of it."

A federal case it would never be. Not even the local courts, it seemed, were interested in a little girl with unexplained bruises and a foul-tempered stepfather. Even a sprained wrist hadn't impressed the courts.

"The courts aren't going to meddle in a custody settlement," Janis Weiss had told him in the clipped, no-nonsense tone she had perfected in the courtroom. "Not based on your inconclusive suspicions."

She had been right. None of the briefs he had prevailed upon her to file had made any difference. And the investigator from Child Protective Services, after spending forty-five minutes searching her cluttered office for the file, had announced in her carefully inoffensive bureaucratese that she had "unsubstantiated" his fears. The system hadn't shown the slightest interest in helping Ben protect his three-year-old daughter.

So he had run. Because he knew he might no longer be able to keep his hands off the man who had done this to Krissy. And because, after months of fighting to stir up a little outrage in an unresponsive system, Ben McKenzie could think of no other way to keep his daughter safe.

And keep her safe he would. If it meant they had to be fugitives, he would guard her. Hadn't she rescued him when he'd thought he was long past deliverance?

Ben's face contorted in a long, deep yawn. He'd been driving all night, ever since he'd picked up Krissy after work on Friday for their weekend together. And the ten-year-old wagon, found through the classified ads and paid for with cash, wasn't as comfortable as his BMW, which he'd left in the parking space outside his condominium. He wished he'd had time to think his plans through before he left, but at least he was doing *something*. His neck and shoulders ached with tension and fatigue. His eyes burned and blurred. He'd wanted to make it all the way without stopping to rest, but he wasn't sure now that he would be able to.

As he passed a highway mileage sign, Ben checked the map on the seat beside him. Ten miles to the next town, which still appeared to be hours away from his destination. It had taken a lot of digging to find the place, the first stop in an underground network for parents who sought to protect their children when the courts couldn't. Or wouldn't. When he got there, he would feel calmer. Then he could breathe again, get his bearings before deciding whether or not to take that final, irrevocable step. Meanwhile, he had his savings, and Krissy would be safe.

How much safer could you get than a place named Sweetbranch, Alabama?

ROSE FINLEY GROANED as soon as she heard the grandfather clock in the foyer strike 5:30 a.m.

"Another exciting morning in Sweetbranch," she said, her voice hoarse with sleep, to the calico cat nestled on her ankles. She nudged Boo awake, tossed off the sheet and dragged herself out of bed before she could think of a good reason not to. *Just like every other morning for the past forty years.*

At least she didn't have to think. Automatic pilot would take care of everything. A quick tub bath—she'd always sworn she would put a shower in the old farmhouse, but she supposed it was too late now—then on to the kitchen for a cup of black coffee. Quietly, of course, so she wouldn't wake Uncle Bump. Uncle Bump thought five-thirty was an ungodly hour to rise in the morning. She supposed he was right about that. Uncle Bump was always right. Just ask him.

On the outside, everything was the same at 103 Dixie Belle Lane. Inside, something felt different.

Boo, perched on the clothes hamper with dainty paw poised in front of her tongue for her morning grooming, accused Rose with a throaty meow.

"I know. Listening to everybody in this town predict how rough it's going to be when I hit forty in a week is making me grumpy. That's all." Squinting through the steam in the bathroom at her reflection in the mirror, Rose dragged a comb through her thick tangle of wavy chestnut hair. She leaned closer to the mirror. "Happens when you get older. Ask Uncle Bump."

A single strand of silver threading lightly through her damp hair seemed to stand up and salute her. "Can't even hide it, Boo. Oh no, this sucker's right there slap in the middle of my widow's peak. What do you think about that?"

Boo merely rumbled musically in her sleek, white-spotted throat.

"Easy for you to say." Rose smiled and ruffled the fur on the cat's head. "If I had orange-and-black hair, I wouldn't complain, either. What have you got to worry about?"

Rose haphazardly brushed her hair back from her delicate, heart-shaped face.

"Face it, Finley," she muttered, slipping cloisonné combs into place to sweep her shoulder-length hair back from her high cheekbones and deep-set eyes. She studied her features—good ones, she supposed, but still... "Everybody in this town's got you pegged for somebody's old-maid aunt."

She grinned wryly. Let 'em think it if it made them feel better. Actually, something contrary in her liked Rose Finley better the older she grew. Liked the self-assurance in her dark, searching eyes. Liked the few extra pounds that softened the face and body that had always been a bit too angular, too sharply thin. And, most of all, liked the greater confidence that came from figuring out the answers to at least a few of life's questions.

Despite a little good-natured complaining, Rose was concluding that forty might not be such a bad place to be after all.

"It's too early for waxing philosophical," she told herself as she dabbed on a quick swipe of makeup. After all, people still said she looked young for her years—and that new choir director at the church *had* asked her out just last week and everybody said he was only thirty-one himself.

Tugging the chain to turn off the light over the mirror, Rose turned away from her reflection. She pulled on the chenille robe looped over the posts of the wooden washstand, which would be a valuable antique if somebody stripped off the yellow paint her mother had slathered on—how long ago? Was it fifteen years already?

Rose shook her head. If she didn't quit totaling up the years this morning, she was going to depress herself right back into bed. Because the truth was, she felt on edge this morning. Jumpy. Unsettled.

She made a face at the imposing grandfather clock, which bonged out 6:00 a.m. as she passed it on the way to the kitchen. Boo impeded her progress by pausing in front of her for wake-up stretches every couple of steps, then waited patiently in front of her bowls.

Cat food rattled into the plastic bowl first. Then Rose poured coffee into the cracked china cup she retrieved from the dish drainer.

Even the cup fed the vague dissatisfaction Rose couldn't quite label. She could see LaFern Finley—tall and thin with a heart-shaped face suspiciously like the one Rose had just frowned at in the mirror—quickly sloshing coffee into that cup. The cup was an indelible part of Rose's memories of morning on Dixie Belle Lane. LaFern had held it in one hand while she hustled little Frank and Caroline and Rose off to school, screeching at them not to leave their raincoats in the locker. Later, LaFern had laughed into that cup on Saturday mornings while she taught her younger daughter, Rose, how to make pancakes. Even later, she had deliberately, solemnly poured coffee into that cup while she repeated the directions Rose had already memorized: what to do if Papa had another stroke.

Rose looked down into the steaming black liquid, watched the crack that began on the gold rim, followed the stem of the pink tea rose and disappeared into the fragrant brew.

Some things never change. Sometimes that was a comfort; sometimes it merely agitated her, stirred that unsettled feeling that was coming more often these days. As if time were running out. As if she should *do* something.

But what?

As Boo followed her on silent cat feet to the screened front porch to wait for the Saturday paper, Rose's eyes swept the still-dark living room. The cream-colored couch with its fading roses and the soft pink armchairs—Uncle Bump's, draped with that gosh-awful green-and-yellow afghan—looked almost exactly the way they'd looked all of Rose's life. The antique china plates and the leather-bound books on the shelf beside the window, the crocheted runner on the mantel, all of it was straight out of Rose's childhood.

Everything was just where it had always been and nothing was here that hadn't been here for years.

Except for the big white envelope edged in crimson.

Three days before, Rose had hastily stuck the imposing piece of mail, unopened, in the library table drawer before Uncle Bump could see it and bedevil her about it. It lay there still, mocking her, goading her, tempting her.

But are you going to do anything about it? Rose asked herself as she pushed open the screen door and stepped out into the cool morning air. *Face it, Finley, it's only too late if you think it is.*

As she sipped coffee and waited for the girl in pigtails who delivered the daily paper from Tuscumbia, Rose previewed the day ahead. After she'd read the latest on Social Security cuts and the new library in Tuscumbia, she would put on one of the six white cotton uniforms hanging in her closet, walk the four blocks to the Picture Perfect Beauty Salon at the end of Main Street and start another day of permanent waves and style-and-sets.

Bunny would gripe about the uniforms and tell the latest on the boy she was dating from Muscle Shoals. And Alma would gripe about what her mother-in-law had said on the phone the night before—ignoring Bunny's advice that, being a widow, Alma no longer had an obligation to be civil to the cranky, complaining woman.

And then she would come home to dinner—either chicken Uncle Bump had undercooked or pork chops he had fried too long—and nag her father's brother about his cholesterol and sit on the porch until bedtime.

Another day in Sweetbranch. Another week, another month, another year. Forty of them on the twenty-first of this month, to be exact.

Rose watched the tall, skinny girl with the old-fashioned plaited pigtails and the baseball cap ride up on her shiny red bike.

"Mornin', Miz Rose." The girl waved and tossed the rolled-up paper over the white wooden fence enclosing the front yard.

Rose winced as she waved back and walked out into the yard after the *Tuscumbia Tribune*. *Miz Rose*. Is that what they were calling her now? Miz Rose—the polite Southern form of address for spinster aunts and old-maid schoolteachers.

"You can't argue with the truth, Finley," she told herself. "Won't be long and you'll be waking up with orthopedic shoes under the bed and blue hair rinse on the bathroom shelf. Miz Rose. Guess that's you, all right."

In spite of herself, Rose chuckled. No wonder Uncle Bump was such a sour old cuss. Reckon she would be the same when the time came.

"Forty." She stopped in the yard and looked around her in disbelieving wonder. Could it really have been so long ago that she'd been a tall, skinny tomboy herself, always up to devilment? Collecting lightning bugs and roly-polies in mason jars in the tree house spanning the limbs of the giant oak in the backyard. Dragging down a line of freshly washed sheets just to see LaFern sputter and fume. Coming home barefoot every day and forgetting where she'd discarded her shoes.

It might have been decades, but most things in Rose's small world looked just the way they always had. The houses up and down Dixie Belle Lane were just the same—white and simple and quiet. Clothes still flapped in the breeze, although Uncle Bump didn't seem to mind mixing brown socks with white sheets. The tree house was still there, although it had been abandoned for years and didn't look steady enough for another generation of Finleys anyway. Main Street had changed the most, with the old movie house now a video rental store and about one-third of the storefronts vacant.

And here, at the sprawling farmhouse Finleys had called home for most of the century, the hedge of salmon pink azaleas lining the picket fence were once again unfurling their delicate blossoms. LaFern had carefully tended those azaleas throughout Rose's childhood, spending hours on pruning and weeding and feeding.

"Beautiful things don't just happen, Rose," LaFern had pronounced every time she had enlisted her younger daughter's help. "You have to *make* them happen."

In the seven years since her mother's death, Rose had barely laid a garden glove on them. But they were like everything else in Sweetbranch—they kept doing the same thing, year after year, whether anybody paid attention or not.

And that, she knew, was what gnawed at her this morning. Turning forty wasn't such a big deal—unless you'd never done anything with your life but watch it pass.

Rose started as Boo tickled her ankles. When she looked down, the cat turned her calico face up in question. Rose smiled and leaned over to pick up the fuzzy feline.

"I know. What am I doing standing out here in my old robe, getting my feet wet in the morning dew?" She hugged the old cat to her, burying her face in its soft neck, and started back for the porch. "Quit looking at me like I've lost my mind. Maybe I'm just trying to figure out how to *make* something happen."

THE PICTURE PERFECT WAS no different this morning, either. The faint aroma of aerosol hair spray fought unsuccessfully to mask the pungent odor of permanent wave solution. The poster pictures on the wall were yellowing and curled at the edges and touted styles that looked as if 1965 had just rolled into town.

Rose stopped and stared at one of the posters. The ruby red smile on the woman with the stiff blond flip was the same one she'd seen the first Saturday she'd come to help LaFern, the summer she was ten. The same one she'd seen the morning she came back from Auburn University, ready to do her duty and help take care of Papa. The same one.

With one swift swipe, Rose yanked the poster off the wall as she walked through the shop's tiny front reception area toward the back.

Alma raised a finely drawn Simply Sable eyebrow at Bunny, then turned back to Rose. "What's with you this morning?"

"I'm tired of looking at it." Rose dropped the offending poster in the large waste bin near the back.

Bunny opened her mouth to speak, then thought better of it. Alma wasn't as circumspect.

"Shoot, Bunny told you last year those posters were scaring

off business. People were afraid they'd leave here looking like they stepped out of 'Leave It to Beaver.' You said that's what they wanted anyway."

Stashing her purse in the back locker, Rose ignored her co-worker.

"What happened to that book of spiked-up hair we got in last week from the styling gel folks in Atlanta?" Bunny started rummaging under the front counter. "I'll tear down the rest and put up some new ones."

Rose pulled the curtain aside and leaned against the door frame. "Yeah. And we'll get a new sign. Call the place The Wild Hair."

Bunny's giggle was interrupted by the ringing of the phone. She covered the mouthpiece. "You getting crazy in your old age, Rose?"

Pointing a no-nonsense finger at her young co-worker, Rose said, "I told you last week, I'm not old. You're just too young to know any better."

"Must be PMS week around here," Alma called out. "Is that what's ailing you this morning, Finley?"

Rose didn't answer. She didn't have to. She and Alma, who had worked side by side since Rose officially joined LaFern Finley at the shop years ago, swapped thoughts with a glance. She reached for a new case of shampoo.

"That's just great!" Bunny slammed the phone back into its cradle. "There goes another regular."

Rose looked through the dividing curtain. The young girl had her face in her hands, her blond hair plopped forlornly over one eye.

"What's wrong?" But she already knew.

"The Rourkes are moving. He got work in Tuscumbia." Bunny stood and smoothed the white smock she wore over her skin-tight jeans. "If I lose one more regular, I'll have to move to Tuscumbia, too."

Rose prepared to start work. The trickle of people moving out of Sweetbranch was turning into a steady stream. Twenty years ago, Sweetbranch had provided the work force for a textile manufacturing plant that made jeans and leisure wear, as well as a plant that made and packaged hair-care products. The textile factory had started laying off people about seven years ago; then, four years ago, it had shut its doors for good. By the time the hair products plant had started cutting shifts, the people in Sweet-branch knew the routine. No one had been surprised when that plant also closed its doors a year ago.

And no one was surprised when people started leaving town, either. People couldn't hang around without jobs.

"Shoot, I'd just as soon live in Tuscumbia, anyway," Alma said as she straightened combs, brushes, mirrors, curling irons and blow dryers on the workstation she'd left in tumbling disorder the night before. "Might meet some men in Tuscumbia."

Bunny giggled and Alma gave her an exaggerated wink. The older woman struck a provocative pose, which was easy given the ample curves she corseted into rigid submission. "I know, you think just because I'm pushing fifty I've got no reason to be interested in men. Honey, after being married to the same man for darn near thirty years, I'm ready to sample some new mer-chandise."

Alma shimmied suggestively to punctuate her claim.

Rose joined the laughter as the two stylists who rented stations from her started in on their favorite topic of conversation: mining for men. Bunny was twenty-one and hungry to settle down; Alma was widowed less than two years and hungry to play around. Talk might be predictable at the Picture Perfect, but it was never dull.

"Then you'd better get out of Sweetbranch," Bunny said. "The merchandise around here's been picked over so many times I wouldn't even have it off a sale table."

"Don't think I haven't thought about getting out of this place while the getting's good." Alma glanced at Rose. "How about it, Rose? We've hung around Sweetbranch too long, don't you think? New pictures on the wall won't make a dang bit of dif-ference. We need a little excitement, a little something to get the old blood pumping."

Rose straightened the divided bin that held the multicolored plastic curling rods she used for perms. "That might be. But you're just like me, Alma. You're not going anywhere. You're just full of talk."

"The heck I am!"

"Finley's right, Alma. You're not going anywhere." Bunny's young, unlined face was playfully smug. "I'm the only one who's going to blow out of this place. I'll be gone before the year's out, and you'll still be here bellyaching about your mother-in-law."

"The heck I will!"

Bunny unlocked the front door and replaced the key that hung on a hook behind the front counter. "That's right."

"We'll just see who gets out of town first." Alma shot another wink across the shop, this time at Rose. "I say *I'll* be gone first."

"Is that a dare?"

"That's a cash-on-the-barrel bet, young'un."

"You're gonna bet me?"

"That's right. I'll bet next week's tips that I make my break before you do."

"You two haven't settled up the last bet yet," Rose reminded them.

"Alma won't admit I'm right. That's why."

"You're crazy. A Baptist preacher is not going to have one iota of interest in a woman like me, I don't care how long he's been a widower." Alma stood tall, shoulders back, inviting her young co-worker to a long look at her figure. "My...features...are way too prominent to be proper. And a Southern Baptist preacher isn't interested unless it's proper."

Bunny laughed. "Quit bragging about your God-given talents. You're just trying to change the subject. I say I'll be out of Sweetbranch while you two are still mixing up blue rinse for the Gilchrist sisters. But I'm not going to take your money again, Alma. You know you can't afford to throw that kind of money away. What'll you use to take your mother-in-law out for Sunday dinner if you start giving away your money like that?"

"Come on, Bunny. Put up or shut up. You willing to bet or not?"

"Sure, I'll bet. I'll bet you're still sitting here trying to talk old Widow Clancy out of dyeing her hair jet black when I'm in the city living it up."

Rose had heard enough. "You're both wrong."

The two women turned toward the decisive voice of the shop owner.

"How's that?" Alma said.

"Neither one of you will be the first to escape." She sat back in her swivel chair and looked at the two women who were her constant companions. "*I* will."

Bunny and Alma exchanged a look. Bunny cocked her hip and

pointed a rat-tail comb at Rose. "I'm not horsing around this time, Rose. I'm serious."

Alma crossed her arms. "Me, too."

"So am I."

But Rose knew it wasn't so. It was the same kind of big talk that filled the air at the Picture Perfect every day. Rose knew that Bunny, as young as she was, might eventually break away. But Alma wasn't going anywhere. And neither was Rose. They knew that and so did she.

Didn't she? The crimson-edged envelope flashed into her mind, again taunting her with its promise of a tomorrow that wasn't merely a reflection of all her yesterdays.

"All right. Let's get official here." Bunny jumped out of her chair and went toward the back room. Alma and Rose followed, knowing what would happen next. Three jars would be found and labeled so they could keep track of their tips—and therefore the amount of the bet—for the week.

Rose barely noticed the jingle of the bell over the front door. Her first customer wasn't due for another half hour. She reached up to the top shelf for masking tape to label the empty conditioner bottles Bunny had found.

"Holy cow!" Alma's whispered exclamation made Rose turn around. The other woman was peering through the curtain. Alma gestured and whispered, "Come here. If this doesn't crank your tractor, nothing will."

Rose and Bunny tiptoed over and peered out to see what had captured Alma's attention.

Standing in the front of the shop was a stranger, which was enough all by itself to attract attention in Sweetbranch. But he wasn't just any stranger. He was a tall, broad-shouldered, silver-haired, made-in-Hollywood stranger. A certifiable hunk in clothes that cost a lot more than the three of them would ever collect in their plastic tip bottles in a month of Sundays.

Maybe it wouldn't be just another day in Sweetbranch after all.

CHAPTER TWO

BUNNY WAS UNBUTTONING her white smock before the bell had stopped jingling, revealing snug jeans and a clingy, scoop-neck blouse.

"In case you don't recognize it, girls, that is class. And money," she whispered, smoothing her blouse and tossing aside the smock. "The money that's gonna buy my ticket out of Sweet-branch. Let me by, girls, I've got a customer."

Alma didn't budge. "No way, child. Look at that silver hair. This one's mine. I'll keep my hands off the young ones if you don't mess with the vintage merchandise."

While the two bickered in whispers, Rose studied the man who stood in the reception area. His eyes were never still, darting around the shop and back out to the street. His clothes were casual, even a little rumpled, but they had a style to them that you didn't see in Sweetbranch. And there was nothing rumpled about the man. He was all clean, crisp lines, from the sharp jut of his strong jaw and chin to the broad slope of his shoulders.

"You're both wrong again," Rose spoke up. "He's mine."

"But I saw him first," chimed in one surprised voice, at the same time another said, "Yours?"

"This is *my* shop and that gives me first dibs on anything that walks through the door." She glanced again at the man. He radiated tension. He looked poised for action, like an actor in a Hollywood thriller. Life wasn't passing this man by. Rose knew the conclusions she was drawing were colored by the fantasies of a bored woman skirting the edges of middle age. But, what the heck, a little fantasy never hurt anybody. "This is *my* shop and that man is *mine*."

At that moment, he leaned over and was momentarily hidden

by the front counter. When he straightened, he had a sleepy-
looking little girl in his arms.

Alma dropped the curtain. "Shoot! He's married anyway.
You're welcome to him."

Rose sauntered through the curtain and toward the front of the
shop. She wanted to check her hair in the mirror, but she knew
she'd never hear the end of it if she did. In fact, she'd probably
never hear the end of this anyway, but that was all right. If running her hands through Mr. Hollywood's hair offered a few moments' reprieve from dull routine, she planned to go for it. So
what if he was married? She could pretend he was 007 on his
way to a rendezvous with death, and hers might be the last fem-
inine touch he would ever feel.

She liked the sound of that. Had a good ring to it. She took a
quick look in a mirror as she passed. Tall, lithe, her thick chestnut
hair billowing around her shoulders, she was a mature beauty that
no shallow youth could match.

What good's a fantasy if you can't take it all the way? she
asked herself.

"Good morning." She turned her brightest smile on the little
girl, finding, once she was closer, that she was too shy to quite
look the man in the eye. The little girl turned wary eyes, dark-
lashed and a startling blue, on her but didn't smile back. Fighting
a sudden sense of unease, Rose forced herself to look at the man.

These eyes were paralyzing. Even more wary than the child's
and as blindingly blue, they warned Rose to keep her distance, to
save her friendly greeting.

The challenge whisked through her, stole her breath, left her
heart pumping at a faster rate than was usually allowed inside the
Sweetbranch town limits. She kept smiling, let her eyes lock with
his. Then reminded herself that the fantasy was hers, not his.

A middle-aged hairstylist in the sticks of north Alabama, that's
what he was seeing.

So much for fantasy.

Her smile faded and she looked away. "What can we do for
you this morning?"

"A haircut. For...for her."

Rose glanced up at the thick, dark hair streaming down the
toddler's back. Her eyes widened before she could check her reaction. "Really?"

His brusque response came quickly and firmly. "Really."

Mr. Hollywood's a little short on charm this morning, Rose decided. Well, a silver-haired hunk might not be susceptible to a big smile from an over-the-hill hairstylist, but she knew how to win over a child.

Rose turned her smile back to the child and held out her hands. "Come on, honey, Auntie Rose will make you so glamorous your daddy won't know you."

Instead of responding to the warmth in Rose's voice, the little girl turned her face into the man's shoulder and huddled deeper into his arms. Rose dropped her hands and shrugged.

"Where do you want her?"

His voice was softer and Rose looked once again into his face. He was looking not at her but at the little girl in his arms. His face was gentle, his eyes tender. Envy stirred in Rose, an envy she never allowed herself to acknowledge when she was around people with children.

She led him to her station and positioned a child's seat across the arms of the chair. The man sat the little girl down, brushing a reassuring kiss on her forehead as he did.

"There you go, sweetheart," he said gently, backing off only a few steps, as if loath to let the child move beyond his touch.

Rose's pique at his earlier brusqueness melted. A man that sweet to a little girl couldn't be all bad. She pumped the chair with her white-clad foot to raise the child to the right height.

"Now, what do we want to do this morning? A little trim around the..."

"Short. Something short." He folded his arms tightly across his chest, gripping his elbows. "With bangs, maybe."

Rose noticed no wedding ring. Not that she'd made a point of looking, but with his hands on his elbows like that... Of course, no wedding ring didn't mean a thing. Plenty of men didn't wear wedding rings.

She turned her attention back to the solemn face in the chair. The big blue eyes were trained on her father's matching ones, as if the little girl, too, didn't like being out of his arms. It was then that Rose noticed the bruise. It was yellowing, fading just under the eye and over the cheekbone that was cushioned by baby plumpness. Rose swallowed hard to keep from emitting the little gasp of sympathetic surprise that rose automatically from her throat.

She pretended not to notice. And decided it was better to keep her opinions about the little girl's hair to herself.

"Okeydokey," she said cheerfully, twirling the chair around and raising the counter to reveal a sink. As she washed the child's hair, she was aware of Alma and Bunny wandering in from the back. "We'll give you a bob this morning. Make you look like a different little girl. And with summer coming on, I bet you'll like it lots better than having all that long, hot hair hanging down your back."

She used her eyes to warn the two women to keep their mouths shut. But she knew that was as unlikely as a Sunday when the church bells didn't ring.

Toweling the excess water out of the girl's hair, Rose tried to keep up a steady stream of chatter, partly to set the child at ease and partly so her co-workers wouldn't have an opening.

"I'll bet your cat won't even know you when you get home," Rose said, clipping part of the child's hair out of the way so she could begin cutting.

She wondered, as she did so, why she hadn't asked about the bruise. The little girl had probably fallen off her tricycle. Or maybe run into a table. Rose had done that herself once, loosening one of her front baby teeth. Why in the world had she decided to ignore it, as if mentioning it would make everyone uncomfortable? "You do have a cat, don't you?"

The question drew the first faint smile from the little girl. She nodded and looked at the man. His smile was reassuring and his daughter's smile deepened. She was a real doll.

Just like her daddy.

"I knew you had a cat. You just look like a little girl with a cat." Rose was surprised to realize that her heart was pounding all out of reason. She decided to keep her eyes off Mr. Hollywood. And to stop acting like old Widow Clancy about the bruise. Old Widow Clancy was suspicious of everything. Being overly suspicious, Uncle Bump always said, was one of the first symptoms that you'd lived in a small town way too long. "What's your kitty's name?"

"Puff."

"Puff. I like that. Did you pick that name all by yourself?"

Rose stilled her scissors, waiting for the bobbing of the head she knew would follow her question. "And what's your name?"

"Kwissy."

From the corner of her eye, Rose saw the man stiffen. "That's a pretty name, too. And how old are you, Krissy?"

The little girl held up three fingers. "And a half."

He was strung far too tight. Just sensing the tension in him was having a similar effect on Rose. She felt ready to snap.

Then Bunny's voice intruded from behind her. "What brings y'all to Sweetbranch this morning?"

Mr. Hollywood's reaction to the question didn't surprise Rose. The grip on his elbows tightened. Those ice blue eyes narrowed. His jaw worked as he clenched his teeth. And the little girl perched in the chair turned her full attention to him.

Rose kept cutting and waited for the silence to end.

"We're on a weekend trip."

Rose hadn't noticed before how low and soft his voice was. Low and soft and deep. You almost had to strain to hear him. She liked the voice, almost as much as she liked the looks of the man it came from.

Anybody who knew Bunny had to know she wouldn't let it go there. "Oh yeah? You got relatives in Sweetbranch?"

"No. No relatives."

Bunny ran her fingers through her hair to give it a little extra fluff. "Oh. Well then, where you from?"

Alma, who was seating her first customer of the morning, glared across the room at Bunny. Rose made one last snip and pulled the blow dryer out of its ring on the side of her station. The whir filled the room, making a response unlikely. From behind, Rose felt the jab of Bunny's toe in her backside. She smiled. And when she glanced up, she saw that he was smiling, too. Right at her. A tight, grateful smile.

Rose had been right. Krissy hardly looked like the same child with the new, short cut. She wondered why that bothered her. And she wondered why she'd known with such certainty that Krissy's father had no good answer to Bunny's questions.

But when Krissy jumped down from the chair and threw herself into the man's arms, something deep in Rose's heart told her she had no reason to be suspicious of this man.

"Look, Daddy!"

Krissy giggled and shook her bouncing, short hair. Her father laughed, a weary laugh that might fool a three-year-old but not a forty-year-old. His heart wasn't in it.

But his heart was in his eyes when he looked down at the smiling child in his arms. And that told Rose all she needed to know about Mr. Hollywood and his touchy mood this morning. There couldn't be anything bad wrong with a man who could look at a child with that much love in his eyes.

BEN FELT ONLY RELIEF as he walked down the quiet Main Street, hand in hand with Krissy. For the first time that morning, she seemed not to notice his anxiety. For the moment, she was too preoccupied with looking in all the storefront windows, more for a glance at her new haircut than curiosity over blue jeans or black iron cookware. He felt a little foolish, now that it was done, for the instinct that had prompted the cut—the instinct to disguise himself and the child.

Ben looked at his watch. Only ten more minutes.

"Da-a-addy."

Ben looked down at the whining protest in Krissy's voice. She was twisting the hand he held.

"Too tight."

He loosened his hold. He was tense all over, without being aware of it. He could remember spending months like that, every muscle and nerve ready. Ready to hear the slightest stirring in the jungle. Ready to see the barest movement. Ready to spring.

He wiped the memory from his mind and smiled down at Krissy. "Sorry, sweetheart. Why don't we go back to that park we saw when we drove into town?"

"With the swings?"

"That's the one."

Krissy nodded and took another look at herself in the post office window. "Will Mommy like my new hair?"

"I hope so."

What he really hoped was that Mommy wouldn't see it. Not for a long time. Not until things had changed.

He told himself he had no reason to feel guilty about that. Cybil had brought it on herself. Cybil had created the problem, and had refused to take action to fix it. Cybil would have to live with the consequences.

And so will Krissy.

Ben swallowed the guilt, knowing it would merely rise up to choke him at the earliest opportunity, as it already had a dozen times since he'd driven out of Winston-Salem, North Carolina, last night.

The spring green park they were approaching didn't seem to fit the rest of the little town. Main Street turned into a state road that twisted its way back to the two-lane state highway by way of a rickety, one-lane covered bridge over a dried-up creek bed. Ben couldn't imagine that too many people made the trip back and forth across the bridge—it looked direly unreliable. The highway led, eventually, back to the interstate. But everything along the way had an air of decay about it. Not quite abandoned, but heading there.

Although it was midmorning on a Saturday, only a few cars and trucks were parked along Main Street. A fading banner drooped over the front of the hardware store, touting a sale on winter fescue seed, which was probably in low demand in early April. A couple of storefronts were vacant, their windows staring out emptily over the quiet streets. Few were as brightly clean and inviting as the little beauty shop had been.

Ben frowned. Being in the shop had made him uncomfortable. It was being around the people, he knew. Especially the woman who'd cut Krissy's hair. Auntie Rose, she'd told Krissy to call her, in a voice that was one part sweet, slow molasses and two parts tart vinegar.

The look in her eyes when she'd given him such a thorough once-over had been the same. The limpid softness in those pools of honey brown had shifted quickly to dark, searching intensity.

She had the look of a restless woman. Ben knew it was one of those sexist thoughts a nineties kind of guy wasn't supposed to have, but he couldn't help feeling it wasn't right for a woman that attractive to be left looking restless.

No, Auntie Rose and her cozy little yellow-and-white shop had looked different from lazy little Sweetbranch.

And so did the park. It bloomed. Pink and white and fragrant, it trumpeted spring with blossoms he knew he should recognize but didn't. The playground equipment looked well tended and well used, with ruts worn smooth on the red clay ground beneath the swings and the aluminum slide shiny with the frequent polishing of tiny backsides. A sandbox was brightly littered with buckets and shovels. Ben saw them in wonder. Did they belong to a forgetful child? Or was life in Sweetbranch so unthreatened by big city problems that community toys could be left out for everyone to enjoy? Either way, it filled him with longing for such a simple life.

He liked the park and wished he felt confident that Krissy could be enjoying such an uncomplicated childhood again soon.

Then he saw the woman, approaching with two small children. It must be her. What was it she had said?

"You will know me when you see me. Sweetbranch has plenty of black residents, but not many like me."

He forgot his circumstances long enough to smile at the woman's slow approach. Built with long bones and strong sinews, she stopped every few minutes to tumble the little boy to the ground and goose him until he squealed in pleasure, or to swing the little girl high overhead. The boy, in tie-dyed overalls, and the girl, in acid-washed denim shorts, were golden, their skin shades lighter than the woman's deep mahogany. Their hair waved, lighter and softer than her thick ropes of hair, which she'd braided with a multitude of bright beads.

She walked right up to him, long hand outstretched, smile broad. "I am Maxine."

Her handshake was as strong as he might have expected. Muscles, sleek and toned, worked in her arms. Her radiant smile eclipsed her crown of uncountable braids and her bright Caribbean clothes.

Ben wondered what this woman was doing in rural Alabama. Then he remembered.

"I'm Ben." He tried smiling back. He had to trust her. He had very little choice.

She knelt to put herself almost on a level with Krissy. "And what is your name, bright eyes?"

Krissy introduced herself, then surprised Ben by sticking her small hand out for a handshake. She had been so timid in recent months, so withdrawn, that her instant openness took him aback.

Now, small hand in Maxine's, Krissy was smiling broadly. "And I've got new hair."

Maxine laughed. "Do you, now? I must say, Krissy, that you look stunning. Listen, would you like to play with Rex and Kesha while your daddy and I talk?"

With very little coaxing, the three youngsters were soon adding to the sheen of the slide.

Ben, feeling awkward and stiff, stuffed his hands into his pockets and stared after the children. Maxine stared at Ben, her eyes almost level with his.

"Are you certain about this, Mr. McKenzie?"

"No, but I don't have much choice."

"There is always another choice." Her voice was soothing, with the lilt of a faint accent.

Her mellow voice didn't soften the words that ate like acid through Ben's thin shell of composure. "Another choice? Like waiting until her stepfather breaks her arm? Waiting until the courts have the *proof* they want?"

Ben was aware that his voice rose with every word, but he didn't seem able to control the rage that suddenly churned within him.

"What kind of proof will do, I wonder? How far is he going to have to go before the courts will agree to protect a three-year-old girl? Do you know what the law in North Carolina says? They want permanent injury or disfigurement before you can get a conviction on child abuse! How insane is that?"

Realizing he teetered dangerously close to losing control completely, Ben paused and took a deep breath.

Maxine nodded and placed a hand on his arm. "So you are certain."

He started to shrug her hand off. Then he felt something more than the strength in her touch; understanding radiated from her and he felt himself calming. "I wish I was. I don't really know what's right."

She linked arms with him and they started walking the perimeter of the park. About halfway around, she started speaking.

"It is not easy, living underground. Krissy will suffer. You must know that." Her voice was gentle but certain. "She will not understand why you have taken her away from her mother. She will need friends and they will be hard to make. You may someday find it necessary to snatch her away from those friends just as she has come to feel at home. She may decide you are not someone she trusts.''

Ben's foot faltered and he started to protest, but she silenced him with a squeeze to his forearm.

''I am not judging you, Mr. McKenzie. If I did not believe that drastic action is sometimes necessary, I would not be here talking with you.'' She gazed out at the children and smiled at their laughter. ''I am simply telling you how she may feel. How this may affect her life. You understand?''

''I understand.''

''Good.'' They kept walking. ''Tell me, now, what has happened to Krissy.''

And he told her the story that gripped his heart with fear and anguish every time he told it. He had told his attorney. His physician. A harried, overworked social worker. His family. The courts. Even Cybil. Complacent, fearful Cybil.

Everyone had listened. But no one had offered any hope of help.

''You'll have to let the courts handle this, Ben,'' his attorney had said.

''I certainly don't like the looks of this,'' his physician had said. ''But it would be difficult to say for sure that this is more than just the bumps and bruises kids are always getting.''

''We've unsubstantiated your complaint, Mr. McKenzie.'' The social worker had spouted her jargon at him. ''We have no foundation for intervention.''

''Get that look out of your eye, Ben,'' his brother Keith had said, wagging a finger under his nose. ''If there's a problem, the courts will take care of it.''

The courts had taken care of it, all right. He still remembered how the judge had averted his gaze when he pronounced, ''Mr. McKenzie, without some clear evidence of abuse, I'm afraid the courts can take no action to remove the child from her mother's care.''

And when he'd talked to Cybil, after the courts had done nothing and Krissy had continued to withdraw, his ex-wife had hugged herself more tightly into the deep collar of her angora sweater and shuttered her eyes. ''You're crazy, Ben. You're letting your save-the-world mentality get the upper hand again.''

But Ben knew Cybil well enough to recognize the lie in her eyes.

"So here I am," he concluded, surprised to find that his rage had dissipated, leaving behind only weariness. "I didn't know what else to do. I couldn't leave her there. I couldn't wait for..."

Ben couldn't put words to the horrors that had gone through his mind every time he'd taken Krissy home.

Maxine gave his arm one more squeeze, then loosened her hold. From the pocket of her full, gauzy skirt, she pulled a business card and placed it in his hand.

"This is an inexpensive motel a few miles down the highway," she said. "You and Krissy can stay there until you decide. But I must know soon. The longer we wait to act, the greater the chances that something will go wrong."

Ben clutched the card in his fist. It felt a fairly insubstantial lifeline. But the friendly conviction in Maxine's eyes buoyed Ben's courage. "And once I decide?"

"Then we find a safe house. I will not jeopardize our network until your commitment is firm. And after that, we build a new life, new identities for you and Krissy."

Ben nodded, barely acknowledging the rush of danger that skittered through his consciousness.

"But, Mr. McKenzie..." Her voice took on a commanding edge. "It is most urgent for you to remember that secrecy is vital. Use cash. Do not tell friends, even your most trusted loved ones, where you are. For anyone to discover you could endanger Krissy and many other children, as well. Children who have already been through much worse than Krissy. Do you understand?"

Discomfort prickled along his neckline. Moving so slightly it was almost undetectable, the fingers of his right hand opened and closed as if seeking to grip something, a move that comforted him in the instant before it flooded him with anxiety. "I understand."

It was only as he walked away, hand in hand with Krissy, that he understood the anxiety that had washed over him. The carefully measured movement of his right hand had once been second nature, almost twenty years earlier. It was the move he used in the jungles of Vietnam to ready his M-14 rifle.

"YOU DID WHAT?"

Ben had known his little brother would blow up when he told him; Keith had always been excitable. That's why he'd talked first about their plans to build a new plant for recyclable paper. They'd already agreed on possible locations in north Alabama and northeast Mississippi and had planned to check out the sites sometime in the next few months. They would simply do it sooner rather than later.

Keith didn't like the unexpected change in plans. But what he really didn't like was Ben's next announcement, that he wouldn't be bringing Krissy home. Holding the receiver slightly away from his ear while Keith spewed out his anger, Ben kept his eye on Krissy. She sat on the black-and-white tile floor of the drugstore looking through the display of coloring books.

"Have you lost your mind? Don't answer that. You have. You've finally lost it. Would you mind telling me what you plan to do now that you've..."

"Could you keep your voice down, little brother?" Speaking in a whisper himself, Ben knew that Keith McKenzie never closed the door to his small, messy office in the printing company they ran. And even on a Saturday, their big-eared secretary was likely to be right outside, soaking up everything Keith said. "I'd just as soon this weren't broadcast over the Nancy Network by lunchtime."

"And you're making jokes. I can't believe you're making jokes." Keith was making a mess of the thick brown curls that were slowly silvering to match his brother's. Ben was so familiar with the gesture he didn't have to witness it to know it was happening. "That's it. This is all a joke. Right? You figure once you've told me this, I can't be mad at you just because you decided to take a Saturday off for one of your silly—you're at the homeless shelter again, right?"

"No, Keith. I'm not at the homeless shelter."

"Then where the hell are you?"

"I can't tell you that."

"Holy Mother, I don't believe this."

"It'll be all right, kid. Trust me. I know what I'm doing." But Ben doubted it. He'd doubted it since he looked into the sympathetic but curious eyes of the tall, slender woman who'd cut Krissy's hair. As he watched Krissy, absorbed in pages of Sesame

Street illustrations, Ben had to wonder if he wasn't on the verge of making the biggest mistake of his life.

"But what about the business? You just gonna dump it in my lap? How long is this going to drag out?"

Ben didn't have the answers his brother wanted, but he searched for something that would calm him. "Listen, I'm going to check out the sites for the paper plant. We've got to do that anyway, right?"

"Who gives a damn about manufacturing recycled paper? That was your bright idea, anyway, if you recall. And if you don't get your butt back to Winston, we may not be producing any kind of paper, recycled or not. I can't run this place by myself."

Ben knew that wasn't true. And he knew that once Keith calmed down, he would know it, too.

"Just cool off, Keith. I'll talk to you in a couple of days. You'll see. It'll work out."

"But how can I get in touch with you?"

"I'll call."

"But..."

"I'll call."

"What about Cybil? What do I tell Cybil? You know she's going to call. She's going to be hysterical and you know I can't handle hysterical women."

"I'll talk to her."

"Bring the kid back, big brother."

"I'll be in touch."

"Ben, promise me..."

Ben severed the connection.

ROSE COULDN'T DECIDE whether she was going to talk about Mr. Hollywood or not as she hurried up the path to the side entrance of the Sweetbranch First Freewill Baptist Church. Best friends deserved to hear the good stuff, of course, but what was there, really, to tell?

A little air of...of what? Not mystery, exactly. Not suspense or danger, to be sure. But there was something. Something besides the sex appeal. That part had been easy to measure, based on the response from Alma and Bunny. No, Mr. Hollywood had brought something into the Picture Perfect besides his silver-haired good looks. A little flurry of excitement had hung in the air all morning, long after he'd walked out.

Rose had still felt it while she did the weekly shampoo and style for Val Murphy, who would now try to maintain that style for a full week by wrapping it in toilet paper every night and adding a new layer of hair spray every morning. It had charged the air around Rose far more than the argument between Rusty Sprinkmann and her precocious adolescent daughter about what kind of haircut the teen wanted. The daughter had won. She always did. But they always argued anyway, involving everyone in the shop and providing more entertainment than the community theater's stilted production of an outdated Broadway musical.

Still, as she walked into the Fellowship Hall of the church for the lunchtime meeting, Rose couldn't decide whether to keep her silly notions to herself or not.

When her eyes lighted on her friend, leaning over a huge box of donated clothing, Rose's excitement bubbled over into a smile. Here was just the tonic Rose needed right now—someone who wasn't typical Sweetbranch. And in her bright, flowing clothes and colorfully beaded hair, Maxine Hammond was anything but typical Sweetbranch.

CHAPTER THREE

MAXINE WAS in one of her moods. Rose knew that right away, from the way she'd drawn her full lips into a long, taut line. One of those silent, brooding moods that came on her every so often.

Rose's exuberance dimmed. Now was obviously not the time to be gushing to Maxine about Mr. Hollywood. Besides, the man was nothing more than a momentary distraction, and Rose knew from experience that such excitement was always short-lived in Sweetbranch.

That was when she remembered the real purpose of her visit with Maxine. And she instantly felt about as sour as her friend looked.

Their project was to come up with ways to keep people from leaving Sweetbranch—especially the young people.

Bad timing for me to be discussing that, Rose thought.

After getting a hug from Maxine's two children, who then dashed back to the corner of the Fellowship Hall to complete a board game, Rose slumped into a straight-backed chair and put her feet up on a folding card table. A flippant mood, she thought, might be her only salvation.

"So, here's my best idea. I say we put up a billboard next to the high school that says Get While The Getting's Good."

Rose saw right away that flippant wasn't playing well in Sweetbranch this morning.

Dropping a flannel gown into the box of secondhand clothes, Maxine drew her ebony eyes away from the children and frowned. "Something is bothering you this morning."

Irritation nudged Rose's mood another step into the dumper. "You and Uncle Bump"

"I beg your pardon?"

"You and Uncle Bump, always reading my mind. You know I hate it when you read my mind."

"Only when you are in a bad mood, my friend. Only when you are in a bad mood." Maxine sat opposite Rose in a metal folding chair. "And what is the cause of your bad mood this morning?"

"I *was* in a good mood."

Skepticism colored Maxine's already grim expression. "Is that so?"

"That is so."

"And I have ruined your geniality?"

The more Maxine egged her on, the more ornery Rose felt. "You and your dumb project," she grumbled.

"Saving Sweetbranch is not a dumb project." Maxine's throatily melodic voice didn't invite disagreement.

That didn't make Rose any less disagreeable, however. "And what makes it worth saving?"

Maxine was quiet for so long Rose thought perhaps she'd stumped her. But when she spoke, it was with a long, almost caressing look at her children.

"Quiet streets with lots of trees. People whose roots go generations deep. No drugs or violence to hurt our children." Maxine's hands were crossed and still in her lap, but her lips trembled with uncharacteristic lack of control. "Sweetbranch is a haven from the world. That makes it worth saving."

Maxine's words stirred a sense of identification in Rose, but she refused to give in to sentimentality. "Easy for you to say. You haven't been here all your life."

"Perhaps it would have been better if I had."

"You don't mean that and you know it." Rose shook her head. "You've lived all over the world. You've marched for civil rights in Alabama and peace in Washington and safe energy in California and feeding hungry children in Florida. Your whole life has been exciting. Not like it would've been hanging around Sweetbranch."

"Those aren't the things that have made my life full."

Maxine always discounted the dedication and accomplishments that had characterized her life. She always said her real accomplishment was finding love.

It was, in fact, love that had brought her to Sweetbranch. Love for Ragan Hammond, who had had the courage to bring his black wife home to the small north Alabama town where his white family had practiced law for generations. It was love that had finally bought Maxine the town's acceptance—her unconditional, contagious love for life and people and everything bright and beautiful in the world.

Rose and Maxine had been friends long before the rest of Sweetbranch had stopped thumbing its nose at the biracial couple. Call it Rose's latent desire, just once, to do what was forbidden. Or maybe it had simply been the lure of Maxine's vibrant and unorthodox life. Whatever the reason, the two had bonded quickly.

And most of Sweetbranch had followed, far faster than Rose would have imagined.

Now Maxine Hammond was one of the people Sweetbranch looked to first for help. She was on the school board. She was active in the First Freewill Baptist Church, which had at first opened its doors to her only out of an embarrassing realization that doing anything else would seem highly unChristian. And she was the driving force behind a community-wide task force charged with revitalizing the town's economy and reversing the town's dwindling population.

"You may play the cynic all you wish, my friend," Maxine said. "However, I know you love the young people of this town. Can you name one other reason that you spend so much time with the youth group at the church and 4-H at the school?"

Rose didn't want to be reminded right this minute of the things she enjoyed about Sweetbranch.

"Maybe we'd be doing them more good if we fixed the old Willow Creek Bridge, just to make sure it's safe when they high-tail it out of town," Rose retorted. "Shoot, maybe I'll offer to drive them to the city myself instead of looking for ways to keep them locked up here."

"You and I have been asked for ideas to keep the town's young people from leaving. Shall we focus on that, my sour-faced companion?"

Maxine's chiding smile was contagious.

"I don't care what you think. Sweetbranch is not a haven." Rose folded her arms across her chest to counter the effects of her answering smile. "It's a prison. And I say we should tell the young people to get out before they wake up one morning and find out it's too late.''

"Ah.''

Rose knew what that long, knowing sigh meant. More mind reading. "Cut that out.''

"Your feet are feeling itchy again.''

"Quit telling me what I'm feeling, Maxie. You know I hate that.''

Maxine laughed, a soft, warm laugh that spoke of delight. Rose felt herself responding with a self-deprecating chuckle. "Okay. So my feet are getting itchy again. Yours would be, too, if you'd spent forty years cooling your heels in the same blasted place.''

"You could leave anytime.''

"Hah! You know better than that.'' Maxine's confident proclamation dampened the rippling beginnings of good humor. "I've been stuck here for years.''

"Because of your father's stroke.'' Maxine raised one eyebrow almost imperceptibly.

"That's right.''

The eyebrow inched up in a look that was clearly skeptical.

"What was I supposed to do? Let Mama take care of him all by herself?''

"She had your brother. Your sister. Your uncle.''

"Frank was already married, living in Birmingham. You know that. And Caroline had...''

"Two children and a husband in Huntsville. I do recall that.'' Maxine smiled softly. "And all you had was college.''

"It made more sense.'' Rose could hear the defensiveness in her voice. It didn't surprise her; she'd told herself too many times that she'd given in too easily. "Auburn University didn't need me to survive.''

"That is true. It was still there six years later when your father passed away.''

"But I was...'' She halted.

"But you were twenty-five.''

Twenty-five. It sounded so young now. But at the time, with all her friends either finished with college and started on careers in Birmingham or Atlanta or started on families in Sweetbranch, twenty-five had seemed awfully late to be starting life. Regret filled Rose and she held it at bay the only way she knew.

"Mother needed me. She was old and worn out and afraid of being by herself."

Maxine looked poised, ready to embark on a sermon, then seemed to think better of it. Instead, she clasped one of Rose's slender hands between her own strong palms. "You have made a wonderful life in Sweetbranch, Rose. You own a healthy business."

My mother's business, Rose reminded herself.

"You make a home for your retired uncle."

Instead of a home for a man of my own.

"You give countless hours to this town's children and young people."

And let the years slip away without ever having the chance for any of my own.

"Many people would be proud to claim all the good you have accomplished in your life, Rose."

"Nice try, Maxine." But she smiled anyway. That was the thing about Maxine—she always made you glow inside, even when you didn't think you had anything to glow about.

"Besides, it is not too late to change, if that is what you want. Have you heard from the university?"

Rose was silent. The envelope sat there in her living room, waiting for her to find a little courage. "Maxie, I don't know..."

"Fill out the application, Rose. The University of Alabama is excellent."

"But what if...?"

"What if you fail?"

"What if I don't?"

The two women laughed together as Rose acknowledged the fears that would come with tackling life head-on.

"Face it, Maxie, I still have my mission here in Sweetbranch. After all, everybody in town's been eager to tell me the last few weeks that I'm well on my way to being the town's eccentric spinster. What would people do without me?"

Maxine gave her friend's hand a playful slap and sat back in her chair. "If you are a spinster, I am a matron and I refuse to be nominated for membership in that society. We are in our prime. Do not forget it."

Rose glanced at her watch. "We haven't accomplished a darn thing today. And it's time for me to get my rear in gear. If I don't get back with lunch before one-thirty, Alma and Bunny will be on a hunger strike. They'd have to stop the press over at the *Sweetbranch Weekly Gazetteer* for the story."

"Then we must do this soon. I want to take substantial ideas to the next task force meeting." Maxine stood and prepared to turn her attention back to sorting the clothes that had been donated for the town's needy families. "You need something to do, Rose. Sign up for the church's aerobics class. It starts in two weeks."

"Eccentric spinsters don't need to stay in shape." *Unless a good-looking stranger shows up in town.* She paused, tempted to tell Maxine about him. But she glanced at her watch again. Maybe later.

"Sign up for the class, Rose. It will do you good."

"You mean it'll do you good to have someone to suffer with."

Maxine pursed her lips to keep from smiling. "If it helps you to think of it as a sacrifice for someone else's sake, go right ahead."

"Just for that, Maxie, I'll run you into the floor. Your muscles will start to ache the minute you see me coming."

Rose left Maxine with a laugh and a hug and started across the Fellowship Hall. Maxine's voice echoed after her.

"Life is always risky, Rose, whether you are twenty-five or forty. But it is never too late."

CYBIL RICHERT McKENZIE Webster couldn't hide from the facts any longer. It was Saturday afternoon and her ex-husband wasn't going to bring her child home. She knew it in her bones.

Her hands shook as she pulled a thin brown cigarette from the slender silver case Colin Webster had given her just weeks after they started dating. She could barely hold the matching silver lighter steady long enough to light the cigarette. The tobacco caught. She inhaled, deeply but raggedly. The smoke filling her lungs didn't calm her as it normally did.

She looked again at the marble clock on the mantel. One o'clock. Colin would be home soon. He wouldn't ask about Krissy. That wouldn't start until tomorrow afternoon. But he would sense something was awry. He always did. He had last night when he had come in from work.

"Krissy already gone?" he'd asked, tossing his briefcase into the Queen Anne chair and heading for the liquor cabinet. He hadn't even looked at her.

"Yes." Then, afraid her clipped reply would reveal things she didn't want revealed, she had started to babble. "They left about five-thirty. Before dark. I'm not sure what he had planned for the weekend. Krissy was...that is, I'm sure they'll have fun. He always takes her somewhere fun."

This afternoon, however, if Colin said something, her resolve would be weaker. Cybil knew that. Her voice would quaver. She wouldn't be able to look him in the eye. Because she knew. Ben wasn't coming back. And she couldn't blame him. Honestly couldn't blame him.

Exhaling the smoke in her lungs on a sob she couldn't control, Cybil stabbed at the ashtray on the coffee table and put out the cigarette.

"He's not coming back. He isn't going to bring Krissy home." In the empty house, she tried the words on for size. Her voice was hoarse, dry and raspy after a morning of silence and smoking. The only real discomfort her admission caused was the edgy anxiety she always felt when she contemplated Colin's reaction to something beyond his control.

Running her hands through her long, silver blond hair, Cybil encountered tangles. She looked down at herself. She was still in the satin robe she'd pulled on at six this morning when she'd dragged herself out of bed to look out the front window and silently dial Ben's number.

There had been no answer. As there had been none all morning.

She had seen Ben's intentions in his eyes when he'd swept Krissy into his arms Friday night. That cold, hard look that was more like the Ben McKenzie she had fallen in love with. She'd always liked that Ben, the one who had shared her own need to claw her way to the top of the heap. Whatever had driven that Ben to achieve, to accumulate, to grab what he wanted at all costs—whatever that was had died in him these past few years. He was different. Making money wasn't that important, he'd said. They had all they needed. His position and his power and his money could do more good in other ways, he'd said.

And as the old Ben McKenzie had died, so had Cybil's love for him. She hadn't been interested in a softhearted do-gooder. But Friday night, the old, hard-edged Ben had resurfaced just long enough to stir a moment of longing for the old days in Cybil's heart. She should have realized right then that something was wrong. But, frankly, she'd been too concerned that he leave with Krissy before Colin came home. Before they had the chance for another of those cold-war confrontations that always led to something more after Cybil was left alone with her new husband. Her new, successful, hard-driving husband.

Cybil tried to anchor her limp hair behind her ears. She had to dress. She had to get a grip on herself. Colin wouldn't like it if he came home from the golf course and found her falling apart. She would wash her face and fix her hair. She would find something in the closet that looked right for the young architect's wife at home and would be lounging on the couch with a brandy when he came in. Maybe he'd putted well and would be in a good mood and they would have a pleasant afternoon.

Or maybe he had putted badly.

Cybil stood on unsteady legs and went toward the master bedroom suite, passing Krissy's bedroom on the way. She had passed the closed door more than a dozen times already, pausing each time to put her hand on the knob, then back away. Krissy wasn't in there. No need to look.

Actually, if not for the apprehension screaming in Cybil's head all day, the silence would have been welcome.

Ben's struggle for custody had been a just struggle—Cybil had realized that all along. She wasn't good mother material, not the way Ben was good father material.

But there was Colin. He'd known how it would look in his social circle for his wife to give up custody of her child. It would be unacceptable. Quite unacceptable, and it would reflect badly on him. On them. Colin had been very clear about that.

Very clear.

Involuntarily, Cybil touched her face. The red, raw mark on her cheek had healed and was no longer visible. But she felt it there, all the time. When she went out to parties, when she lunched with friends. It was funny. She'd hidden in the house for weeks, refusing to go out where she would have to make lame excuses. But now, long after the mark was gone, she still felt it would give her away.

Her hand shook. She dropped it to the doorknob, where it hovered for a moment before gripping the knob and turning.

Shadows filled the pink-and-white room. Cybil crept in and stood flattened against the door frame while she glanced around the room. The purple bunny rabbit caught her eye. Another sob escaped her throat. Pushing the door closed behind her, she crossed the room, snatched the fuzzy toy off the bed and slumped to the floor with it clutched to her chest.

"Krissy? Krissy, baby, where are you?"

And the answer came to her, harsh and unwanted, but undeniable.

Safe. That's where Krissy was. Safe with her father. Far away from the abuse that her mother had forced herself to ignore. Far away. But safe.

ROSE WANTED TO DAWDLE, the way a child dawdles on the way to school, pausing to study cracks in the sidewalk and broken twigs—things whose only intrinsic value was their ability to delay the moment of walking through the schoolhouse door.

She paused outside the church, for the second time that day taking in the sights and smells that had become such second nature she barely noticed them anymore. The red bricks of the church were old but sturdy, they'd housed worshippers in Sweetbranch for more than a century. The spreading oak in the front lawn, its newly sprouting leaves fluttering pale in the breeze, had sheltered more community dinners than anyone could count—tomorrow's would be little different from the ones Rose remembered as a child. Or the ones her mother had no doubt remembered from her own childhood.

"Work, Rose," she prodded herself. "You've got to get back to the shop."

Rose pointed her white-shoed feet down Main Street to the Clock—only outsiders called it Around the Clock Diner, since it had been at least fifty years since the highway was rerouted and there was no longer any need for twenty-four-hour service. Saturdays the lunch special was chicken-fried steak with two vegetables, biscuit and tea, and her three orders were probably cooling on the counter in their white boxes right now. She'd already dawdled too long with Maxine. But she felt like dawdling some more.

She sniffed the early hothouse strawberries in the little green cartons on Mr. Whitley's sidewalk display. She fingered the packets of flower seed in the bins in front of the hardware store. She studied the new sundresses in the window at the Sweet Bou- tique.

"Better have one," Agnes Sauter called to her as she followed a customer out and paused to prop open the door. "They're straight from Atlanta."

"You think?" Rose fingered the soft, mint green rayon and imagined the warm sunshine on her shoulders.

Ida Clancy clutched her Sweet Boutique shopping bag to her rounded front and grunted. "Agnes, don't you talk this girl into any foolishness, you hear?"

The town gossip's voice intruded unpleasantly into Rose's enjoyment of the afternoon.

Agnes wrinkled up her well-lined face. "What're you getting at now, Ida?"

"Rose isn't getting any younger," the Widow Clancy pronounced in the tight voice that pronounced much of what she felt needed pronouncing in Sweetbranch. "I'm not sure she's at the age any longer when it's wise to show that much shoulder."

The words stung, but Rose refused to let her face reveal it. Was everyone in town counting down to her birthday?

Agnes's eyes widened in outrage. "Ida, that's the worst I ever heard, and I've heard plenty from you over the years."

Rose smiled gratefully at the shopkeeper, who had been her mother's best friend since the two women had planned their weddings for the exact same day in June approximately sixty years earlier. Agnes and LaFern had feuded for three months until their fiancés got so tired of the arguing that they'd both taken their rings back. Just long enough to make Agnes and LaFern realize that June 6 wasn't the only Saturday in June. They both switched dates and everybody in town got to attend both weddings. June was a big month in town that year.

Agnes Sauter's reprimand didn't seem to faze Sweetbranch's self-proclaimed arbiter of good taste. Ida Clancy merely raised her chin and smiled serenely. "All I'm saying is she's a maiden woman of a certain age. People will talk. That's all I'm saying."

"Who'll talk, Ida? You?" Agnes cackled and turned to Rose. "Besides, girl, you might not get to be an old maid after all if you'd show a little shoulder."

"I'll remember that, Mrs. Sauter." And giving one last caress to the soft fabric, Rose shook off Ida Clancy's words and continued down the sidewalk.

Now absolutely certain that the gravy was congealing on the chicken-fried steak, Rose walked through the door at the Clock. The bell jingled overhead and Mellie Hawkins came out from the kitchen, a tray of baskets filled with piping biscuits on one shoulder.

"Eighteen minutes late," Mellie calculated as she dropped baskets of hot bread onto the four occupied tables and booths in the diner. "I figured the world must've come to an end and somebody forgot to tell us."

The short, squat waitress stopped at the last booth near the door, drawing Rose's attention away from the three boxes stacked on the counter. She opened her mouth to respond to Mellie, but the two people in the booth knocked the wisecrack she had prepared right out of her head.

It was Mr. Hollywood and the little girl. His plastic glass of iced tea paused on the way to his lips and his eyes locked with Rose's. And Rose knew right then that Maxine might be right, maybe it wasn't too late to make changes.

And she was going to start right now—by seeing just how long Mr. Hollywood would be passing through Sweetbranch. Who knows? If he was here long enough, maybe they'd both have time to unbend a little.

CHAPTER FOUR

BEN HAD the eeriest feeling that this woman he knew only as Rose had his number. Which, of course, wasn't possible.

You're nuts, McKenzie, he told himself. *Out of your tree.*

This woman knew nothing about him. She couldn't possibly begin to understand who he was and what his life was about. But he felt his mouth go dry and his blood pound out of control as a slow smile crossed the woman's lips and she moved toward his table.

"Well, I'll be Sleeping Beauty if you two haven't found the best eating establishment in the entire metropolis," she said, propping a hand on the slender hip she cocked at a saucy angle. "And I'll bet you did it completely without the aid of the *Visitor's Guide to Sweetbranch.*"

Ben laughed, as much in response to the flirty little twinkle in her eye as to her flippant remark. And before his laughter could fade, in fact even before he could pull his gaze from her deep-set brown eyes, his smile widened at the sound of Krissy's tiny hands clapping.

"Auntie Wose!" her voice chirped happily, and Ben's heart warmed with gratitude to the woman who prompted that joy. He'd seen all too little of it lately.

Rose looked down at Krissy, perched in the booth beside Ben in a red-and-blue booster seat, her smiling mouth ringed with spaghetti sauce.

"Well, hello there, cute stuff. That spaghetti looks mighty good."

Krissy smiled and nodded her concurrence, then thrust a spoonful of the pasta—carefully cut into little-girl-size bites—into her mouth, pointed across the table at the empty side of the booth and ordered, "Sit there."

"Krissy!" The mild protest escaped Ben's lips before he could check his alarm.

Krissy looked up at him, confused. Then she swallowed, smiled and looked back at Rose. "Sit there, pwease."

Rose laughed and, without waiting for any other invitation, slid onto the vinyl bench. "Now how could I turn down an invitation like that?"

Then she turned her dark eyes back on Ben and he knew he had to take defensive action. He glanced away for a moment, then returned her frank gaze. "Krissy, I'm sure Ms. Rose is too busy to visit with us right now. She probably has to get back to her shop. I'm sure other little girls are waiting for haircuts today, too."

A moment of indecision flickered in Rose's eyes, then she propped the dimpled point of her delicate chin in her hand and smiled. "No, actually, you know, I'm just starving for some lunch and I believe the next little girl needing a haircut isn't coming in for a good long while yet."

"Oh. Well..."

Her smile dared him to search for another way to run her off. But Ben found he couldn't think that clearly. He was too caught up in the way her smile transformed her delicate features into something lush, almost sensuous. Her face was heart-shaped, her chestnut hair rising in a dramatic widow's peak from a broad forehead. Her eyes were wide and long-lashed, her nose slim and straight—not a hint of upturned cuteness about it.

But her mouth, small and echoing the heart shape of her face...ah, that was what he kept coming back to. Kissing that mouth would be one devil of a dangerous thing.

"So, where you folks headed?"

He turned his attention back to the chicken-fried steak on his plate and reminded himself that he had to be very careful with this woman. He tried to form a safe answer, then looked up from his plate to discover that Krissy had also turned a questioning gaze in his direction. His throat constricted. Now what?

"We're...um...just sightseeing." He reached over and tweaked Krissy's nose, noting with increased discomfort that she had puckered her forehead in a confused frown. "Right, Kris?"

He barely risked a glance at Rose, whose brows arched high on her forehead. "Sightseeing? Well, I can sure see how you ended up in Sweetbranch. Guess you're checking out the old abandoned blue jean plant. And there's always a crowd of tourists down at the strip mine swimming hole. Shoot, Sweetbranch is a real mecca for tourists, especially this time of year, Mr....?''

Her voice trailed off in a question. Ben was grateful when the waitress zipped past, pausing long enough to refill his iced-tea glass and frown at Rose.

"You gonna sit here and jaw all afternoon or you gonna take them lunches back to the shop? Alma's on the phone. Says she's so hungry her belly thinks her throat's been cut. What you want me to tell her, Rose?''

"Tell her I'm having lunch with a client, Mellie." Rose smiled up, serenely unperturbed by the waitress's sharp tongue. "Tell her to have a pack of cheese crackers and keep her shirt on. And the first chance you get, maybe you could bring my take-out box over here."

Mellie stopped, stared, raked a quick glance over Ben and Krissy, nodded and started back toward the counter. "Gotcha."

Ben could barely swallow a bite as he watched Rose, an unconcerned smile on her face, wave to someone else across the diner. When she turned her attention back to him, he busied himself buttering a roll for Krissy.

"I guess Sweetbranch is one of those places you've been meaning to see all your life. Is that it?''

Ben cleared his throat and was spared answering when Krissy piped up, "We went to the park."

As Rose engaged Krissy in a detailed discussion of the many delights the small town park held, Ben relaxed enough to get down a few bites of his lunch. There wasn't much Krissy could say that would endanger them—she knew nothing to reveal, he assured himself. Some of the tension that knotted his shoulders and stomach eased away as he half listened to her babbling about the giant stuffed Pooh Bear in the church nursery at home and the goldfish that had died last week and the alphabet song her Uncle Keith was teaching her.

He had almost convinced himself there was nothing to be wound up over when Krissy at last ran out of steam and Rose turned to him and said, "I'm sorry, we haven't really met. I'm Rose Finley. And you're..."

And she held out her hand and he took it in his. It was small and warm and fine-boned and gentle and he forgot everything except the feel of it in his hand as he blurted out, "Ben. Ben McKenzie."

She held his hand just a moment longer, giving it an extra squeeze before letting it go. "That's good, Ben McKenzie. I was beginning to wonder if you were going to be evasive about that, too."

Damn! Here he'd done the one thing his contact in the park had clearly told him not to do. Ben felt the prickle of perspiration down the middle of his back and, with an effort of will, forced himself to relax. It was done. There was no undoing it. And how much harm could it be, anyway? It wasn't likely that the big news of his disappearance would make its way to Sweetbranch, Alabama, anytime soon. He wasn't famous or anything. Big deal.

But one thing was certain. He had to change the direction of the conversation. This Rose Finley was asking all the questions. That had to change.

"So, where'd you come here from, Ben and Krissy?"

Krissy opened her mouth to reply and Ben knew he had to forestall any more inadvertent revelations.

"We'd rather know about you, Ms. Finley. Wouldn't we, Krissy?" Without waiting for a reply, he fired a question at Rose. "Have you lived in Sweetbranch all your life?"

Rose laughed as she opened the white carry-out box the waitress set in front of her. "I have lived in Sweetbranch forever. Although some folks would say that it just seems like forever. Even a weekend in Sweetbranch seems to last forever. You know what I mean?"

The good humor flashing in her soft brown eyes reached out to him and he relaxed slightly. He smiled back at her and found himself picturing a young Rose Finley, growing up a little cheeky and a little itchyfooted in this small town. And he could see her now, still a little cheeky and a little itchy. What he couldn't see was what had happened in all the years in between.

"So why are you still here?"

Some of the light went out of her eyes for a moment. Then she seemed to recover and resumed splashing vinegar over her collard greens. "Oh, you know how it is. The bright lights. The glamor. That feeling of being on the edge of something big about to happen. Why, I was here when they dedicated the new annex at the

Sweetbranch First Freewill Baptist Church. And the year the high school wrestling team came in third in the entire state." She paused. "Sometimes the pace is breathless."

Ben realized he had been paying less attention to what she was saying than he had been to the soft, flowing cadence of her voice. In the cities of North Carolina, the Southern drawl had been so diluted it melded comfortably with the other varied speech patterns heard these days in the Sun Belt.

In Rose Finley's voice, the South had, indeed, risen again.

"Don't knock it. You have things here a lot of cities would envy."

Clicking her fork against the edge of her carry-out box and narrowing her eyes, Rose pursed her lips and studied him closely before she spoke again. "What is it this morning? Somebody declared sainthood for small towns, right?"

The friendly challenge in her voice swept through Ben and he remembered what he'd missed about women in the two years since he and Cybil had divorced. City women, professional women, were just like city men—so pressured, so serious, so focused on the economy, on the crime rate, on the issues of today. To them, a conversation that was only half-serious—while the other half was fun—was hardly worth the having in a world where every second had to count.

In that world, he reminded himself, the small business owner wouldn't have had the time to toss her plans out the window and stop for an unexpected lunch.

He grinned, barely noticing the lightening of his mood, it felt so natural. "You mean you missed the news? Congress held the vote last night. They're limiting metropolitan populations to ten thousand. Cities have two years to comply or all federal funds will be withdrawn. The president is threatening to veto and the street gangs are behind him one hundred percent."

Rose laughed. "Another brilliant move from Washington. No more symphony orchestras to worry about or art galleries or lecture series on college campuses. We can concentrate all our attention on the important things in life—country craft shows and church bake sales."

She was teasing, he knew, as he had been. But he also knew she was gently complaining about life in a town so small and quiet and out of the way that it hadn't even warranted a freeway exit.

"Actually, it might not be such a bad plan." As he looked around, Ben found pleasure in the soothing quality of a diner full of people who knew one another by first name. People whose families had no doubt known one another for generations. "Big-city excitement is vastly overrated."

"Which big city are you speaking of?"

"Most of them."

"Including the one you're...getting away from for a while?"

And he knew from the way she phrased her question that Rose Finley was not so small-town gullible that she hadn't raised her suspicions. He'd been entirely too evasive, too leery of her interest and her friendliness. It was just the kind of thing that was likely to stand out in a place like Sweetbranch. He would have to remember that. Being careful was one thing. Being mysterious was something else entirely.

He shrugged away her question and countered with another of his own. "You must like *something* about Sweetbranch."

"Yeah. I like knowing at least a dozen people who'll lend a hand when something goes wrong. Walking home after dark without having to worry about it. Watching the babies grow up and start Little League." She chuckled and looked around. "And the gossips. Why, do you realize that by the time church lets out tomorrow, everybody in town will know more about our lunch together than we know?"

With instant comprehension, Ben knew she was right. It didn't even matter if he was extra careful not to look over his shoulder. Just being a stranger in this town meant everyone would be talking about him. He shifted uneasily in the booth. None of this was going exactly the way it was supposed to.

"Yep, you've got to watch out for us small-town gossips, Mr. McKenzie." And with a wicked twinkle in her eye, Rose closed the lid over her lunch, wiped her fingers on the paper napkin in her lap and leaned closer. "Now, how long y'all going to be in Sweetbranch? You never did say. And I'm going to have to have something to tell all these nosy folks when they start asking tomorrow."

With the sound of imagined gossip ringing in his ear, Ben knew he needed a good story. Now. She might be joking around, just giving him a playful poke in the ribs. But he still had to tell her something that added up.

"Actually, I'm not sure. We're...I'm thinking of relocating. Somewhere out of the city. I'm not sure the city's a good place to bring up a child these days. So, we're looking around. We might stay awhile and...see how we like Sweetbranch."

She leaned back in the booth and leveled her brown eyes on him. He couldn't quite fathom the look she gave him; it flitted too quickly from disbelief to mistrust to acceptance. "What business are you in, Mr. McKenzie?"

Another flimsy answer would be one too many, he knew. He deliberately retrieved his glass often from the table and took a long swallow. Thinking time. Just a moment to collect his wits. That's all he needed.

"Sales." He breathed a sigh of relief. Sales. Simple. Open-ended. Nonspecific. Safe.

"Sales?" Her stare didn't waver, although he caught a glimpse of stifled humor in her brown eyes. "Shoes or office equipment? Just in case somebody asks me, of course."

He stared dumbly. Now she grinned outright. He was making a botch of this. A good thing he hadn't said he was in the CIA. It was painfully obvious that intrigue wasn't his game.

"I said, what line of goods do you peddle, Mr. McKenzie?"

She was teasing him, giving him a taste of small-town nosiness. If it hadn't made him so damned nervous, he would've paused to consider how much he was drawn to her ability to make her point. She should've been a lawyer.

"Sporting goods." The words spilled out without his giving them much thought. It didn't seem to matter. Very little, it seemed, was safe around Rose Finley.

She let the silence settle between them. Even Krissy was silent, her attention now shifted from the half-eaten plate of spaghetti she had pushed out of the way to the paper placemat and crayons the waitress had brought when they took the booth. Ben waited, nervously, for Rose's next salvo. But she said nothing, just kept her unwavering brown eyes directed on him, those perfect lips softened by an enigmatic smile.

The silence finally got to him. He was uncomfortable wondering just what she was thinking about. He needed to fill the silence, to get her mind off whatever it was speculating on so shrewdly.

"Of course, not strictly sporting goods. I mean, I've sold other things, too. Like office supplies. I have sold office supplies." Cracking under interrogation. That's what he was doing. "Of course, right now I'm sort of between jobs."

And that, he realized as he saw her expression change, was at last the correct answer. Her eyes softened, the mocking half smile left her face. He had deftly, brilliantly—and completely by accident—explained away his uncertainty and his evasiveness and his obvious discomfort.

"I see." Her voice was soft, too. He almost expected her to reach over and pat his hand. Her instant concern was almost his undoing—he felt the most absurd urge to confess his lie. "Well, I'm sure things'll look up soon, Mr. McKenzie. Although you ought to know, Sweetbranch isn't exactly booming, jobwise."

"Well, we'll probably hang around awhile. See what comes up." His eyes darted around the diner. Where was the waitress? Where was his check? How soon could he extricate himself from this discussion before he was in so deep that...

"Where are you and Krissy staying while you're here, Mr. McKenzie?"

He quickly regrouped. Did this question need yet another lie in the sticky web of falsehoods he was weaving? No, he decided. This one needed the truth. Because in Sweetbranch, word would travel fast once he and Krissy checked in at the motel his contact had recommended. He gave Rose the name of the motel.

"Mr. McKenzie, I don't mean to stick my nose in this, but that's not the best place to stay with a little girl. Especially if you might be here for a while. It's...well..." She glanced at Krissy, who was vigorously creating a blue-faced fairy princess on her paper placemat. "Well, it's sort of a local rendezvous spot, if you know what I mean. And the walls are thin."

Suddenly, her face darkened in a blush. "At least, that's what I've heard. That the walls are thin. I personally wouldn't know."

Ben found himself smiling again. Here he'd had her pegged for someone who could brazen out anything and she was turning red-faced over the reputation of the local rent-by-the-hour motel.

"Well, I appreciate your concern, but there really isn't much else to choose from in Sweetbranch, is there?"

"The best thing to choose in Sweetbranch would be the highway out of town."

Ben shook his head.

"But if you're determined to stay..." She paused. He saw her eyes widen with an idea, then saw her struggle to suppress it. The idea won out. She tapped the table with her fist. "I'll tell you what, Mr. McKenzie, you and Krissy can stay with us."

"Us?"

"Uncle Bump and me. We've got a big old house and it's just the two of us and we've been talking about renting out a couple of the upstairs bedrooms and..."

"Oh, we couldn't do that. Why..."

"Sure you can. This isn't the city, Mr. McKenzie. This is just Sweetbranch. It makes a lot more sense than being cooped up in a dingy old motel room all day."

"No, I really don't think..." He felt the tug on his sleeve and glanced down at Krissy, who was staring up with a gleam of excitement in her big blue eyes. He shook his head at her. "No, we really couldn't do that."

"Why not, Daddy?"

"Well, because..." Why not, indeed? Because they were supposed to be keeping a low profile. Because a three-year-old might not remember she wasn't supposed to mention her mommy. Because it was dangerous to get involved with the charming Rose Finley and her uncle. What kind of name was Uncle Bump, anyway? What was he, a retired Mafia hit man? "Your uncle might not appreciate the intrusion, and besides..."

"Uncle Bump? Shoot, he'll love it. He loves kids." She waved at the waitress for their checks, as if the issue were decided. "Besides, he could look after Krissy while you scout around for a job. You'll like Uncle Bump. Well, maybe not right away. But once you get used to him, you'll realize he's just an old softie acting tough. He and Krissy'll get on great together. What do you say?"

"Pwease, Daddy. Pwease, I want to stay with Auntie Wose. And Unka Bunk."

He looked down into Krissy's persuasive eyes, thinking how nice it would be for her to stay here, that it might help her face the times when she missed her mother and her toys and her own pink-and-white bedroom. Ben knew he was sunk. Right now, the sadness and accusations he feared seeing in Krissy's eyes were a lot more threatening than the stern look of his contact in the park a few hours ago.

What was it she'd said? That the day might come when Krissy would hate him for what he was doing. He let out the breath he'd been holding.

"Well, I don't want to be a bother..."

THE OIL in the old cast-iron skillet was so hot it would be smoking any minute, but Rose still had to toss the chicken pieces in flour and right now she was up to her elbows in potato peelings. Uncle Bump was right—she should've let him do the cooking while she aired out the two extra rooms upstairs. With five pounds of chicken to fry for dinner on the church grounds tomorrow, along with a big bowl of potato salad, what on earth had possessed her to pick this afternoon to try to prove she knew her way around a kitchen when everybody was well aware...

The loud bang was right over her head and she ducked instinctively, looking up through squinting eyes to make sure the ceiling wasn't coming in on her. It wasn't, but it might be before long.

Dropping the potato peeler into the sink, she stepped up to the stove and gingerly pushed the skillet off the burner. Then she walked into the hall, wiping her fingers on the terry-cloth dish towel she had tucked into her jeans for an apron, and peered up the stairs. "Are you still alive or should I send for the undertaker?"

Much thumping and thrashing and muttering ensued before Uncle Bump's face appeared at the top of the stairs. It was red—except where two days' growth of snowy whiskers obscured the view—clear to the top of his head. The fringe of white hair over his ears and the wisps that were all he had left on top were scattered helter-skelter. The tail of his red-and-black flannel shirt was dribbling out of his pants on one side and his bright yellow suspenders were flying at half-mast.

His thin face was—of course—engaged in a furious scowl.

Rose smiled. "I said..."

"I heard you. Now, where the hell did you say you kept the goldang sheets for the..."

"In the cedar chest in Frank's old room." Rose wiped her face with her sleeve to hide her deepening smile. Wouldn't do for

Uncle Bump to see her smiling when he was having so much fun being irascible. "Uncle Bump, you'll have to watch your language now that we're going to have a little girl in the house."

"Watch my language? In my own home?" He gripped the worn newel post at the top of the stairs and leaned toward her. "If I wanted to watch my language, I'd go live in one of those old folks' homes with a bunch of prissy old women who could have a mouthful of horse poop and still wouldn't say…"

"Jacob Ebeneezer Finley!" Rose hastened to interrupt him. She knew the phrase that followed from many hearings and it was just the kind of homespun profanity that she wanted to nip in the bud. "You be nice, now. I mean it."

"What do we need with a bunch of strangers moving in with us, anyway? They'll probably rob us blind. City folks. And a young'un. I'm too old to put up with a young'un running around making a racket. Rosie, you're not going senile on me, are you?"

Rose had wondered about that herself. In fact, she hadn't even been able to tell Bunny and Alma the big news when she'd finally made it back to the Picture Perfect. She'd just listened to them fume about their late lunch and clamped her mouth shut when they'd bugged her for an explanation.

They'd hear all about it soon enough.

"You listen up, girl!" Uncle Bump's growl demanded her attention. "Have you got any idea how the tongues are gonna wag in this town when word gets around you've invited a man to live here with you and your doddering old fool uncle?"

Rose merely laughed at that. "Since when do you care what people in this town wag their tongues about?"

That stopped him cold. His scowl faded. His grunt turned into a chuckle, which he quickly stifled and swallowed. "*I* ain't supposed to care. *You* are."

"Me being the maiden niece, you mean?"

Uncle Bump screwed his face up in displeasure and waved a gnarled finger at her. "If you tell me one more time that you're not a maiden anyway, I'll eat a dozen eggs for breakfast all by myself tomorrow morning. Send my cholesterol right through the roof. Some things you're just not supposed to bring up, you hear me, girl?"

Rose merely laughed. "Uncle Bump, if Sweetbranch wants to talk, let it."

Satisfaction welled up in her as she tossed off the flippant words. Truth was, that was half the reason she'd made the offer to Ben McKenzie in the first place. The thought of shocking some of the narrow minds in Sweetbranch gave her a little thrill on a day when she'd had it with her hometown—had it all the way up to the starched white collar of her uniform.

The other half of the reason was to assuage her guilt over being one of those nosy small-towners when it came to Ben McKenzie, when the truth turned out to be simple. He was out of work. Who wouldn't be edgy?

Then there was the way Ben McKenzie made her feel a little reckless every time she looked into those bottomless blue eyes. But that would really give Uncle Bump—and the Widow Clancy and half the Women's Auxiliary of the First Freewill Baptist Church—apoplexy.

"Now, I've got chicken to fry for dinner tomorrow. Get those sheets on the bed. And don't forget to put towels out in the bathroom."

"Towels? Where in the..."

"In the chifforobe right behind you."

He turned away, grumbling and snarling over the disruption in his day. Before Rose could get back to the kitchen and return the skillet of oil to the flame, the trill of the front doorbell froze her in her tracks.

She stared at the door. Through the crisp white lace over the oval window, she could see the shadow of someone tall. And someone short. Her breath caught in her throat.

What in the world had she done?

"What're you staring at, girl? Open the blasted door. Ain't getting cold feet, are you?"

Rose didn't have to look over her shoulder to recognize the wicked teasing in Uncle Bump's voice.

Every instinct in her body told her to straighten her hair, check her face for flour dust, yank the red-and-white-checked towel from the waistband of her jeans. But she didn't. Couldn't, with those sharp brown eyes boring into her back. So she merely walked to the door and flung it open, mustering a smile.

What had she done, indeed?

He looked uncomfortable standing on the wooden porch, a battered gym bag in one hand and a Raggedy Ann backpack draped over his shoulder. Krissy clung to his other side, one hand in his, one thumb in her mouth, head lowered, eyes wide and peeking beneath the fringe of her new bangs.

As the early spring day had warmed, Ben had shed his cotton sweater and tied it around the straps of the backpack. The sleeves of his white cotton shirt were rolled halfway up his arms. His forearms caught her eye—solid and tan and dusted with sandy brown hair.

Rose swallowed hard and tried to dampen her lips, but her tongue, if anything, was drier yet. He was here. And what was she going to do with him?

And what was she going to do with herself and these crazy, wild ideas he stirred up in her? Well, Uncle Bump always said if you were going to make a fool of yourself, you might as well have a juicy tale to tell out of it.

And wouldn't Ben McKenzie—solid arms, ice blue eyes, silver curls and all—make one heck of a juicy story to tell around the bridge table when she was sixty-two?

CHAPTER FIVE

ROSE WILLED HERSELF to ignore the foolishness that was warming her body. She looked Ben straight in the eye and smiled. "Well. So you're here."

He looked as nervous as she felt. "It's four o'clock. You said four. If you've changed your mind..."

She stepped back quickly to gesture them in. "No. Oh, no. It's fine. Come on in."

But Ben didn't move. Krissy tugged on his arm, gesturing for him to pick her up. Ben didn't respond. His eyes were on Rose, a spine-tingling blue and direct.

"No, I mean, if you've changed your mind...we could still check in down at the motel." He made a slight move in the direction of the yard. "You don't have to explain. This probably wasn't a good idea in the first place and..."

Rose barely listened to him stumbling his way toward retreat. With a few more awkward phrases, he would be backing off the porch toward the nondescript station wagon she saw parked in the drive. He would be gone and this wild notion of hers would disappear and not haunt her anymore.

Life would go on as usual.

"No, we've been waiting for you. Please don't go."

She saw his hesitation and doubted this was a man who was accustomed to being at the mercy of people's kindness. He might not be a Hollywood secret agent, but he had the air of a man whose decisions went unchallenged, who never had to ask anyone for anything.

Did he feel she was offering charity? she wondered, noting the grim hardness of his lips while she tried to ignore the welter of goose bumps that quivered over her skin.

"Really, Uncle Bump and I have just been talking about how

grand it's going to be to have some life in this old house again.''
Grateful for an excuse to turn away from the man who was making her do and feel such unlikely things, she looked around at
Uncle Bump, who had made his way down the stairs. ''Weren't
we, Uncle Bump? Just the two of us, it's downright empty-
feeling. Isn't it?''

Uncle Bump didn't respond. He stood a few steps behind her,
his wrinkled shirttail billowing out unevenly, his wiry white hair
floating wildly, his arthritis-knotted, tobacco-stained fingers rubbing the whiskers on his chin so roughly Rose could swear she
heard the rasp. Her stomach gave a little turn. He looked totally
reprehensible. She was used to it. But it suddenly occurred to her
that Ben McKenzie might not be overly eager to have his daughter
in the same house with a seventy-two-year-old man who looked
like he slept in the barn.

Worse even than his appearance, which resisted all efforts at
grooming, was the look he was giving Ben McKenzie—a look
that always preceded some outrageous remark. Rose started to fill
the silence, but it was too late.

''You ain't after my niece's money, are you?''

Rose grabbed a fistful of his shirtsleeve. ''Jacob Ebeneezer
Finley, I thought I told you to behave!''

She glanced back at Ben and Krissy and saw that, surprisingly,
a reluctant grin was spreading across Ben's face, softening those
strain-stiffened lips. She felt the shiver again. She released her
hold on her uncle's shirt.

''No, sir, I'm not.''

Uncle Bump smothered his own grin behind a stern nod.
''That's good. She ain't got none, you know.''

Rose threw up her hands. Well, at least Ben was getting a good
dose of Uncle Bump before he even walked through the door. He
could decide for himself whether to put up with the sharp-tongued
old cuss.

She glanced apologetically at Ben, too embarrassed to look him
full in the eye. ''You can see for yourself what it's like around
here. If you'd like to stay, we'd like to have you.'' She jabbed
her uncle in his bony ribs with her elbow. ''Wouldn't we?''

''Yeah, sure.'' Now he smiled, an angelic, grandfatherly smile
that belied his causticity. ''I'd like a younger woman around the
place for a change.''

He stepped to the front door and started to squat in front of Krissy, but Rose could see that his stiff knees and even stiffer back wouldn't let him lower himself. Instead, he reached into his hip pocket and pulled out a bit of feather and fluff and opened his palm to hold it down for Krissy to examine.

"Know what that is?"

Krissy huddled closer to Ben's leg for a moment, looking up at her father for some sign that this scruffy-looking old man was safe to approach. At Ben's nod, she loosened her grip on his knee and leaned over to peer into Uncle Bump's palm.

"Ever seen one of those?"

She looked up at him. As she peered at him with those deep blue eyes she had inherited from her father, she obviously saw something that struck a chord. With a timid smile, she said almost inaudibly, "Nosir."

Uncle Bump nodded and held out the fuzzy item so she could take it from him, which she did, turning it over and over in her pudgy hands.

"That's a streamer fly, young lady. Use it for fishing. Looks like a minnow wigglin' around in the water. 'Course, that one ain't got a hook on it. It's broke. You ever been fishing?"

Krissy stared, then blew on the feathery article and watched it flutter. She giggled at the motion, then again looked up at Ben for reassurance. When he smiled—a tender smile that somehow reassured Rose, too—Krissy looked back at Uncle Bump, her expression now less tentative. "Nosir."

Uncle Bump put his hand on her shoulder. "But didja ever catch lightning bugs and put 'em in a jar to light up your room at night?"

She giggled again. "Nosir."

"Eat honeysuckle?"

"Nosir."

Uncle Bump shook his head, a mock-serious expression on his face, and slowly led Krissy into the house. "Well then, young lady, you and me's got a lot to work on. A lot to work on. That's quite a shiner you had there. I'll remember not to cross you. Now, how about fried chicken? I know you've eaten it, but didja ever cook it? I've got some in here right now that Rosie's been trying to cook to take to the church tomorrow. But she's not much of a cook—don't hold that against her, now—and I think you and me's going to have to save the day. What do you say to that?''

And they disappeared into the kitchen, leaving Rose staring at Ben across the threshold. His eyes followed the two, the timid little girl and the garrulous old man, with a look of gratitude that seemed strangely out of proportion to Uncle Bump's simple act of welcome. After the two disappeared through the kitchen door, Ben continued to stare for several seconds before he turned his gaze slowly to Rose.

She smiled and shrugged. ''Well, I guess it's settled, then. Come on up and I'll show you your rooms.''

He nodded and she led him up the stairs to the big, airy room that had been her brother Frank's.

It wasn't much changed from the day almost thirty-five years ago when Frank left home for college in Tuscaloosa. It was clean and neat, with faint triangles faded into the yellow walls where school banners had been taken down a few years ago. The single bed with its brown chenille spread looked short and narrow as she imagined Ben McKenzie crawling into it tonight.

''This was my brother's room. I hope it'll be all right.'' And with the image of Ben McKenzie sprawled on the bed, she backed out of the room quickly, stumbling against him and springing away as if burned. ''Uncle Bump and I, we use the bedrooms downstairs now. So we won't...we won't get in your way much.''

''I just hope we won't get in your way much.''

He set his gym bag inside the door and she gestured down the hall to the next door. ''I hope you don't mind Uncle Bump...he's really sweet. But if you don't think it's a good idea for him to spend much time with Krissy, I could...''

''I like him already. Anybody who can make Krissy smile is okay by me.''

She nodded and opened the door to the next room. Her room when she was a little girl. The window beside the bed overlooked the backyard, had a wonderful view of the path to the creek and the falling-down doghouse where Scout had lived his thirteen years. The room was still pink and ruffles—LaFern Finley had never acknowledged that daughter Rose would be a tomboy no matter what frilly trappings were forced on her. A shelf of dolls lined the wall over the white chest of drawers.

Rose was self-consciously aware as she studied the room she

hadn't really looked at in years that it was old-fashioned and outdated.

"Krissy can sleep here if you think that's okay. It was…it was my room." She laughed nervously, almost apologetically. "Mama always wanted me to be a girl."

Ben laughed with her and the sound encouraged her to turn around and look at him. Fine lines crinkled around the eyes that had so mesmerized her. His smile was gentle, and again she was struck by a look of gratitude that seemed to far outstrip the little bit of hospitality she was extending. Ben looked around the room and Rose would almost have sworn she saw his eyes glistening with moisture.

"I think she'll feel happy and…safe here. Thank you, Rose Finley."

ROSE FELT RESTLESS. Cooped up. In the dim glow of the overhead light in the entrance hall, she stared at the living room, at the chintz, high-backed couch she should have recovered years ago— or replaced. Why not replace it altogether? she wondered. Where was it written that nothing in your life ever got to change completely? And then there was the carved mantel, overpopulated with family pictures, and the threadbare afghan her mother had labored over decades ago, spilling now over the back of the bentwood rocker.

She could easily have been ten years old again, she thought. The only changes in the big living room were the soft pink she'd painted the walls a few years back and the waist-high weeping fig shedding its leaves in front of the side window. Other than that, it was the same sweet and homey room that had made her ache to break out when she was ten.

Rose smiled as she turned back to lock the front door for the evening. Some things, she thought, never change. Like restless Rose Finley, always wishing she could go after whatever was waiting around the bend in the road.

The calico cat curled around her ankles and took two steps toward her bedroom, beckoning her with a soft trill.

"Okay, Boo. I'm coming."

As she hooked the screen, she heard footsteps creak overhead. Her eyes went up automatically. Okay, so there were momentary changes. But not real changes. Not the kind of changes that re-order your life.

The smells of spring from outside and the fading echoes of the afternoon and evening from behind her made Rose pause. She couldn't quite shut out the balmy night air, couldn't quite close the door on this day, which had, after all, turned out to be quite unlike any of her other days in Sweetbranch. Instead of closing the big oak door and following Boo to bed, she unlatched the screen and walked out onto the porch.

The April air was a cool caress on her skin. She raised her face to it, then followed it into the yard. It was almost ten o'clock and no one else was stirring on Dixie Belle Lane. Up and down the wide, oak-lined street, houses were dark or lighted only with the soft glow of reading lamps peeping through lace curtains. Sweetbranch was curling up for the night.

Tempted by the taste of fresh air and solitude, Rose wandered through the yard. She thought of slipping off her shoes to see if the grass was still dew-wet, night-cool. But she didn't.

"That's not a forty-minus-a-week kind of thing to do," she whispered to the ten-year-old she felt stirring in her.

She walked through the yard, pausing to lean over the hedge of azaleas to see how much they had unfurled during the warm, sunny day. Quite a lot, actually. Maybe this June after the blooms had faded, she would trim and shape the bushes and fertilize them. Anything that kept blooming after so much neglect deserved to be cared for.

She continued her wandering around the side of the house. Her eyes strayed upward to the room that had been her brother's. It was dark, as it had been for years, except when Frank and his brood came for holidays or rare visits. Now she wondered if Ben lay in the bed, looking through his window at the star-flecked sky. Was he asleep? Or was he, like her, feeling restless?

More fantasies, she told herself. *This is Sweetbranch, not Hollywood, Finley.*

She kept moving, into the backyard, where she remembered for the second time that day her childhood delight in vandalizing her mother's clothesline. There were no clothes on the line now, although she was suddenly immersed in the clean, fresh fragrance of a shirt that had dried in the summer breeze. With that fragrance in her nostrils, she suddenly laughed and loped under the clothesline, batting at an imaginary towel, sending it billowing over itself to wrap around the line and arouse her mother's irritation.

Rose was surprised, as her pace slowed, to realize she had laughed out loud at her foolish pantomime. She was also surprised to find herself at the foot of the century-old tree that housed the Finley tree house.

The boards nailed into the massive tree trunk as footholds looked wobbly, as indeed the tree house itself did in broad daylight. Rose reached out to wiggle the nearest foothold and found she couldn't move it. Nor could she move the next one. They held staunchly, as if in readiness for the next generation of Finleys.

Which will be a long, long wait, Rose thought. She stared up into the tree, which was just beginning to fill out with new leaves. The tree house, she realized, wasn't as far from the ground as she had remembered.

Without thinking it through, she placed one foot on the first foothold and hoisted herself off the ground. Then up to the next foothold, and the next, her heart beginning to thud and her grin growing wider the closer she came to the platform spanning four sturdy branches. She had a hand on the floor of the tree house, checking it for rickety boards, when a voice at her feet startled her.

"So this is what you do for excitement in Sweetbranch."

With a muffled gasp, Rose jumped slightly, one foot almost slipping off its foothold before she regained control. It was Ben. Sneaking around in the dark. She remembered the look of hard mistrust in his eyes when he'd first walked into the Picture Perfect.

"I scared you. I'm sorry."

His voice was as soft as the night. Rose shivered, and reminded herself how Ben's eyes softened when he looked at Krissy.

"No, just startled. That's all." And because she could think of no more reasonable action, she finished her climb into the tree house.

As she sat on the edge, legs dangling over the side, a freshly sprouting limb tickling the top of her head, the stars a few feet closer than they had been just minutes before, Rose laughed again.

"Come on up. It's the best spot in town for a panoramic view of Sweetbranch."

When she looked down, he was peering up at her, his face mostly shadows, his hair shining moonlight silver. It looked soft. As soft as his jaw looked hard. She shivered again in the cool air.

"Is it safe?"

She laughed again, this time a breathless, skittery sound. *Is it safe?* "I'm wondering that myself."

He bounded up the blocks, quickly, agilely. Only when he reached the top and scrambled onto the wooden platform beside her did she notice that his left knee seemed stiff, less limber than the rest of his lithe, muscular frame.

He looked around the tree house and seemed to decide it was more than satisfactory.

"So, can you see the tallest building from here?"

Rose laughed again. So much laughing. If she didn't watch herself, she could get used to the idea of laughing. It felt so...young. "I think this *is* the tallest building."

And he laughed with her. His laugh was soft, rolling up from somewhere deep in his chest and spilling over her like a fuzzy blanket. This time, she knew, the shiver wasn't from the cool air at all. She pulled her arms tightly around her but knew they offered no protection from what was coursing through her body.

"Is this your nightly bedtime ritual? Communing with the stars?"

"I haven't communed with the stars like this since..." She hesitated. She wasn't sure she wanted to tell him how long it had been, then realized how foolish that was. He could see for himself that she'd hardly been born yesterday. "It's been almost twenty-five years, I guess. Not since Arnold Turner followed me up here and kissed me on the lips and I pushed him out and broke his arm in two places. And smashed his glasses. Mama grounded me all summer. But at least I figured out I was more interested in Arnold Turner than I was in climbing trees. I was fifteen—I guess I should've already figured that out. Uncle Bump said us Finleys have always been late bloomers."

"That explains it, then."

She blushed in the dark, his voice suddenly reminding her that she wasn't just reminiscing into the night or blabbing to Alma

She was sitting here in the darkness with Ben McKenzie, a perfect stranger. A very perfect stranger. Yakking on about some foolishness that had happened a lifetime ago.

She tried to shrug off her concern. As if it mattered what he thought of her, anyway. "Explains what?"

"Why you look ten years younger than any other forty-year-old woman I've ever met. Being a late bloomer has its obvious advantages."

He is not flirting with me, she told herself. *He's being polite. Gallant.* After all, his slight drawl told her he was a Southerner—and therefore no doubt a gentleman—even though he was, as Uncle Bump called him, a city slicker.

She almost giggled at the phrase, then remembered what Ben had said.

"And you have a silver tongue, Mr. Ben McKenzie."

They lapsed into silence, listening for night sounds. A dog howled in the distance. A few early crickets tuned up for the chorus that summer would bring.

Rose was surprised to realize that she felt comfortable in the silence, in the darkness, with Ben McKenzie at her side. Not the way you would expect to feel with a stranger, much less a man whose presence seemed to vibrate through the peaceful evening. She was so aware of him, so aware she was tempted to reach out, touch him, test the power of that presence.

"Tonight was nice, Rose."

"A little dull, I know." She was glad she couldn't see the evening through his eyes. For her, it had been better than the typical evenings in Sweetbranch. After the four of them ate dinner—after frying chicken for Sunday dinner, Uncle Bump and Krissy had discovered they had a real way with ground beef and noodles and cream of mushroom soup, too—they had sat in the living room. Uncle Bump taught Krissy to play checkers while Rose read. Ben had simply watched his daughter and Rose's uncle, although he had stood from time to time and paced the room uneasily. He had to be bored, Rose knew. But despite her restlessness and Ben's boredom, there had been laughter in the house. And Uncle Bump had even coaxed their new housemates into coming for dinner on the grounds at the church tomorrow.

Maybe, she thought, that would be a little less boring than a long Sunday afternoon at the Finley home.

"Not dull. There's a difference between dull and peaceful."

"I know."

"Do you really not know how special it is here, Rose? If I lived here, I'd never want to leave."

The dreamy, almost wistful tone of his voice made it impossible for Rose to deliver one of her usual flippant comments. "I know you're right. It's just... You've been other places. Seen other things. You aren't here because you have to be."

A hint of bitterness crept into Ben's voice. "I guess you could say that. I guess..."

He didn't say more. And Rose knew she didn't know him well enough to ask what he meant. Knew it was one more of those secrets he seemed to keep under lock and key. Like where he was from. Like why in the world he was looking for work in a place like Sweetbranch, which didn't have enough jobs to go around for the people who were already here.

And here she was, mooning over him, trying to turn him into some kind of mystery man, when the plain truth was he was nothing but a single father who'd lost his job to hard times like lots of other folks and was running scared, looking for a way out, looking for a better place.

And he thought Sweetbranch was it.

Well, who was she to tell him any different?

But all her hard-nosed skepticism didn't seem to make any difference when she sat here next to him in the darkness, thinking about the hard line of his lips earlier today and the faint furrow that stayed in his forehead even when he wasn't frowning any longer. Thinking about the pale hair dusting those hard, tan arms.

Yes, she was ready to make a fool of herself, all right. It was time to get stern with herself. "Well, it's getting late. Guess I'd better get myself inside."

He didn't move as she backed over the edge of the platform, seeking the first foothold with her toe.

"Good night, Rose."

"Good night, Ben."

As she walked through the yard, she let herself imagine that his eyes were on her, that he followed her movements through the yard, that his eyes lingered on her with longing.

She lay in bed for a long time that night, listening for his footfall on the steps when he came in and climbed the stairs to his room. Listening to the creak of the floor overhead, realizing with dismay that his room was directly over hers. She stared into the darkness, her eyes trained on the spot where he stood, moved, undressed.

Finally, unable to sleep, she eased out of bed and walked to the kitchen for a glass of juice. It was then that she heard his voice, whispering into the darkness. She realized he must be at the telephone table around the corner in the living room. She moved on until his next words registered.

"I'm not going to tell you where I am, Keith. What you don't know can't hurt you. Or me, either."

Eyes widening, heart thumping, Rose told herself she could hardly make judgments based on one side of a conversation. Nevertheless, she whirled silently and scurried back to her room, closing the door soundlessly behind her.

When she heard him climbing the stairs again a few minutes later, Rose wondered about the blind faith with which she'd accepted what little Ben McKenzie had told her about himself. Just because he and Krissy seemed so close, just because she automatically trusted the love she saw between them.

But the words he'd whispered into the telephone sounded so...suspicious. Could she have been wrong about him?

And she remembered the cold, hard look she'd seen more than once in Ben McKenzie's blue eyes. Soft voice aside, those eyes were telling. And, as much as she wanted to, she didn't trust what they told.

CHAPTER SIX

TWO TEENAGE BOYS PULLED off their choir robes, rolled up their starched white sleeves and propped open the double doors of the old brick church with stacks of Baptist hymnals. Music spilled onto the lawn, the sweet sopranos and round baritones and here and there a hearty bass. Joyous singing mingled with the wonderful smells of fried chicken and buttermilk biscuits and sweet potato pie.

It was homecoming at the Sweetbranch First Freewill Baptist Church, a day for rejoicing and welcome and dinner on the grounds.

Ben McKenzie felt as if he had, indeed, come home.

"Afternoon, neighbor!" A man not much older than Ben, wearing a plaid, short-sleeved shirt and an unraveled bow tie sticking out of his front pocket, thrust a hand in Ben's direction. "Believe you're new to town. I'm Melvin Smallwood. Run the garage down on Main. Welcome to Sweetbranch."

The first time it had happened, Ben had been taken aback. His first inclination had been to retreat, to tighten up and go stiff-lipped and back away as quickly as possible. But he had quickly learned it was just Sweetbranch's way. Whether motivated by curiosity or just plain friendliness, everyone seemed eager to meet a stranger in town.

"Nice to meet you, Mr. Smallwood. Ben McKenzie." The words were like a weight on his chest. He'd screwed up. He knew that. He'd known it the instant he told his real name to Rose Finley in the diner the afternoon before. But what could he do about it? Except keep blundering along.

"What brings you to Sweetbranch, Mr. McKenzie? We don't get many visitors."

Ben had to remind himself that the question was frank and

open; there was not a shade of distrust in Melvin Smallwood's hazel eyes.

"My daughter and I are...thinking about moving to your town." He'd grown a little less uncomfortable with the lie, although he was not quite so at ease that he would handle it glibly. Especially here, in the shadow of the church spire. He half expected to be struck down each time he perpetuated the lie.

"And that must be your little one." The mechanic pointed toward a cluster of children holding hands in a circle. Krissy, eyes closed and giggling, was spinning around unsteadily in the middle of the circle.

Ben felt the warmth enveloping his heart again. The sight of his little girl laughing and playing, instead of staring solemn-eyed and unspeaking as he had seen her so often lately, convinced him the lies were excusable. "That's her."

He talked a few more minutes with Melvin Smallwood, who promised to ask around about anyone looking for a salesman. Then they drifted apart, Smallwood toward the gospel singing in the church and Ben up to wooden tables where desserts were spread out invitingly.

And what'll you do if someone like Smallwood actually finds you a job offer? Ben wondered as he filled a paper plate with a generous slice of frothy coconut layer cake. *Good thing you didn't say you were a schoolteacher or a carpenter.*

It was hard to see, now that he was mired in fabrications, how anyone managed to keep up the charade. He supposed you got more adept as you went along. He could only hope.

As a bite of coconut icing and rich yellow cake melted in his mouth, Ben roamed the shady churchyard. He'd been reluctant to come to this event. He'd sensed Rose's ambivalence when her uncle first brought it up and hadn't wanted to do anything to upset her. But Uncle Bump—who was now sprawled in a folding chair under the biggest of the shade trees with a small enclave of old-sters—was persuasive. And when the old man had started filling Krissy's head with promises of chocolate cake and children's games and a choir that sounded just like angels from heaven, his daughter's big blue eyes pleading in Ben's direction had finished him off. Ben had no resolve these days when it came to refusing Krissy anything.

Mere minutes had passed this morning before Ben had sin-

cerely wished he hadn't given in so easily. One of the first faces
he'd seen was a glowing dark one topped with a crown of thick,
ropy braids. Maxine, the woman from the park, had looked
strangely out of place in this church full of ice-cream colored
linen suits and beflowered straw hats and not just because of the
wild splash of color in her wardrobe, either.

The stern set of her eyes and mouth as she'd visually castigated
him had been far different from the friendly, curious and open
gazes he'd received everywhere else.

Ben had looked down, acknowledging guiltily that he hadn't
followed her very explicit instructions. When he looked up, she
had moved away.

Well, he guessed that settled the question of whether he should
call her about his change in address. She knew. Or would very
soon.

Seeing her now, climbing the steps back into the sanctuary,
Ben felt once again the nagging unease. He hadn't meant to endanger the secrecy of her efforts. In fact, at the time he'd felt he
was doing the smart thing to blend right in. Now, plagued with
the memory of her accusing glare, he wondered if he hadn't simply chosen the easy route.

As he glanced across the lawn and saw a familiar form, Ben
realized that the whole truth might be more complicated than that.
Rose Finley had drawn him to her completely against his will and
his better judgment.

She sat with her back against the trunk of an oak that was older
than the church building, legs curled up around her, eyes closed,
face raised to the afternoon sun that peeked through the just
emerging leaves. The soft skirt of her dress was a circle of pale
green covering her legs and feet. The dress, he knew, wasn't
something he would find in one of the stylish catalogs or trendy
boutiques where Cybil did most of her shopping. It was decidedly
old-fashioned, in fact. But on Rose it looked just right, especially
with that chestnut hair pulled back from her face with two fancy
clips. She looked like someone's World War II sweetheart, the
all-American girl.

You sound like a romantic sap, he warned himself. *And this
isn't the time or the place for that.*

But even as he told himself to turn back around and lose himself in the crowd, Ben kept moving toward the woman who had opened her home to him.

"You haven't quit eating already, have you?"

Ben watched as she responded to his question with a slow smile. She didn't open her eyes.

"You aren't *still* eating, are you?" she countered.

"I sure am. I haven't seen food like this since the last time I went home to Mother." He dropped onto the ground beside her. His knee was almost touching the fabric of her skirt. He remembered the way it had swished over her hips when he'd walked up the church steps behind her. She was softly round, firm, all woman. And the sight of her had roused a hunger in him. A hunger that was part simple lust and part longing for something untouched by greed or ambition or sleek sophistication.

The hunger, he knew, must go unsatisfied.

So why are you sitting here at her knees like some fawning suitor?

"Enjoy it. You aren't likely to see cooking like this anytime soon on Dixie Belle Lane." Her eyes swept over him now, searching him for that unadorned truth he couldn't give her. "Uncle Bump hasn't won too many blue ribbons at the county fair for his home cooking."

"I don't know. He won Krissy over last night."

"I thought it was the other way around."

Ben smiled. "That's what she does best."

Rose pulled her knees up to rest her chin on them, tugging her skirt primly down around her ankles.

She looks like somebody's tomboy little sister, Ben thought, *the one who doesn't yet realize she's a heartbreaker.*

"I know. I saw right away she had you wrapped around her little pinky."

"I confess. I'm a besotted old dad. Putty in her hands." He licked the last of the sticky coconut icing off his fingers. "I was born again the minute I laid eyes on her."

Rose raised a slim eyebrow in question.

"I mean, she made me feel like I'd been given a second chance in life." Ben decided he'd better stop there. He hadn't meant to get into this. Just as he hadn't meant most of the things that had happened since he showed up in Sweetbranch. As if the town had taken charge of his life.

But Rose turned questioning, honey brown eyes on him and he wanted her to understand. The way he'd wanted *someone* to understand for three and a half years. And the openness in her eyes seemed to promise that she would. That promise wiped out the wariness he was supposed to be exercising.

"She was...I was almost forty when Krissy was born, you know. Long past the time for being a...I knew I wasn't cut out for all that family and fatherhood business." Ben read acceptance and understanding in her smile. "I was in business." He warned himself to be careful. "I was out for the fastest buck and the slickest deal. I didn't care who got squeezed, as long as I came out on top. I'd...I'd learned the hard way that nice guys finish last."

Ben pulled a piece of clover from the ground at his knee and twisted it in his hand. That Ben McKenzie seemed so unreal to him, but it was the Ben McKenzie he'd been for almost twenty years. The Ben McKenzie that came back from Vietnam. The Ben McKenzie who knew better than to trust.

"One little girl changed all that?"

Looking up into her face, Ben was captured by the uncomplicated curiosity in her eyes. He wondered if one look at Rose Finley's face in those days might not have worked a miracle, too. He doubted it. That Ben McKenzie would have looked at this woman and seen someone who couldn't fit into the tony life he had envisioned for himself.

"When I saw Krissy, some part of me..." Ben struggled for words. He'd never yet been able to make anyone understand. "It was like a part of me died...the ugly part, the aggressive, bullying, greedy part. And all that was left was this man who melted a little more every time he held his daughter in his arms. I was never the same after that. I turned into a real softie."

"And that changed a lot of things in your life?"

Ben felt his throat constrict. Any minute, his new landlady was going to find out just how big a softie he'd turned into. He swallowed hard and cleared his throat. "Yeah. A lot of things."

"Are you glad?"

Now Ben smiled. "Yeah. I'm glad. I wouldn't go back. I'm just sorry it took me forty years." Rose's answering smile faded and Ben knew he'd touched a nerve. "Do you have children, Rose?"

"No. I used to figure I would, but life had different ideas. And now...well, now it's way too late for me to be thinking about playing mama."

She didn't look him in the eye, but he heard the effort it took for her to put a touch of flippancy in her answer. Chin still propped on her knees, she faked a wry smile.

"Not so late." He wanted to touch her, to ease the fingers that had tightened on a fistful of her skirt, to smooth the fine, taut lines that had appeared on either side of her mouth. *Oh Lord, this isn't good. Not good at all.*

But her response wasn't what he expected. She treated him to one of her sharp grins and said, "If you think I'm going to saddle a poor little child with a middle-aged mama, you definitely are soft in the head."

Ben almost laughed out loud. But he saw a hint of something serious in her eyes and squelched the urge. "Now wait a minute. I happen to think us old-timers make great parents."

"Maybe." She shrugged, as if the whole conversation really mattered very little to her. "I guess my perspective's a little different from yours."

"Oh?"

She didn't answer right away. He studied her smooth face, looking for clues. But she kept her eyes carefully averted and everything else about her expression was completely serene and noncommittal.

He waited for the silence to get to her. Eventually it did.

"I guess I know what it's like to be an afterthought in somebody's life, Mr. McKenzie."

"An afterthought? Now what makes you think you were an afterthought?"

"My mother was forty-five when I was born, and in those days that didn't happen very often. Except by mistake." She grinned that what-the-hell grin, but he saw the vulnerability in the tight set of her lips. "Anyway, she didn't have much patience for chasing a young'un around the neighborhood. And then..."

Rose took a deep breath and he saw her shifting her skirt in preparation for standing. He put a hand on her arm and held her still. "Don't go. I'm not trying to pry. I just...I'm interested."

Her eyes rested on his and Ben was suddenly, painfully aware of the heat where their flesh met. The crook of her elbow, where his fingers rested, was warm, leaping with her pulse. Ben thought for a moment that he would shatter into a million pieces if he didn't lean close to her and cover her lips with his.

And didn't she feel the same way? Didn't he feel the pounding in her blood beneath the pad of his thumb? Didn't he see her longing in that fleeting moment when her eyes blurred and lost focus?

He dropped his hand. Then dropped his eyes long enough to break the spell. When he looked up again he gave her a shaky smile. "I don't think this is covered in the book of Southern Baptist homecoming etiquette."

Her soft laugh shook, too, and he was grateful she didn't try to pretend that whatever had happened between them hadn't happened.

"If it is, it's probably listed in the deadly sins category, Mr. McKenzie." She gathered her skirt safely around her knees and pushed herself off the ground.

He looked up at her as she stood over him, an uncertain smile on her lips. From this angle, the swell of her breasts beneath her fitted bodice struck him as the most alluring thing he'd ever seen. Silently, he blew out a quivering breath and stood. "No, Ms. Finley, sins get much deadlier than that."

He heard a little hiss of sound and realized Rose had gasped. Or sighed. From the look in her eyes, he wasn't sure which.

"I'm sure they do."

She took one step backward, then turned and walked away.

MAXINE HAMMOND WASN'T prone to fits of temper or flights of fear. But when she saw the looks—and the touch—exchanged between her best friend and this man with things to hide, she was both angry and fearful. She wasn't aware, however, that either showed until her husband put a gentling hand on her shoulder.

"Maxie, you're going to snap that serving fork in two as clean as a whistle if you're not careful."

Ragan's whisper, in his gentle drawl, eased some of the tension from her shoulders. She loosened her grip and dropped the fork onto the platter of baked ham.

"What's wrong? You've looked like a thundercloud all day."

She turned to him, drawing calmness from the familiar sight

of his ash blond hair and fair, freckled face. The happiness welled in her even as she could almost see disaster brewing.

She watched Rose walk away from the man who was living a lie. She saw the little skip in her walk, saw the half smile trembling on her lips. She remembered the bored impatience she had seen in Rose's eyes just the day before.

Her friend wouldn't be bored much longer, Maxine feared.

And you'd have to be strong, indeed, to fight against that. Maxine leaned against her husband's shoulder and felt the strength pour into her. Yes, love could be strong. And fighting against it could be futile. Even racial hatred and small-mindedness—even violence—hadn't been strong enough to defeat her love for Ragan.

But their love had a foundation of truth. He knew all her secrets and loved her anyway. What could you say for a love that started with untruth?

She must speak to Rose. But what could she say without jeopardizing the work she did? And that she could not do. She would not have the blood of another young one on her hands ever.

BEN STOOD IN THE MIDDLE of the whirl of wicker baskets and cardboard boxes being filled with plates and platters and bowls of cake crumbs and stray chicken wings and a smattering of casserole. He looked around for Krissy, seeing plenty of small heads dodging here and there. Car engines were coming to life. Trunks were being opened to receive the remains of the day's activities.

Homecoming at Sweetbranch Freewill Baptist Church was breaking up.

All afternoon, the sprawling church lawn had been alive with activity—running children, laughter, milling people. And in a few moments, Ben knew with a certainty that bordered on apprehension, the lawn would be empty. A crumpled napkin here, a child's lost shoe there would be the only signs of life that remained once the cars pulled away.

Ben's vision faded, then quickly refocused.

The crowd buzzed with preparations for leaving. And in the crowd, Ben couldn't see the familiar dark head of his daughter.

Light perspiration broke out just along his hairline.

She was so short. So tiny. She would be hard to spot. But if he didn't find her, if he didn't get her out of here before...

Once again, Ben's vision blurred. The scene before him shifted. The sounds hitting his ears changed cadence. Slow, cheerful drawls merged into new sounds, singsong, nasal sounds that were foreign yet familiar, voices staccato with fear rising into panic.

Ben knew the village now. Recognized the people. They should have left before now. He had told them days ago. Take the children. Take the babies. Run. Leave. He felt the urgency pounding fiercely in his blood. And knew it was too late. He could barely draw a breath. His lungs were running out of air. A small hand tugged at his pant leg, asking for protection. Ben drew deep, gulping breaths and it wasn't enough. A baby cried. He should have made them listen. Should have been able to...

Something exploded in Ben's left ear.

He couldn't cry out, but a strangled gasp rose in his throat. He wheeled in the direction of the sound, knowing what he would see, not wanting to see it, knowing he had to see it. Perspiration poured down his back and sides as he turned toward the sound.

Melvin Smallwood had taken a hammer to the metal joint that held up one of the picnic tables. He would knock the now empty table down and stack it away in the church storage room with all the others.

Ben stared, willing his eyes to refocus, waiting for his heart to stop roaring in his chest, waiting until the fear subsided enough to permit him to move again.

He started at the tugging on his pant leg, pulled away, determined to brush it off, to get away from it. His bad knee twinged. Then he heard the voice.

"Daddy? Time to go, Daddy?"

Relief washed through Ben, leaving him weak. He looked down at Krissy and sank to his knees beside her, wrapping her tightly in his arms. His voice was a hoarse rasp. "Yes, sweetheart, it's time to go."

But where? Where could he take her that was safe?

BEN STARED at the pay phone. He had to use it. And wasn't sure he could. He was still shaken by the strange lapse of sanity that had taken place at the church. And what he had to do now, he knew, would shake him even more.

Krissy was with Uncle Bump, back at the house, deeply engrossed in another checkers game. But Ben felt vulnerable, insecure. Dialing Cybil's number merely intensified the feelings.

When his ex-wife answered the phone, her cool, dignified voice restored some of Ben's sense of control. He and Cybil had always been, if nothing else, in control. He remembered that feeling now and drew a long, slow breath to let it take root.

"Cybil, I don't want to frighten you, but I...I'm not going to bring Krissy home tonight."

"Where are you?" Her voice was still calm. Ben drew strength from it. He had loved Cybil at one time, when they both wanted the same things. She had been strong and savvy and smooth and so had he.

"I don't think it's a good idea for Krissy to be there. We both know she isn't safe. I won't have her hurt. Do you understand, Cybil?"

There was a long silence, long enough for Ben to look up and down Sweetbranch's deserted Main Street and be grateful for Sundays at dusk, when the small town was occupied with Sunday night prayer meeting and heating up leftovers for supper.

"I want to talk to her, Ben."

He was grateful there was no hysteria in her voice, although he did wonder at a mother who could be so calm. "Not now. I don't think that's a good idea right now."

"How long? How long will you keep her?"

"As long as I have to."

"Ben..."

He heard the crack in her voice then and it was almost his undoing. Maxine had been right. This wasn't going to be easy. Wasn't fair to anyone, really. But what else could he do?

"I'll keep in touch."

"Let me talk to her. I want..."

He cut off the beginnings of fear in her voice by easing the receiver down into its cradle. As he walked back to the tidy white farmhouse, he couldn't silence the voice of guilt in his own head. He simply did his dead level best not to listen to it.

CHAPTER SEVEN

ROSE RUBBED the last beads of water from Krissy's tummy, wondering how to contain the splashing, wiggling bundle of exhuberance.

"Be still, Krissy," she cautioned softly, asking herself whether a firmer tone was called for. "You're going to squirt right out the window."

Krissy giggled, kicking at the soapy water draining from the tub and ignoring Rose's warning about the danger of her imminent and unscheduled departure. Rose smiled and kept toweling. Marveling at the child's silky young skin, she tried not to show her trepidation over this thoroughly mundane task of motherhood. She didn't want to scare Krissy by revealing her anxiety. Surely real mothers did things wrong, too; or was knowledge born with labor pains, burned into the brain with each rending contraction? Pretending it was all in a day's work, she wrapped the fluffy pink towel around the girl with a bear hug and a playful growl.

"I've got you now!" Rose scooped her towel-encased captive into her arms and dashed across the hall, where a fresh nightgown waited on turned-back sheets. "I'm taking you back to my cave to gobble you up."

Krissy squealed her pleasure as Rose dumped her onto the bed. "You're not a mean bear, Wose. You're a good bear."

Nightgown in her hand, Rose paused and assumed a wounded expression. "How do you know I'm not a mean bear?"

Krissy stood on the bed, dropped the towel and held up her arms as Rose slipped the nightgown over her head. "Mean bears aren't pretty."

Rose reached for the tiny white panties dotted with pink bunnies and made the fiercest face she could muster. "There. Now am I a mean bear?"

Krissy merely dropped back onto the bed and smiled. "Only a pretend one."

Rose sat on the edge of the bed that had once been hers. The little girl snuggled against her hip, eyelids already drooping. After her father's death, Rose had come to bed in this room every night and allowed her heart to dream of days when a little girl of her own would lie here. One day, even in Sweetbranch, she had told herself, she would find the man who would sweep her off her feet. The man who would make her feel passion and fill her with life.

It wasn't to be, Rose now knew.

Krissy shifted to cradle her face in one pudgy hand. The movement turned the left side of her face to the light and Rose saw again the faint discoloration under her eye. She winced. Her suspicions mingled uncomfortably with her awakening desire for Ben McKenzie.

"Would you like a story while you wait for your daddy to get home from his walk?" *Where, pray tell, is there to walk to on a Sunday evening in Sweetbranch?* she wondered. *And why had he been so insistent that Krissy stay here?* She wanted to know more about him, about his ex-wife. About what he was doing here in Sweetbranch when he so obviously had a very different life elsewhere. And she knew she'd never ask. The less she knew about Ben McKenzie, the safer her heart would be. That other life would certainly reclaim him sometime soon.

"Uncle Bump said he has a story," Krissy said, interrupting her thoughts.

Rose smiled. "I'll just bet he does. You snuggle up under the covers and I'll go see if Uncle Bump has on his storyteller's hat."

The phone was ringing by the time Rose spotted Uncle Bump, shoes off, belt buckle loosened, slumped down in his favorite chair in the living room. "Krissy is awaiting the Finley family's resident storyteller in her chambers."

He grumbled and groused as he readjusted his clothes and dragged himself out of the comfort of his chair. "Young'uns! Always wantin' something. I told you this wasn't gonna work. But I guess you've got it all figured out. Shove all the extra work on old Bump. That'll solve everything."

He continued muttering as he stiffly mounted the stairs, but Rose could see in his eyes the little gleam of pleasure he couldn't quite hide as he passed. She grinned as she grabbed the phone on the fourth ring.

Maxine's melodious voice carried an unfamiliar tone, a tone Rose couldn't quite pinpoint as the two friends exchanged greetings.

"You have certainly aroused the interest of the good people of Sweetbranch."

"Oh?" The grin that Uncle Bump had left her with deepened into a full-fledged smile.

"You need not play coy with me, Rose Finley. You seem to have found a solution to your discontent."

Rose would have sworn that Maxine's own words held a touch of discontent. But that must be her imagination; Maxine Hammond was the last person in Sweetbranch who would harbor any small-town narrow-mindedness. "Now, Maxie, you're the one who told me it was never too late to get out there and shake things up a little."

In the silence, Rose could almost see Maxine pursing her lips the way she did when she was carefully formulating the words she wanted to say.

"I did not tell you to open your home to the first handsome stranger who captured your fancy."

"He is handsome, isn't he?"

"Rose, I am serious. Have you considered the consequences of this action?"

This was strange, indeed. Maxine Hammond, urging caution and mistrust. Yes, this had definitely been an out-of-the-ordinary weekend in Sweetbranch. Rose leaned against the wall, inordinately satisfied with herself. If Maxine was this perturbed, the rest of the town must be fit to be pickled.

Good!

"Of course I've considered the consequences." She used a soothing voice. "I promise to take precautions against pregnancy—Doc Newman said that wasn't a hot flash last week. It's way too early for that, so it's conceivable... Oops, that's a bad pun, isn't it? Anyway, I'll be careful not to get myself in trouble. A girl can't be too careful about her reputation, after all. Although I believe most people in town will be sympathetic to my plight, grabbing my last chance for a fling and all that. I think I need that aura about me if I want to be one of those truly legendary spinsters one day. You know, the kind with a tragic past. Really, I see this as my opportunity to dress up my story a little, don't you think?"

This time when Maxine spoke, there was no ignoring the strained tone of her voice. "Have you quite finished?"

"Aw, Maxie, lighten up. I'm not going to ruin my life with this guy. I'm a big girl. And he seems like a perfectly nice man. What's the harm?"

"You know nothing about him."

Maxine's warning prickled Rose's conscience, but she ignored it. "He's out of work like lots of other folks. He's looking for a new start. And he's got a little girl who needed someplace better to stay than a smelly old room in the Atlasta Motel. It's that simple, Maxine."

Maxine emitted an exasperated sigh. "Rose, you have been well sheltered here in Sweetbranch. In this world, you simply cannot..."

The sound of a footstep on the front porch stole Rose's attention. He was back. Her blood ran a little faster as she waited for him to walk through the front door.

"...sympathy for the little girl lead you to actions you might one day regret."

The screen creaked and he walked into the hall. His eyes were clouded, a frown etched into his forehead. He looked lonely, even a little afraid. Rose wanted to run right over to him and put her arms around him and tell him everything would be all right.

Maxine was right. This was a dangerous situation. But not entirely for the reasons Maxine thought.

Although she had to admit Maxine could be right about those things, as well.

"Rose, are you listening to me at all?"

"Hmm?" At the sound of Rose's voice, Ben looked up. Rose smiled at him. His returning smile wasn't at all convincing. "Yes, yes, I'm listening."

Mostly, however, she was watching. Watching as Ben trudged up the stairs. Watching until he disappeared.

"Yes, I'm listening," she repeated, turning her full attention back to Maxine. "But I think you're overreacting."

"Think about it, Rose. Very carefully. That is all I ask of you."

And think about Ben was all Rose could do as she turned out

the lights except for a small table lamp in the living room and wandered onto the front porch. Curling up in the porch swing, listening to the cricket concert, which was occasionally punctuated by the pop of the porch swing chains, Rose stared into the dark evening.

Maxine was worldly. Maxine had seen and done many things. Normally, Rose took advice from Maxine almost as seriously as if it had been carved in stone about the same time Moses came down from the mountains with his tablets.

But this time her instincts told her differently. And she was willing to trust those instincts if that's what it took to grab life by the throat and make things happen.

BEN STARED AT THE CEILING in the bedroom that felt like a prison of his own making, his mind spiraling with fragments of thoughts unpleasant and unsettling.

The call to Cybil had played over and over in his mind while he walked back to the Finley house, had dogged him even as Rose had turned away from her own telephone conversation long enough to bestow upon him a welcoming smile.

A smile, he told himself, *that you don't deserve.*

His guilt had receded to the back of his mind when he'd climbed the stairs to Krissy's room, where Uncle Bump was just wrapping up an incongruous bedtime story about a magical tadpole who helped a little girl catch her first fish. Hearing Krissy's gleeful reaction to the homespun tale and seeing her unconditional trust in the grizzly old man, Ben allowed himself a moment's reprieve.

He had done the right thing.

But when Krissy was safely tucked in and the house below lapsed into dimness and silence—except for the rhythmic creaking of the porch swing—and Ben was once again alone with his thoughts, the demons returned.

Krissy might be safe, but what kind of price would she pay for it? Could he ever hope to give her a normal childhood? And what about Cybil? He had loved her once. She had given him the most precious gift in his life—Krissy. And if her weakness had surfaced, well, did any of them lack weakness? Should she have to pay by having her only child snatched out of her life?

Yes, dammit! Yes, she does! If she couldn't, wouldn't keep that child safe from pain and fear, yes, she did.

But Ben's soft heart—the soft heart Cybil had scorned so much she had ended their marriage—made it hard for him to wish that kind of punishment on the woman who had shared his life for most of a decade.

And as if being softhearted wasn't bad enough, it seemed he had even been stricken with a serious case of softheadedness. What else could explain his infatuation with Rose Finley? All that lush hair waving down to her shoulders, hair his fingers itched to touch, didn't excuse the way he had allowed himself to wallow in schoolboy daydreaming. Neither did those big brown eyes that wavered between tempting invitation and naive uncertainty. Or the voice. The long legs. The slender hips. The pale skin.

Or the warm heart.

If anything, it was the warm heart that would compel a better man to keep his distance. Any woman who would invite a strange man into her home simply because she wanted to shelter the child at his side deserved better than to be seduced by a man who could only tell her lies.

A man who's breaking the law.

The thought burst into his consciousness, startling him to alertness. Now that he had spoken to Cybil, the idea that he might soon be a wanted man was more than an abstract notion. The search for Ben and his kidnapped daughter could begin anytime. A frantic call to the police. An overwrought interview. Would the FBI be called in? Would they search his home? Question his family? Would everyone he knew in Winston-Salem read the story in tomorrow's paper?

Ben's stomach roiled. His head throbbed. What had he done? And was it too late to call the whole thing off?

Can the melodrama, McKenzie. Ben jumped off the bed. Plunging his hands deeply into his pant pockets, he paced to the window. *You've watched too much TV.*

But he didn't believe it. He believed Maxine Hammond and her zealousness for secrecy. She knew the dangers if he was caught. He had been living in a fool's paradise when he let his guard down with Rose Finley. She knew his name. She knew Krissy's name. The only thing she didn't know was just what she'd gotten herself into when she gave her trust to Ben Mc-Kenzie.

Ben clenched his fists in his pockets until they were balled up as tightly as his stomach.

Then he heard a noise, a soft, ragged sound from the next room. He walked to his door and looked down the hall toward Krissy's room.

Krissy was crying. Not the loud, demanding cries of a child seeking comfort, but the low, muffled cries of someone old enough to want to hide her sadness. The sound wrenched Ben's heart, but not as cruelly as the knowledge that his three-year-old daughter felt she had to cover her tears.

Misery in his heart, he rushed to Krissy's room and pulled her into his arms.

"Sweetheart, what's wrong?"

Her sobs escalated. She buried her face in his chest and curled herself tightly into his lap. "Sad, Daddy. I'm sad."

Ben squeezed his eyes shut and held her close. "Poor sweetness. Why didn't you call Daddy when you felt sad?"

She merely snuffled out an unintelligible answer and he waited for her sobbing to die. When her crying had quieted, he patted her head and whispered, "What makes Daddy's baby sad?"

"Where's Mommy?" Her voice was thick with tears and so quiet Ben knew she asked her question with misgivings. Guilt poured over him, rivers of it.

"Mommy's at her home, sweetheart." And what else could he tell her? What else would a three-year-old understand?

"I miss Mommy."

Ben wondered, for one piercing moment, if Krissy had ever cried for him after she and Cybil moved out. Had she ever wanted him in the middle of the night, cried into Cybil's arms because she missed her daddy?

He hoped not. He hoped so.

"I know you do, sweetheart. But right now we have to be here. Don't you like it here with Uncle Bump and Aunt Rose?"

Her head nodded against his chest. Then she wiggled herself free enough to look up at him in the light coming from the hallway. "Maybe Mommy can come here, too."

The temptation to lie to her was strong. If a lie would soothe her, make it easier for her to have sweet dreams... No, he was lying to enough people. And he wouldn't do it, if he could help it, to Krissy. Not to his daughter.

"I don't think so, sweetheart."

Fresh tears glimmered in her still-wet eyes. "We'll go home soon?"

"I don't know, Krissy. We...do you know why Daddy brought you here?"

She shook her head.

"So your new stepdaddy won't hurt you anymore. So he won't make you cry anymore or feel sad." She looked down. "He hurt you sometimes, didn't he?"

Her only answer was to raise her hand and slowly slip her thumb into her mouth. She hadn't sucked her thumb in more than a year. Ben fought back rage at Colin, at the courts, at everyone who had stood in the way of protecting Krissy.

"It's okay to tell me. He can't hurt you anymore. You can tell Daddy." He lifted her chin and raised her eyes to his again. "Didn't your stepdaddy hurt you sometimes?"

Reluctantly, almost imperceptibly, she nodded, then leaned her face into his chest, where his anger and frustration festered.

"Well, he won't anymore." He cradled her head in his hand and crooned softly to her. "That's why we're here, sweetheart. So no one will hurt you anymore."

He rocked her in his arms until she fell into a deep, sound sleep. Then he laid her back in the bed, covered her and walked out of the room.

The prospect of sleep was no longer even a faint glimmer in his mind.

WHEN THE SCREEN DOOR creaked open, Rose started out of her reverie. Uncle Bump had said goodnight an hour ago, and sitting here with the darkness drowsily settling in around her, Rose had almost forgotten the two of them were no longer alone in the house.

Then Ben walked out onto the porch, hands in his pockets, face staring rigidly ahead, his lean body looking taut, coiled.

Her own body responded to his presence with an instant softening. She tried to remember the last time she had wanted a man. Had it felt this way? Had it filled her with this maddening combination of weakness and strength? Had it hummed and shivered through her so distractingly? She thought not. In fact, as she tried to conjure memories of the only lover she'd had since returning to Sweetbranch, all she could remember was drifting into his arms the same way she'd drifted through life year after year in Sweetbranch. A nearing-middle-age schoolteacher, he had been little more than a way to fight the boredom.

No, that wasn't the way she felt about Ben McKenzie at all. Ben McKenzie made her feel hungry. Agitated. So filled with urges she could barely sit still in his presence.

She jumped up. He started. His right hand went to his waist, seemed to convulse into action even before his eyes darted in her direction. Rose drew back involuntarily. She had been right. The first moment she saw him, glancing around the Picture Perfect, she'd thought he looked ready to spring.

"Sorry if I scared you." She smiled a bit uncertainly and waited for his eyes to lose their wildness.

"No, that's..." He looked down at his right hand, flexed it, shoved it back in his pocket. "That's okay. I didn't know anyone else was up."

"Just me. Putting off..." *Wrong, Finley.* She could hardly go telling him she was putting off crawling into that lonely bed of hers for another long night. Could she?

He didn't seem to notice that she hadn't finished what she'd started to say. He walked to the porch railing, leaned onto it and stared out over the yard. "Yeah, me, too."

Rose drew a long breath for courage and walked over to stand beside him. "Worried about tomorrow?"

His lips twisted in a grin so wry it was almost a grimace. "Tomorrow. Yesterday."

"It'll work out. Something always comes along." She wasn't sure why she said that. She certainly didn't believe it. But she gave in to her desire to comfort this man.

"Does it, Rose?" He turned to her. His eyes were hard and filled with futility. They twisted her heart.

"No. Not always."

They stared at each other in silence. Finally, some of the intensity in his eyes seemed to ease. He smiled, a faint smile that didn't go deep enough to reflect much real happiness.

"Good. I wouldn't like you nearly so much if you started acting like one of those people who said what they think other people want to hear."

She laughed softly. "And what else would make you not like me nearly so much?"

She was startled by the brazenness of the question. But she wasn't sorry she'd asked it, especially when she saw the interest flicker in his eyes. In a flash of inspiration, she realized what it was she had seen—a moment when he considered kissing her.

She wondered, her heart both racing with excitement and pained by disappointment, what had changed his mind.

"I don't think I'd better answer that question."

"You don't have to hide anything from me, Ben." Knowing she was acting like a foolish, desperate woman, she leaned just a breath closer to him. Close enough to feel his heat.

His voice was lower, gruffer. "I wouldn't like you nearly so much if you weren't so trusting."

Her voice was almost a whisper. "I'm not. It's you. You make me do strange things. Like remember who I used to be."

"And who was that?"

Her eyes half closed. Her smile was half dreamy remembrance of the past and half sweet drowsiness that belonged completely to this moment. "Somebody...somebody who felt life held... possibilities."

Rose wasn't surprised when his face lowered hesitantly to hers. She raised her lips another fraction of an inch, felt herself ready to burst with aching.

His lips brushed over hers, tentative at the same time they were masterful, testing her response at the same time he warned her what he intended. A sigh escaped her and he grazed her lips again. This time, the tip of his tongue teased against her slightly parted lips. Rose trembled. A wave of sensation traveled down her body, rendering her legs unsteady. She clutched his arm as fiercely as her waning strength allowed. He covered her lips completely, then pulled her slowly but fully against him.

She was drowning in her own weakness. His lips played over hers. Soft. Forceful. Hot. Something started unfurling deep within her, but she didn't have time to focus her attention on it. Too many other things were happening. Too many other sensations were bombarding her. Her legs felt as limp as one of the rag dolls on the shelf in the upstairs bedroom. Her breasts were in flame, tight and tingling with crying need. Low in her belly, sensations teased at her, stealing her breath.

His hands played over her back. Urging. Cradling. Seeking. All tenderness and trembling constraint. The unfurling deepened, began to fill her.

Then she sensed him pulling back, braking to a slow stop before they neared the precipice looming before them, a precipice Rose had not yet begun to acknowledge. But as Ben's lips lightened on hers, as his hands released her and became only the whisper of a touch at her back, she saw where they had been headed.

Drawing a long, ragged breath as their lips reluctantly parted, Rose wasn't sure whether she was grateful to Ben for his good judgment or peeved at him for his ill-timed ability to rein himself in.

Face it, Finley, came that infuriating voice in her head, *he might not have been quite as famished for this kind of thing as some of us. Could be he's used to feasting on better things, anyway.*

Could be he wasn't exactly carried away.

What had begun to blossom inside her curled tightly upon itself and burrowed deeper. Stung by the thought that her desire might have been paired only with Ben's mild interest, Rose nevertheless forced herself to look him in the eye.

Her heart was pounding so hard, her breath coming in such short, sharp spurts that she wasn't sure she trusted what she saw. The hardness seemed to have disappeared from his face—gone from his eyes, gone from his lips, gone from the tight set of his jaw.

And bless her if he didn't seem to be breathing just as hard as she.

Rose laughed. It came out an unsteady rasp. "Well..." She swallowed hard and backed away from him. Backed far enough away that she no longer felt his heat. She was both grateful for and resentful of the cool night breeze that whispered over her skin, stealing the heat she had stolen from him.

"Well, I guess that was an interesting experiment, wasn't it?"

"Don't do that."

His gruff voice crackled through her, almost frightening her. Maxine was right. What did she really know about this man? He could be anyone. Anything. She tried to force a nonchalant firmness into her voice to show him this was no big deal to her, that he hadn't reduced her to jelly.

"Don't do what?" It came out a breathless whisper.

"Try to turn it into something...unimportant...meaningless. It wasn't."

She saw the hunger in his eyes even as she heard it in his words. "It wasn't?"

He pursed his lips into a tight, thin line. But she still remembered their softness, the gentle way those lips had provoked her into giving what he had wanted to take. Abruptly, swiftly, he turned away. She saw that his back, too, was now even more rigid than it had been when he'd first walked onto the porch. She raised a hand to reach for him, to soften him again.

"Go to bed, Rose."

Hand raised in his direction, Rose trembled from the weakness he had induced in her. Her hand slowly dropped. He was right. It was late. Too late for this foolishness.

Hugging her arms to her chest, she walked inside.

"WHAT WE NEED ARE JOBS!" The earnest voice rang out in the crowded school gym.

Ben peered around the cavernous room lined with hundreds of metal folding chairs and accommodating a standing room only crowd. Many of the faces he recognized from the church dinner just two days earlier. A few he recognized from his own aimless wandering yesterday and today, while he tried to reconcile the conflicts in his heart.

Rose sat near the front. He could see her straight back, her thick chestnut waves. And damn him, he could still taste her lips whenever he let himself. Or, more accurately, whenever he wasn't able to stop himself.

She had gone out of her way to stay away from him the past two days. She hadn't looked him in the eye, she hadn't said his name, she hadn't allowed herself within an arm's length of him.

Ben was glad. And he was damned frustrated.

"That's right—jobs!" Another voice rang out and muttered assent rumbled through the crowd, ignoring the town council representative pounding his gavel on the table in the front of the room. Ben forced his attention to the irate voice. "Industry. If we don't get some kind of industry, we ain't got a prayer of keeping our young folks in town."

"Or the old folks, either," came the rejoinder from a woman standing at the back.

"All right! We hear you!" The gavel against the table cracked through the dissatisfied rumblings. "But we've got to keep some order here. Now, we've got a proposal before us to set up an activities program for the young people. Can we stick to that?"

Ben looked around the room. Some faces were angry, others merely discouraged. Others seemed frozen, guarded against revealing whatever emotion lurked beneath.

"Hec, I've got something to say."

Her voice prodded him to instant attention. He looked to the front, where Rose was now standing. Her hands, he noticed, had tightened in a death grip around the clasp of the corduroy handbag she clutched to her stomach.

Hector Griffin, whose chin had been forsworn for the sake of an extraordinarily prominent Adam's apple, was the town's mayor and funeral parlor director. He smiled, the vacuously pleasant smile of the mayor, not the somber smile of the funeral parlor director. "Go ahead, Miz Finley."

"Hec, there's no point in trying to impress anybody here," she responded with the drawling irony that was just a little out of kilter in this polite small town. "We're all neighbors. You can call me Rose."

Hector Griffin's smile evaporated into ill-disguised irritation. Ben could sympathize. This monthly meeting of the Sweetbranch Town Board hadn't gone well. It had been interminable. And it had been subject to plenty of volleys and snipes from the audience.

"You know, Hec, that I've been working with Maxie's group to come up with this youth plan." Rose's voice was measured and just tight enough that Ben realized she was nervous speaking before the group. Neighbors or no, normally outspoken or no, Rose Finley clearly wasn't comfortable in the public eye. "So I don't mean this to be...I'm not trying to say we shouldn't do something for the young people in town. But..."

She took a deep breath. Ben wished he were close enough to cover her hand with his to show his support. But there was too much distance between them. Physical distance, necessary to enforce the emotional distance.

And Rose was right to do that, he knew. Being around Rose Finley for the past two days without showing—much less giving in to—his urge to touch her had been one of the most rigorous exercises in self-control he'd ever been subjected to.

"But I think these folks are right," Rose continued. "We can entertain our kids all day long, but we've got to give them a concrete reason to stay. We've got to give them some assurance that they'll be able to raise a family and make something for themselves if they stay here." Her breath seemed to run out and she paused again. "We've got to give them jobs."

Hector's response was drowned by the applause that followed Rose's outburst. Ben joined in the applause, mostly for the courage of her words. And for the color creeping into her cheeks as she remained on her feet, color he could see even at this distance. Rose Finley obviously wasn't finished.

"Well, Miz—Rose—that's fine. But how do we do that? We can't exactly hog-tie some big old company from down in Birmingham and drag it up here by force, you know."

The color in Rose's face deepened. Ben saw her ease backward and thought she was simply going to sit down, silenced by Hector's condescending tone. Then he saw her delicately pointed chin jut out.

"I know that, Hector Griffin. I'm a businesswoman in this town, too, don't forget." There was no reticence in her voice now. An involuntary grin stole over Ben's face. "I don't know what the answers are, exactly. But other towns have done it. And I think what we ought to do is find out what they've done. Make a study of it. And put together a plan for recruiting industry. If other towns can go out and sell themselves to big companies, I don't see why Sweetbranch can't do the same thing."

The rumble had started again, a rumble with the sound of rallying support. Hector pounded his gavel and looked up and down the table for help from his other board members. "There's some merit in that, I'm sure, Rose. What do y'all think?"

The members of the board looked around, waiting for someone else to speak first. At last it was Maxine Hammond who spoke, her gentle but resonant voice commanding instant silence in the room.

"I would have been happier if attention were not diverted from the plan before us," she started, smiling at Rose. "But since it has been, I must add my agreement to what Rose has said. Sweetbranch has much to offer—an eager work force, low property taxes, available land at reasonable prices, an abundance of natural resources. Perhaps now is the time to assign an economic development committee and..."

Ben's mind focused on what Maxine had said, only half listening as the crowd debated the idea. All the assets she cited—ample workers, low taxes and low land prices, natural resources—would certainly serve as drawing cards for industry.

A printing company, for example, looking to establish its own environmentally sound paper plant.

Of course. Sweetbranch might be exactly what he and Keith—well, he at least; Keith was still lukewarm about Ben's idea of producing their own recycled and recyclable paper—were looking for. Excitement welled up in him; he was half-tempted to jump up right now and tell these people what he was thinking about. Why launch a big search when...

Then he remembered. His excitement soured. Yes, building his company's plant might solve Sweetbranch's problems. But right now, Sweetbranch was his hiding place. His and Krissy's.

And tipping others off to his location, he reminded himself, might jeopardize not only his own daughter but a network committed to protecting others like Krissy. Innocent children with nowhere to turn.

Ben sank back in his chair, the sickness in the pit of his belly overwhelming the noisy enthusiasm of the crowd, from which he felt suddenly and irrevocably isolated.

CHAPTER EIGHT

ALONE AND RESTLESS, Ben wandered Sweetbranch the next day on one concocted errand after another.

He sifted through children's clothes at the general store. He tucked a pair of denim overalls under his arm, then another, taking a certain satisfaction in the thought of his city-bred daughter in the old-fashioned clothes. He bought a paperback novel at the drugstore and a can of shaving cream he didn't need but was on sale. He peered in the window of a secondhand store at an old manual typewriter. He could use it to type résumés for the job hunt Rose Finley no doubt expected him to start any day now.

The dusty old keys mocked him. And how, exactly, could he launch a job search? He had a name he couldn't use and experience he couldn't brag about. And he didn't even need a job. He had a job. A job he couldn't go to.

Frowning at his reflection in the window, Ben turned away abruptly, right into the path of a tall, brightly dressed woman.

"Excuse me." Maxine Hammond turned her dark, expressive eyes on him. "I should not be in such a hurry, Mr....McKenzie, is it not? It seems all of Sweetbranch has your name on their lips."

His mouth went dry. It didn't take much to read the chastisement in her innocent words. "I guess that's true."

Her lips smiled, but her eyes didn't. They were troubled and intense. "At any rate, it was careless of me to stumble into your path. One should be more careful. I was heading for the park. Have you visited our town park, Mr. McKenzie? It is usually empty this time of the day. Perhaps you would permit me to show you around?"

He wanted to say no, because he understood this was no mere friendly invitation. He didn't want to talk to Maxine Hammond

He was already confused and miserable and guilty. But he knew he deserved her displeasure.

"That's very neighborly." And he turned to walk beside her, his feet heavy with dread. What if she ordered him out of town? Threatened to turn him in? Where would he go then?

"I see you are patronizing our local establishments." Maxine gestured toward the bag in his hand. "You have made yourself at home quickly."

He wanted to defend himself, wanted to make an excuse. But he understood her caution. They would talk of nothing on this public sidewalk, nothing that could be interpreted as anything more than casual conversation.

"Yes, I have. I've...the people in town have been so friendly. It's been...they make it almost impossible to say no to their hospitality."

"I see." She turned a searching look on him. "How nice you have discovered so many trusting, open souls in your visit to our town."

Ben was growing angry with this calm, accusing woman. It wasn't his fault! Couldn't she see that?

Maxine turned her eyes to the sidewalk ahead. She pointed toward a bright awning over a storefront. "Our newspaper. Harley Wilcutt is the editor. A fine man. His father founded the *Sweetbranch Weekly Gazetteer* in 1928. Harley's son lives in Nashville, so townsfolk speculate that tradition will not continue. But Harley is still diligent in his pursuit of the truth. People say those with something to hide should stay away from Harley. And, I would add, away from anyone in a small town who might take an untoward interest in a stranger."

Again, Ben heard the warning she imparted.

She turned her attention across the street now, to another storefront, one Ben recognized.

"The Picture Perfect Beauty Salon is another of our longtime local establishments. Rose Finley inherited it from her mother." She paused. "But, of course, you already know about Rose Finley, don't you?"

He stole a glance in her direction. "Not...not much."

"Rose Finley is one of those special people who has spent most of her life living for others. A selfless person." She turned a pointed gaze in his direction. "She quit college to help her mother care for her father after his stroke. He lived for many years. And when he died, Rose gave up her dreams of starting a new life to care for her mother, who by then was old and frail and afraid of being alone.'' Maxine paused. ''Do you understand?''

Ben thought about the deep well of dissatisfaction he had sensed in Rose. He remembered the trace of irony when she talked of being born late in her parents' lives. And he remembered how willing she had been to take him in when he led her to believe he was needy.

''Yes. I understand.'' He understood more, too. He understood that Maxine Hammond wanted him to know that Rose was not a person whose willingness to give should be abused.

''Good.'' There was, for the first time, a hint of emotion lilting through Maxine's voice. ''There is one more thing you must know about Rose Finley.''

''Okay. Shoot.''

''It would make me unhappy to see her hurt or deceived. Apart from my husband, Rose Finley is my best friend.''

The words so stunned Ben that, after a long moment of silence, he found himself laughing. ''You do have a flair for the dramatic, don't you?''

He caught a glimmer of humor in her eyes as they stepped off the sidewalk at the end of Main Street and turned toward the park. ''So I have been told.''

Maxine said nothing more as they walked between the stone markers at the park entrance. A young mother was at the swing with her toddler. Maxine waved and veered away from the twosome. When they reached a pond at the far end of the park, she sat on its edge and looked into the mossy water. Still she didn't speak. When he didn't speak, either, she looked up at him with a question in her eyes.

Ben understood she was offering him a chance to explain. He wasn't sure he deserved it.

''I'm sorry.'' He sat beside her and looked her directly in the eyes. ''I know I screwed up. It just...things just happened. We...Krissy and I...met Rose and she sort of overwhelmed us. She was so friendly and likable and...dammit, there's no excuse. I just forgot. Before I knew it, I was telling her my name. And then she wanted to know why we were in town. And then she told me how people would talk if Krissy and I were staying out at that motel. And...I don't know...I just got swept up in this idea of living with her and how safe Krissy would be and..." He stared at his hands. "I screwed up. I'm sorry."

A measure of understanding warmed Maxine's voice. "Rose is not an easy person to resist."

Ben wondered if Maxine knew exactly how true that statement was. He hoped not. Knowing what had passed between him and Rose might wipe out what little bit of compassion her voice had recovered.

"But the fact remains, Ben, you could jeopardize many things with your action. If you decide to take that final step, you must do it soon or make arrangements elsewhere. If you are identified and connected with the network, you will endanger the work we do, the safety of many children, even Rose." Ben darted a confused look at her. "Yes, Ben. Even Rose. Do you suppose if the authorities seek you and find you at the Finley home they will not find her actions suspect? Do you suppose they will be gracious in their treatment of her simply because she was motivated by generosity?"

"But she doesn't know."

"That is true. You must, of necessity, deceive her."

Ben winced at yet another gentle accusation.

"You must make your decision, Ben. If you want the help of the network, you must let us know and we will help you." She put a hand on his arm. "We want to help. But we must know you are committed. If you are discovered, I can no longer guarantee the safety of your daughter through our network here in Sweetbranch."

"I know." What he didn't know was how he would be able to make that decision. "I'll...I'll decide soon. And I'll move. I'll get out of Rose's house right away."

Maxine sighed. "I wish it were that simple."

"What do you mean?"

"If you move now, you will do nothing but call more attention to yourself. Too many people know you are here." Her eyes filled with worry. "You must stay where you are."

Ben nodded, relief mingling with his growing anxiety.

Maxine stood. "But, Ben, you must not involve Rose in this any more than you already have. Do not entangle her with your life. Do I make myself clear?"

"Quite clear."

But he wondered, as he took a different route out of the park from the one Maxine followed, how he was supposed to stop something that had already begun.

ROSE PEEKED into her purse, then snapped it quickly shut before either Alma or Bunny could notice.

The big, fat envelope was addressed to the Office of Admissions Services at the University of Alabama in Tuscaloosa. She'd put four extra stamps in the corner just so she wouldn't have to run over to the post office for Leila to weigh it and ask what in the world she was mailing off to the university. Leila saw it as part of her Christian duty to see to everyone's business, just to make sure no one was straying off the straight and narrow.

Like I might be writing off to the college for a degree in illicit sex, Rose thought as she shoved her purse in her locker and went out front to face her two co-workers.

Maybe a little education on the subject would help, she mocked herself. *You don't have much natural knack for it.*

It had been almost a week, but Rose still hadn't stopped stinging from the crisp, efficient way Ben McKenzie had turned the heat down just when things were starting to sizzle. He'd gone out of his way to steer clear of her, but it hadn't made her less aware of him. The longing hadn't stopped. She melted into something hot and helpless every time she thought about the way his lips had felt on hers, the way her body had zinged to life when she'd leaned into his chest.

Living on daydreams wasn't turning out to be as much fun as she'd thought when Ben McKenzie walked through the shop door almost a week ago.

Alma was teasing Gayla Watkins's frosted hair into a nest of knots and Bunny was straightening magazines in the waiting area when Rose entered. Conversation paused. Rose checked the book to see when her first client came in.

"So, Rose, how's the landlady business?"

Rose had wondered how long it would take Alma to bite into that—the topic was too juicy to steer clear of for long. She had backed off after Rose's adamant refusal to answer questions on the Monday after dinner on the church grounds. But permanent silence on the matter was asking too much, Rose knew.

"I don't know," she said, continuing her casual study of the appointment book. "Ask Uncle Bump. He's the one doing most of the landladying."

Mostly it was true. Uncle Bump still did the cooking. And Krissy stuck to him like a wet sucker to a new dress. After Sunday night, Rose had tried not to get too involved with the little girl. No more help at bathtime, although she listened to the splashes and giggles wistfully. Sometimes the memory of hugging that little towel-wrapped body in her arms was as deep an ache as the memory of how desperately she'd clung to the other McKenzie.

Alma filled the room with a breathtaking cloud of metallic-smelling hair spray, then deposited the metal canister at her workstation.

"Listen to me, Rose Finley." She pointed the tail of her comb at Rose. "If you mean to tell me you've got that fine-looking specimen living in the same house with you and you're making no attempt to lure him into something the Women's Auxiliary could gossip about, well, you ought to be ashamed of yourself."

"Alma, the world does not revolve around men."

All three women in the shop cast suspicious looks at Rose. Alma turned her comb to the task of smoothing Gayla's tightly teased hair into a frosted helmet. "You have been alone entirely too long, Finley."

Bunny held up a stack of magazines. "She's right, Finley. I read last week in one of these magazines that sex is like Mother Nature's own narcotic. It'll cure headaches and PMS and all that stuff."

"I don't have headaches." *Except the one I get every time I think about making a fool out of myself with Ben McKenzie.*

"You might as well drop it, Bunny." Alma adopted a sage tone of voice. "It's clear as that gray in her hair that Finley's never really been loved. If anybody'd ever really set fire to her, she'd be itching for it just like the rest of us. You can't miss what you've never had."

Rose snapped her jaw tightly shut. Alma was too close to right to suit her. One inept college boy, no matter how ardent, and a lukewarm high school science teacher hardly constituted vast experience in being set fire to.

"What do you mean, as clear as the gray in my hair?" It wasn't that obvious, was it? She leaned into the mirror.

"You got gray hair, Rose?" Bunny peered over Rose's shoulder into the mirror. "Golly, you do. Rose, I'd get rid of that. Ain't much. If old blabbermouth here'd keep her trap shut, nobody'd notice. But shoot, why chance it?"

Alma stood back and surveyed Gayla's hair for any errant spots of softness she could tease or lacquer into submission. Obviously satisfied that everything had been sufficiently conquered for another week, she applied another layer of spray. "She's right. We could take care of that for you if you'd let us, Finley."

Bunny ran her fingers through the ends of Rose's shoulder-length waves. "Wouldn't auburn highlights be a killer? With a little shaping here and there, just to soften it up around her face?"

"Sure thing. We could take five years off her in a couple of hours." Alma held out a mirror to Gayla and turned a wicked smile on Rose. "Unless you *like* the notion of getting middle-aged."

"I am *not* middle-aged. I'm in my prime." Rose echoed Maxine's words as she studied her reflection. A new look, huh? It was tempting. With a little razzle-dazzle in her appearance and a college degree, she could go places. She could do all the things she'd dreamed about. She could...

Shoot, by the time she got that college degree, she really would be middle-aged.

And if the truth were known, knocking a few years off her age probably still wouldn't give her what it took to attract a smart, sophisticated man like Ben McKenzie.

Face it, Finley. Your life is mapped out for you right here in Sweetbranch. And Ben McKenzie is not the road to a whole new life. He isn't even a temporary detour.

BEN PICKED HIS WAY down the overgrown path leading to Uncle Bump's favorite fishing hole. Vines and stumps and an occasional low branch raking his shoulders made him uneasy as he forged his way through the bush. Sunlight filtered through the sparse new growth of spring, but the lack of openness squeezed Ben's lungs.

He hated the forest.

He moved faster. His heartbeat picked up, roaring through his body. He wanted to run but worried that a vine would grab his leg, hurl him to the ground. What if he couldn't find his way out? What if...

He burst into the clearing. He paused a moment to fill his lungs, to slow his heart, to refocus his darting eyes. The overgrowth was behind him now. The clearing was warmed by late afternoon sun and the creek ahead glistened silver in the light. On the creek bank, familiar figures completed his reorientation. The thin, stooped back of an old man with wildly scattered white hair was bending close to a shiny dark head. On steadier legs, Ben moved closer.

"Now, all you do is poke that little point right through his squirmy little tail once," Uncle Bump was advising, his fingers guiding the worm and hook in Krissy's pudgy hands. "Then twist him around again and give him another good jab."

Krissy squealed in disgusted delight. "Yuck!"

"Yeah, yuck just about covers it, little lady." Uncle Bump chuckled. "Now you're all set. Let's toss that sucker...er, that feller...out there and see if anybody's hungry. What do you say?"

"Won't he swim away?"

"Nosiree, he's not going anywhere. You've got him but good." And Uncle Bump guided Krissy's arm in tossing her baited line into the creek. "Now remember what I said. Your fingers are a mite...sticky. So fisherpeople can't be sucking their thumbs. Got it?"

"Got it."

Calm swept through Ben as it did each time he caught another glimpse of Krissy fitting into life in Sweetbranch. Her new overalls rolled up to reveal bare, dirty feet, her bare shoulders growing brown from hours she spent outdoors, Krissy was not the same child she had been a week ago. Her rare, shy smile had been abandoned in favor of an almost constant grin. She chattered continually and laughed almost as much. She ran and played and seemed to have forgotten that TV existed. Her days were spent fishing and playing games in the park and tagging along behind Uncle Bump. She played in floury dough and turned out misshapen biscuits. She hunched down beside a gallon jug of water and watched, fascinated, as the sunshine turned it into tea. She made red mud pies from the iron-filled Alabama earth. And the bumps and bruises she brought home now were from running too fast or learning the hard way that her arms and legs couldn't quite yet manage the task of tree climbing.

This Krissy was not the sedate, serious, unsmiling toddler who played so quietly she almost disappeared and flinched when adults noticed her. This was not a fashion-conscious youngster already responding to her mother's compulsion to teach her the alphabet and dress her in the right labels.

Krissy was a little girl again, plain and simple. Sometimes it was all Ben could do not to weep with gratitude.

Other times, the guilt still gnawed at his gut.

Shrugging off the thoughts that were sure to spoil his mood, Ben walked to the creek bank. "They biting?"

"Daddy, sh. Don't scare the fishies."

"Oops. Sorry." He settled down on the flat surface of a rock beside the two anglers. "I didn't know these were 'fraidy cats."

Krissy shook her head. "Not kitties. Fishies. I caught two fishies."

"Two? Already? I guess we know what's for dinner."

The look in his daughter's eyes told Ben that it had never occurred to her that the slippery, shiny creatures darting through the clear water might be considered edible.

"Well, we ain't actually had any keepers yet," Uncle Bump acknowledged, carefully baiting his own hook. "But we're getting lots of experience. Right, little miss?"

"Lots of 'sperience." Krissy nodded and jiggled her fishing pole. "Do we got a bite, Unka Bunk?"

"Could be. You want to drag 'er in and take a gander?"

Krissy nodded. Ben smiled at the old man's patience. It was clear that, for Krissy, catching fish was less the purpose of the sport than baiting and tossing and reeling in and rebaiting. But Uncle Bump showed no sign that the continuous process interfered in the least with his own attempts to make a catch.

The next hour, while he sat back and watched his daughter and the grizzled old man who had appointed himself surrogate grandpa, Ben wondered if Maxine Hammond could find a permanent place for them that was just like Sweetbranch. By the time the three went home, with Krissy's prattling and Uncle Bump's gruff responses taking the anxiety out of the trip through the woods, Ben almost forgot his guilt.

They walked up the wooden back steps, scattering their fishing

gear around the porch before they trailed through the screen door
into the cheerful kitchen. Ben smiled as Uncle Bump spearheaded
a trip to the washroom to cleanse Krissy's hands of any bait-
related stickiness. As Ben left the kitchen and walked through the
hall, the front door opened.

It was Rose, in one of her prim white uniforms and utilitarian
shoes, nevertheless managing to look anything but prim and utilitarian. Her hair swung freely to her shoulders, her cheeks were
rosy from the afternoon sunshine, her eyes were bright.

Until they saw him. Then she shuttered them, pulled the shades
down and shut out the light.

His guilt came back, full force. And so did the futility of asking
the underground network to find a place like Sweetbranch. Because it wasn't only the small population and the lack of big-city
amenities that made Sweetbranch the perfect place to raise his
daughter and get his own life on an even keel again.

It was Rose Finley and the way she had made a home for them.
And he would have to betray her. There was no other way.

CHAPTER NINE

FORTY.

Rose made a displeased face at herself in the mirror, then reconsidered, smoothing extra moisturizer into the little crinkles the face making had caused.

"Forty's not the end of the world," she told her reflection as she completed her morning ritual. "Not anymore. Look at Jane Fonda. Liz Taylor. Cher."

As she shrugged into her chenille robe, she wondered if something in silk wouldn't make her feel a little less dowdy, a little less screamingly middle-aged with a capital *M*.

Rose yawned as she trudged to the kitchen for her morning coffee. Or maybe she wouldn't have coffee this morning. Maybe tomato juice. Something to break the routine. Something to prove old dogs *could* learn...

Her eyes popped open from the yawn when she turned the corner into the kitchen and plowed right into a wall of something warm and hard and human. The sleep went right out of her eyes when they opened on Ben McKenzie, standing there in dress pants and a white shirt still open down the front.

Open down the front. Rose's mouth turned to cotton as that little bit of reality took hold. A narrow strip of flesh showed between starched cotton, a narrow strip of hard, tanned flesh sparingly furred with hair that sparkled silver in the overhead light. Rose listened in mortification as a tiny gasp that could be labeled a sigh escaped her lips.

She looked up a tad too late to avoid being caught at her voyeurism. She was grateful there was no smugness in his face. He started buttoning up, from the bottom, as if he hoped she might not notice.

"You're—" she paused to clear the hoarseness from her throat "—up early."

"I've got some...job possibilities to check out. Out of town."

If only he didn't look as flustered by all this as she felt. If only he acted cocky, cool, even a little insufferably confident in his power to set her heart racing. That might have made it easier to remember that Ben McKenzie had no place in her life. But he didn't have the good grace to look that way. He looked as if his fingers were fumbling over the buttons and sounded as if his tongue were obeying only reluctantly.

And that made her want to smooth the front of his shirt where his awkward hands were rumpling it.

She turned away abruptly and headed for the coffeepot. She forced her mind into reverse to respond to his previous remark. "Job possibilities. Good. That's great. Good luck."

"Thanks."

He hovered behind her. She wondered how soon he would leave so she could safely get on with the routine. Boo was rubbing her legs, quietly reminding her that an empty bowl needed attention. But Rose was reluctant to turn around, reluctant to have Ben stumble into her line of vision again. She stared out the window, barely noticing the daylight creeping pinkly into the sky. She was waiting. But he didn't budge. It was as if Ben were as paralyzed by this unexpected morning meeting as she.

"Krissy said she's helping Uncle Bump get ready for a party tonight. You're having a birthday."

She burned her tongue on a big gulp of hot coffee. "Yeah. The big one."

"I'll try to get back in time."

"No, that's not necessary. I mean, it's just a little party. Not a big deal. Don't go out of your way."

Please be here. That's what she wanted to say. *Be here to help me celebrate. Be here to make it feel special.*

He reached over to put his empty cup into the sink at the same moment she reached across the sink for a saucer from the dish drainer. Their arms crossed and brushed. They both froze, staring at the point where their bodies touched, a point that seemed to be made of flame and smoke. But neither moved. Until they raised their heads to lock eyes.

"Rose..."

His whisper was as flammable as his white sleeve against her pink chenille. The flames licked through her, wickedly slow but insidiously thorough. No part of her was spared the heat, from the taut tips of her breasts to her thrumming lower regions.

"Ben, don't..."

But he did anyway. He leaned nearer, his face close to hers. His lips brushed hers, the start of another quickflash brushfire. His shoulder brushed her breast. Another gasp escaped her lips. His tongue flickered, seeking the source of the sound. Damp and hot, she opened to him.

Her fingers loosened. Her coffee cup shattered in the sink. Her quivering, heated body ordered her to ignore it. But her mind demanded that she snatch the only opportunity she was likely to be offered. She backed away.

His eyes still held no smugness. They were as glazed and unfocused as hers when he whispered, "Happy birthday, Rose."

ROSE COULDN'T BELIEVE she was spending so much time staring at herself in the mirror on her fortieth birthday. This time, wet hair touched her shoulders. Alma and Bunny hovered over her cape-wrapped shoulders, arguing.

"Auburn number forty-three," Alma was insisting.

Bunny held another swatch of synthetic hair against Rose's head. "Nope. Got to be Blaze twenty-seven."

"That's gonna be too red. She don't want to end up looking like a stand-in for 'I Love Lucy.'"

Rose moved to stand. "That's it. This is ridiculous. I'm calling this off before it goes any..."

The women put restraining hands on opposite shoulders and shoved her back into the chair.

"Keep your drawers on, Finley." Alma winked at her reflection in the mirror. "You're in good hands."

Bunny patted her reassuringly. "You said yourself, forty's a good time for a fresh start."

Rose drew a deep breath and decided to let the two conclude their bickering and get on with the make-over. At least it was taking her mind off some of the more disconcerting aspects of the day—like the way it had started.

They agreed on Auburn thirty-six, which the literature assured would "lend a subtle fire to ordinary brown." As she closed her eyes, leaned back in the chair and let them begin, she muttered, "Birthdays ought to be suspended after twenty-nine anyway. Or definitely after thirty-nine."

Alma snorted her agreement. "So write your congressman. Remember that pudgy little fellow with the veins in his nose who came through here last October. He said call him in Montgomery anytime. Bet you he could legislate something if you called him up."

"Shut up, Alma."

"No, you shut up, Finley. You're gonna be a new woman when we finish with you."

Rose wasn't entirely sure she wanted to be a new woman. But the old one was bored and restless and on the verge of doing something extremely reckless. Maybe this would serve to squelch that urge.

And maybe not.

THE SMALL TOWN in northeast Mississippi, just a few miles from the Alabama border, had everything Ben's printing company needed to establish a paper plant.

He and Keith had pinpointed the area a few months ago, along with another possible location in Tennessee, and apparently their information about Waco, Mississippi, had been right on target. Ben had spent the day quietly gathering additional information without revealing his identity or his purpose. At this stage in a fact-finding mission, that wouldn't be wise even if he wasn't worried about whether or not the law was on his trail.

After nosing around all day, Ben had determined that Waco might be perfect. The determination didn't make him happy.

He kept looking for ways to knock the small town off the list of possibilities. Was the population aging a little too quickly? Was the railroad spur a few miles too far to the south? Were there too many other healthy industries in town competing for workers? Was there some way to turn to disadvantage the fact that paper manufacturing was already one of the state's leading industries?

Or was it simply that Ben had his mind made up to build his paper plant in Sweetbranch, Alabama? Ben shoved the thought aside. It was out of the question. He couldn't even consider it. And that was that.

On his way out of town, Ben turned off the highway down the private road leading through the piece of wooded property he had heard was available for a good price. The property had sounded right—the right size, the right amenities, the right zoning, close enough to the right price to encourage negotiation.

But when Ben pulled his car off the highway and drove down the narrow dirt road, he was looking for things that didn't satisfy him.

About a quarter mile down the road, Ben stopped the car and got out. It had felt good today just to be working again, doing something constructive. His enforced inactivity, his isolation from the work he enjoyed, had been harder on him than he had imagined. Today, asking questions, weighing options and calculating advantages, he had felt a renewed vigor.

That couldn't have anything to do with kissing Rose Finley in her bathrobe, could it? he quizzed himself.

The truth was, the kiss had been like the cherry on a sundae, the sweet topping on a day that had made him feel normal and useful and productive again.

And it should make you feel like the lowlife son of a bitch that you are.

Ben refused to let his conscience work on him today. Later maybe. Tonight. No, not tonight, either. Ben glanced at his watch. Tonight he planned to get home in time to celebrate Rose's birthday.

He tramped over the land, checking to see what kind of forestation grew naturally and whether there were signs of disease. He calculated how much clearing would be required to widen and pave the road and whether an appropriate spot for the actual physical plant existed or would have to be carved out of the forest. He breathed in the warm air and the scent of the woods and smiled.

He walked and made notes for more than an hour, hardly noticing that the sun was sweeping low in the west until it dipped below the line of towering shortleaf pines. In a matter of moments, the woods he had been cheerfully assessing darkened. Overhead, the sky was still light, but the denseness of the foliage and the sudden obscuring of sunlight cast the woods in a different mood.

The back of Ben's neck prickled. He shoved his notebook into his back pocket. He started walking toward his car. The prickling traveled down his back. He picked up his pace. The car was just ahead. He couldn't see it yet, but he remembered. All he had to do was veer off to the left when he got to that ivy-covered stump and...

Or was it to the right? Perspiration tickled the middle of Ben's back.

His throat closed up. He pushed more aggressively through the woods, shoving branches out of his way, trampling wildflowers beneath his feet, snapping off a branch without a thought if it didn't willingly clear the way before him. His eyes began to glaze. His breathing grew labored, seemed on the verge of shutting down altogether. He coached himself not to gasp for breath. And did it anyway.

Then the oaks and cottonwoods and pines disappeared. Kudzu vines vanished. The notebook in his pocket and the loafers on his feet disappeared. No more Mississippi woods. No more forty-three-year-old Ben McKenzie.

The jungle choked him. Held him back. He slashed through it. Hurry. Hurry. He might still make it in time. He might beat the guns. The grenades. He might beat death.

The jungle suffocated him. Squeezed the breath from his lungs. Grabbed his feet and slowed his running, stumbling gait. Snagged his arms, his weapon, his shoulders. Would make him late.

It was forbidden, this running back to cheat death. Even caring was forbidden. Telling the villagers—sharing intelligence—had been forbidden, but he had risked it.

They had not listened. They had stayed. And they would die.

The guns were closer. The smoke was closer. The stench he had come to know too well was closer. His boots grew heavy, slowed. But his heart drove him forward. If there was one life to save, one old man, one young mother, one baby...

He broke into the clearing. Chaos. Thatch roofs smoldered. Cook pots were scattered. And bodies. Bodies he might have recognized if he had the courage to look closer. But he staggered through the noise, the heat, the stinging smoke, looking for a familiar body that still moved, still had voice, still had breath.

Someone to save. Someone who would now listen to his warning, accept his protection.

The body found him. Wahn-Lei on pudgy, unsteady legs, chubby fingers grabbing at Ben's camouflage pants. Tears tracked through the gray ash on the plump baby face.

"Help, Joe! You help, Joe!"

Relief and rage shared space in Ben's heart. He reached down to sweep the child into his arms. And run. Run back to safety. Find a safe place for this one baby, away from massacre and fire and vengeance. A safe place.

His fingers closed on Wahn-Lei's little chest. Short arms came up to grasp Ben's neck as they had welcomed Ben many times. But before he could lift the toddler, Wahn-Lei jerked in his arms, slammed against Ben's knee with numbing impact. Ben crumpled to the ground, confused.

Then he saw. He saw the damp, dark circle on the tiny back. Saw bloodstained fabric clinging to the knee of his camouflage pants. Felt the aftershock pounding his knee. He looked up into the cold eyes of a Vietcong who was not too many years older than Wahn-Lei.

It was a gaunt face, pale with fright and wild with the kind of vengeance the jungle gave birth to. A teenager turned madman. The face of death, Ben had known with chilling certainty.

"He need no more help, Joe. Now you need help." With a malevolent grin, the adolescent raised his weapon and pointed the barrel at Ben's face.

The gun misfired.

His face now twisted in fury, the boy soldier turned the butt of the rifle toward Ben and raised it. But before he could lower it, before Ben could even flinch away, another young boy in ragged uniform ran up, shouting shrilly, pulling him by the arm.

And they disappeared.

As Ben knew, even in his numbness and fear, that he must. He could no more afford to be discovered here than these young Vietcong could.

Ben pulled little Wahn-Lei to his chest. He must get them both to safety. The numbness in his leg began to dissipate, replaced by searing pain. Ben tried to run, but his knee wouldn't hold him. So he crawled, scrambled, Wahn-Lei held tightly to his chest. He crawled on one arm through the jungle, sweating, sobbing, whis-

pering against Wahn-Lei's ear as he went. "I've got you now,
Wahn-Lei. You're with me now. It's going to be okay. Don't cry."

Wahn-Lei hadn't cried. And when Ben was far enough from
the noise and the smoke and the stench of flesh to stop, Wahn-
Lei was growing cold in his arms, the stain from his shattered
chest now branded into Ben's broader one.

Ben sobbed, arms wrapped tightly around the narrow trunk of
a young sycamore. His heart threatened to burst with the racking
of his sobs as the world came slowly back to him. Vietnam receded once again, leaving him in Mississippi and the gentle air
of springtime dusk and the confusing pain of twenty-year-old
tears.

Shaken, Ben sat with his cheek against the rough sycamore
bark, waiting for the tears to dry, his heaving chest to still, waiting
for the moment when he could open his eyes without fear of what
he would see. When he was certain the visions were gone, certain
that Vietnam had returned to the dark recesses of his soul, he
pulled himself painfully, slowly to his feet. On trembling legs,
holding to trees for stability, he staggered back to his car.

AS HE WALKED onto the front porch an hour later, Ben was grateful for the brightly lit house and the sounds of celebration pouring
through the windows. His limbs were steadier, but his mind still
felt vulnerable and weak. Happy noise and people were welcome
distractions.

The rhythms of a big band album came from the living room
stereo. Ben saw Uncle Bump and Krissy's less than expert hands
in the black streamers awkwardly draped across doorways and
swirled around stairway newel posts. A bouquet of black balloons
hung from the overhead light in the entrance hall. And from the
kitchen he heard the strains of a dozen voices singing the familiar
birthday tune. He wandered to the door and peered in.

"You're growing old...." Everyone laughed aloud as someone
tacked the lament onto the end of the tune.

Ben tracked the next singing voice to one of the women who
worked with Rose. "You've got gray hair."

"Not anymore I don't," Rose retorted, flinging her head to
bounce the waves glancing off her shoulders and drawing another
laugh from the small crowd.

Indeed she didn't. Her chestnut hair now had the glow of deeper, richer auburn, a complement to the glow of her fair skin and dark eyes. The combs that usually pulled her hair severely back from her face were gone. Now it waved softly around her temples before cascading to her shoulders. Her lashes seemed longer, the deep set of her eyes more sultry, the color in her cheeks higher, her lips glossier and brighter. Even her clothes looked different—a soft sheath in vibrant teal clung to her slender curves in place of the comfortable jeans and shirts she usually wore.

She looked younger. And more vibrant. More sophisticated in a way that didn't turn its back on her old-fashioned womanliness. She took his breath away.

"Girl," barked Uncle Bump, "you better blow them candles out before the volunteer fire department gets wind of the blaze."

Krissy scrambled into a kitchen chair for a closer view. "Yeah, Auntie Wose. Bwow 'em out."

"Okay. Okay."

Rose filled her lungs and was about to blow when someone yelled, "Make a wish! Don't forget to make a wish!"

"A wish? Do you still get wishes at my age?" She looked up and around the room, her eyes glittering with fun as her friends encouraged and needled her. "Okay. A wish. Now, let's see, what in the world would a woman who's just reaching the prime of life wish for? Hmm."

Her eyes raked the room, full of mischief, landing at last on Ben, who still stood in the doorway at the edge of the room. There they paused, the humor dying, replaced by the look of stunned desire he'd seen in them this morning.

She slowly turned her attention back to the candles. She drew another deep breath and blew.

One by one, the candles flickered out, all but the one under Krissy's curious nose. As Rose emptied her lungs, Krissy saw the single candle twinkling and added her own puff of air. The light flickered out. The room erupted in cheers.

Wondering what she had wished, wondering if it matched the wish in his own heart, Ben let his eyes sweep the clutch of people huddled around the table. All eyes were on Rose, smiling, filled with fondness. All eyes except one pair.

Maxine Hammond's eyes were fixed on Ben McKenzie. They

were not smiling. They were not fond. They were challenging. And they warned him that she didn't like the look she had seen him exchange with her best friend.

CHAPTER TEN

ROSE WALKED BRISKLY down Main Street, checking her watch. She had agreed to meet Maxine at the Clock for dinner.

"So, my friend, you have survived almost a week of your fortieth year." Maxine smiled and stirred artificial sweetener into her glass of iced tea. "Tell me, is it as bad as you envisioned? Or were the reports of your slide into senility greatly exaggerated?"

"Oh, it's been a grand week, Maxie." Let's see, there was the night she had screwed up her courage and followed Ben onto the porch, only to have him dash off for one of his mysterious walks. And the night she had insisted on cooking, only to learn that Ben and Krissy had other unspecified plans. "Just grand."

"Good." Maxine's wry smile said she hadn't missed the irony in Rose's voice. "Then I am certain you are eager for the first aerobics class on Monday night."

With a sinking feeling, Rose remembered the day Maxine had nudged her into signing up for the class. "Monday?"

"Monday. Shall I meet you for the walk over?"

"Is it too late to withdraw?"

"Far too late. To withdraw now brings the risk of certain cellulite."

Rose laughed.

"Good. You are in a pleasant frame of mind. For a change." Maxine spread her napkin in her lap and smiled pointedly. "I bring with me tonight another opportunity for you to broaden your horizons. Now that you have officially reached adulthood..."

"I did that a long time ago."

Maxine waved off Rose's interruption. "Now that you have the wisdom that comes with true maturity," she said, rephrasing her words carefully, "I have a proposition for you."

"Well, you're the only one."

Rose caught a momentary flicker of disapproval in Maxine's dark eyes. "I must say I am glad to hear that. Now, I am here tonight to offer you a position on the town's new Economic Development Task Force. Well, that is not exactly true. Actually, I have been empowered to offer you the chairmanship of that task force."

Rose's hand paused in reaching for the wedge of lemon on the rim of her glass. She stared at her friend. "What?"

Maxine hid her smile behind a swallow of tea. "An excellent cadre of local business owners has been suggested for membership in your task force and..."

"*My* task force? Hold your horses, Maxie. I don't know anything about being chairman of anything."

"Certainly you do. It is widely agreed on the town board that you have been bossing people around for years. We now expect to harness that natural ability and put it to work for the fine people of Sweetbranch."

"Who said I'm bossy?"

The two women sat back and waited for the waitress to set plates in front of them. As she did, Mellie raised her eyebrows at Rose's question. "Honey, I reckon everybody in town knows that. How else did you manage to turn that cantankerous old uncle of yours into a cook all those years ago? Now I hear you've got him baby-sitting. Shoot, you're not just bossy. You're a dang miracle worker. After all, once you nab your fella and get yourself a new stepbaby, you'll have a baby-sitter already broken in."

"What?" Rose's mouth dropped open. The very thought...the very word...stepbaby. Something close to terror yet skirting the edges of anticipation skimmed across the surface of her emotions. "I am not...Mellie, well, all I can say is that's quite an imagination you've got there."

Mellie propped her hands on her broad, aproned hips. "You telling me you're not out to nab that fella?"

Rose felt the color flying to her cheeks. No matter what she said, everyone in Sweetbranch would have heard it by lunchtime tomorrow. Mellie dispensed a lot more than free refills on iced tea with every meal she served.

"Mellie, I am not out to nab a fella. Any fella. Or a..." She almost choked on the next word. "Or a stepbaby."

"Reckon she means it?" Mellie turned from Maxine to Rose with a wicked grin. "Rose, I never had you figured for the type to want to keep things loose. But, heck, at your age nobody's going to pass judgment if you want to do a little dallying. Well, nobody except maybe the Widow Clancy and her bunch over at the Women's Auxiliary. Hazeline Cloninger was in here yesterday and she said..."

"Mellie?" Maxine's gentle but firm voice stemmed the flood of words from the waitress. She pointed to another table across the diner. "I believe Roscoe needs some vinegar for his turnip greens. Perhaps you should attend to him."

Mellie shrugged, reached across their table for a bottle of hot peppers steeping in vinegar and walked away.

Rose turned studious attention to unwrapping the paper napkin from her utensils and spreading it in her lap. She hazarded only a quick glance across the table at Maxine before busying herself applying extra salt and pepper to the corn and squash casserole on her plate. Maxine's piercing eyes were trained on her, demanding, insisting.

"Well, where were we?" Rose picked up knife and fork and started slicing the thick grilled pork chop on her plate. "Oh, yeah. You were trying to con me into another thankless job for the town board. And I was getting ready to tell you how I don't have time for any more extra work right now."

From beneath her lowered lashes, Rose watched as Maxine also started eating with measured, careful movements.

"Of course. You do have extra duties these days, do you not? Your uncle is certainly helping, but having extra people in your home necessarily creates extra work."

With an exasperated sigh, Rose had to admit she had only herself to blame. If she'd wanted to stir up everyone in Sweetbranch by bringing Ben and Krissy home to live with her, she had certainly done the job.

"You're not starting on me, too, are you?"

Maxine didn't say anything for several moments. "I believe your determination would be put to good use in finding ways to revitalize this town's economy. Shall I report back to the board that you have agreed to chair the task force?"

Grateful for the change in topic, Rose capitulated. "All right.

Tell them I'm in. But I don't want a bunch of sour old men to work with.''

Maxine named the other business owners who had been suggested for the task force. Rose was pleased. In addition to the requisite number of sour old men, there were also a fair number of enthusiastic, imaginative people.

"Good. We might just stir up some things."

"Of that I am confident."

When Rose glanced up to share the wry smile she felt certain had accompanied her friend's remark, she was surprised by the troubled frown on Maxine's face. Slowly, Maxine laid down her fork and reached across the table to rest her hand on Rose's.

"Rose, please be careful. Do not do something you may come to regret.''

"Make up your mind. Do you want me to chair this task force of yours or not? If you're having second thoughts..." As she looked into Maxine's eyes, it dawned on Rose that the task force was not the source of Maxine's concern. "Oh."

"Exactly. Oh." Maxine gave her hand a little squeeze before letting go. "You do not know this man, Rose. Stay away from him. Protect yourself.''

"I'm a big girl, Maxie. Forty now. All grown up. You said so yourself."

Maxine expressed her skepticism with an uncharacteristic grunt of displeasure. "You are naive."

"And you've got a cog loose. What happened, Maxie, did one of those beads in your braids get hung up in the little wheels of your brain and get things out of whack up there?"

"My beads have not interfered with the cogs in my brain in the least." The faint smile returned to her face and voice. "But about you, my friend, I am not so certain."

"You think I've gone off the deep end because I had another birthday this week."

"I believe you feel that life has passed you by and that many other opportunities may not present themselves."

Rose didn't want to hear any more. "When I need somebody to explain me to myself, I'll let you know."

"And I believe that is leading you to do things that you would not do if you were more satisfied with your life. But, Rose, please do not let that dissatisfaction lead you into decisions that could ruin your life. Do not throw away your life for the sake of a little excitement."

Rose yanked her napkin out of her lap and tossed it onto the table, gathering up her purse as she did so. "Don't tell me what's going to ruin my life. For your information, there isn't much to ruin. And if I decide to grab a little excitement, I don't need your permission to do it."

She stood to leave, but as she looked down at Maxine's dismayed face, her anger dissipated. She dropped back into the booth and stared beseechingly at her best friend.

"Maxie, you have a wonderful life. Two pretty little children call you mommy and hug you every night at bedtime. A husband who loves you so strong even I can see it in his eyes. Don't tell me my life's too good to risk. My life is a big old empty house and an uncle who doesn't shave every day." She paused to clear the sob that was collecting deep in her chest. "I don't even have any memories to keep me warm at night. If I want to make some memories, I don't need you to tell me it's not a good idea."

The understanding in Maxine's eyes was still clouded by a fear that seemed unreasonable to Rose, even when she remembered all the things that didn't add up about Ben McKenzie.

KRISSY BOUNCED on the front seat so impatiently it was all Ben could do to keep her still long enough to fasten her seat belt.

"Hurry, Daddy. Hurry."

"We have to fasten your seat belt, kiddo. Even if you're in a hurry. Now, you mind Uncle Bump. Do everything he tells you. Okay?"

She grabbed him around the neck and gave him a wet kiss on his cheek. "I do. I do. Hurry, Unka Bunk. Hurry."

Uncle Bump settled in behind the steering wheel of Ben's car and looked around to familiarize himself with the vehicle. The old man looked uncommonly dapper. In honor of their outing to Tuscumbia to play miniature golf, he had shaved and slicked his flyaway hair back and found a red bow tie to wear with his plaid flannel shirt and yellow suspenders.

"Hurry," he grumbled under his breath. "Hurry to play golf. Poor substitute for fishing, if you ask me."

Krissy reached over to pat the wrinkled hand on the steering wheel. "Itta be fun. You'll see."

"Well, just remember our deal. You lean over and pick up all the balls for old Uncle Bump. And, ah—" he patted his front pocket to check for his glasses "—stand by the hole so I can see where I'm aiming. Right?"

Krissy nodded. "And I get the red ball."

Uncle Bump knotted up his forehead and pretended to consider that carefully. "I don't know. What's that leave for me? I don't want some sissy color."

Krissy giggled. "Green. You can be green."

"Green?" He feigned outrage. "Do I look green to you?"

Ben leaned through the car window and kissed his daughter on the cheek, then whispered loudly, "Think you can get Uncle Bump to behave, Krissy?"

"He'll be good," she pronounced solemnly. "Else he has to go to his room tomorrow."

As he watched the car glide down Dixie Belle Lane, Ben fought the restlessness festering in him. He knew it was pointless to sit around wondering if Rose would be home soon. Besides, he was more than merely restless. His mind needed work, needed challenge. Even his body needed occupying—it and his mind were so preoccupied with his recurring fantasies about Rose Finley that he sometimes felt he would explode if he didn't find something to do with himself.

But he'd found no place in town to work out, to burn off the excess energy and the emotions he needed to expend. So he had decided to try jogging. He'd tried it years ago and discovered that the knee shattered in Vietnam hadn't been up to the constant pounding of the pavement. But that had been years ago. Perhaps, with the years of working out and weight training since then, his knee was stronger.

And he had to do something or lose his mind.

After putting on the knee support he always used when he worked out and lacing up the jogging shoes he'd picked up at the general store earlier in the day, Ben started slowly down the road, trying neither to favor his knee nor to strain it.

For the first few moments, he enjoyed the excitement rushing through his body. He was moving again. Feeling the wind in his hair, feeling his muscles heat up. His legs tingled as the blood rushed through them. The sidewalk rose up to meet his feet and a gladness rushed into his lungs with the fresh air he breathed.

But Ben discovered that his mind was less willing than usual to empty out and let his body take over. His legs and arms and lungs pumped cooperatively, but his mind also continued to pump.

Cybil pumped through his mind. He had called her earlier in the day, after a call to his brother had revealed the unexpected news that no one seemed to have noticed that Ben had spirited away his daughter.

"Nothing?" Ben had stared at the cracked sidewalk beside the pay phone on Main Street. "What about the police?"

"If the police are asking, they're not asking anybody I know," Keith had insisted. "Not a word, Ben. Nothing in the paper. Cybil hasn't called. Nothing. It's weird."

It had given Ben a weird feeling, too, as if he might have stepped off the earth while no one was watching and ceased to exist. You don't take a woman's child without triggering a response. The old prickling feeling that something was about to go wrong had seized Ben. After he finished telling Keith about the Mississippi site—which somehow sounded less promising in the telling than it had seemed in reality—Ben had stared at the telephone for several minutes before turning and walking away.

But after his visit to the general store, shoebox under his arm, he had passed the phone again.

He had dialed Cybil's number from memory and held his breath while it rang. Twice. Four times. He let out his breath. She must be out. Good. That would save him from bruising his conscience again and...

Her voice when she answered on the seventh ring had sounded fuzzy. When she heard his voice, it had sharpened to an overly careful preciseness. And Ben knew, with a sharp jab to his midsection, that she had been drinking.

His fault, too, of course.

"Well, all-American hero Ben McKenzie surfaces again." The sarcasm in her voice called to mind the haughty tilt to her head, the minuscule lowering of her eyelids. "Are you getting tired of playing your little rescue game, Ben?"

Ben struggled with his response. His inclination was to answer her sarcasm with sharpness of his own. He had to remind himself that his goal wasn't to get back at Cybil.

"Are you all right, Cybil?"

Her laugh was brittle and humorless and, it seemed to Ben's familiar ear, verging on out of control. "What an absurd question. You've stolen my child. You've ruined my life. And you want to know if I'm all right?"

"She's fine. She smiles a lot more these days."

He had intended only to reassure his ex-wife, but he realized his words also held the sting of accusation. But it was too late to retract them.

"You're lying!" The barest edge of hysteria crept into her voice. "She's not fine! She wouldn't be happy away from me. Away from her mommy."

"She does miss you. That's true."

"Bring her home!"

Ben rubbed his temple. He hated to bring it up, but he had to know. "You haven't reported it, have you?"

Cybil was silent.

"Why not, Cybil?"

Still she was silent. He discovered he couldn't quite imagine what she was thinking. They had been married for nine years. He had loved her even after he had stopped liking her. But now, he discovered, he could no more fathom her than he could fly.

Still, he hazarded the only guess that made any sense to him. "You know she's safe with me, don't you?"

A weak, whining sob came over the line. "Bring her back, Ben. It won't happen again. Please. I need her. I really need her. Bring her back. Okay? Colin's furious that I let you take her. He... Please, Ben, give me back my baby."

At the mention of Colin, Ben's sympathy waned. But as he jogged, a queasiness spread through his stomach at the memory of her thin, boozy pleading. When there had been little else to admire about Cybil, there had at least been her dignity, her regal manner.

And is that your fault, too? he asked himself, now suddenly conscious of the sharp discomfort in his left knee. Slowing his gait, Ben tried to ease the strain on his knee without halting completely. But within half a block, he realized his knee was stiffening and growing more painful with each stride.

He stopped and limped back to the house on Dixie Belle Lane, feeling as dejected as he knew he must look.

ROSE HELD THE NOTE in her hand and stooped to sit on the front steps. The house was empty. Uncle Bump and Krissy were on an excursion to Tuscumbia.

So she was alone. Just a month ago, being alone had felt comfortable. Commonplace. Uncle Bump was one of the mainstays of Sweetbranch's clique of widowers and longtime bachelors who served as the counterparts—but not the companions—of Ida Clancy's church auxiliary women. So Rose was accustomed to nights when her uncle was out playing checkers or other unspecified males-only activities.

But this was different. Now she was accustomed to a house that hummed with people. A house with a child always hummed, she was learning. And even though she had tried to steel herself against involvement with Krissy, even though she had tried to distance herself from the little girl who had no real place in her life, she had discovered it was an impossible task.

Little girls stole your heart. They smiled and you smiled back. They came to you with their scraped knees and you kissed them. They gave you a hug and a crumpled dandelion and you took them with a lump in your throat.

Rose tried to convince herself that the long, solitary evening ahead held appeal. But she knew it wasn't so. She would miss the noise of Uncle Bump's grumbling and Krissy's merriment.

And Ben. She tried not to picture his face, imagine his presence. But it was impossible. She would miss him, too. Would miss the sparks that filled the air when he was around.

"Stop mooning, Finley." Shoving the note into her pocket, she pulled herself up and walked into the yard. The grass was already creeping up to her ankles. Time to pull the lawn mower out and nag Uncle Bump into getting it oiled up and ready for the season. Rose felt herself wilt in anticipation of the long summer stretching ahead of her. Soaring temperatures and smothering humidity and the necessity to appear enthusiastic when somebody suggested splitting open an icy watermelon or handcranking some ice cream—summer was one more thing to endure.

She supposed Uncle Bump would want a garden, too. Rose

wasn't sure she had the heart for the weeding and fertilizing and watering necessary to coax another crop of tomatoes and okra and cantaloupes out of the backyard.

She leaned over the hedge of azaleas, which were finally in full flower some two weeks after all the others in town had faded and lost their blooms.

"Late again," she chided her mother's handiwork, recalling with a smile how LaFern Finley had defended the recalcitrant hedge.

"That's okay," she had assured her impatient daughter. "They're stragglers. When all the other spring color is faded, these'll jump right out to brighten everything up again. Nothing wrong with late bloomers, Rosie."

Rose straightened in time to see a familiar form turn the corner onto Dixie Belle Lane. She thought at first it was her imagination. But it was Ben, dressed in jogging shorts and T-shirt. Perspiration trickled in a vee down the front of his gray T-shirt and his silver hair was kinked with dampness. His legs were long and hard, corded with strength. He was favoring one leg, the one that was snugly bandaged at the knee.

And he looked dejected. His head was down, his shoulders slumped. He looked like a man whose battles with the world were weighing him down.

Maxine's warning came into her head. What did she know about this man, really? Nothing, except that he seemed to need her. And his need was difficult—impossible?—for her to reject.

Rose leaned on the white picket fence and watched him limping up the sidewalk. In spite of everything, a smile curved her lips as she watched.

"I could've told you if you'd asked me," she said as he drew nearer.

He looked up, his expression first startled, then softer when he saw her face. "Told me what?"

"That running's for kids whose bodies don't mind the abuse." She swung open the front gate as he approached.

He gave her a weak grin as he entered the yard. "I guess you're right. I just needed to do something. Back home...I usually work out at the Y. But..."

She nodded at his gesture of surrender. "I know. No fancy

fitness clubs around here. But that's no good reason to ruin your leg.''

He slapped at his left thigh. ''Running didn't do this. This leg's been ruined a long time.''

''Oh?''

She saw his hesitation and knew that, once again, he didn't want to elaborate. He looked up into her questioning eyes, then away. His answer, when it came, was abrupt.

''Vietnam.''

Vietnam, she knew, could explain a lot about Ben McKenzie. But his curt answer, delivered in that tone of voice that precluded further discussion, didn't diminish the vague suspicions gnawing at the back of her mind.

Attempting to lighten the conversation, she smiled. ''Too bad you're not female. If you were, you could join the rest of us in town who are stiff-jointed and out of shape when the church starts its aerobics class next week.''

Ben responded to her smile with a distracted one of his own. ''Women only? Not very broad-minded of you.''

''Nobody ever accused Sweetbranch of being broad-minded.''

He nodded. He would turn and walk away in another moment. Rose searched for a different topic.

''Having any luck with the job hunt?'' She sensed him stiffen at the question and told herself that was natural.

''Not much.''

He moved on toward the house. She watched him, knew he was doing all he could to minimize his limp. He wasn't a man who liked his weaknesses to show. He wouldn't want anybody commiserating over his unemployed status any more than he would want anybody clucking sympathetically over his bad knee. But still...

She caught up with Ben as he reached the steps.

''You asked around town much?'' She clamped down on her urge to put a hand under his elbow as he took the steps.

''Not much.''

She might have known that, of course. If he'd asked around town, she would have heard. She ignored the voice that wondered how hard Ben McKenzie was looking for a job, because that didn't add up. Ben seemed like anything but shiftless.

''Maybe I could help. My friend Maxine...''

"No!" The word that burst forth was no longer simply abrupt. Now he sounded harsh, almost angry. He turned at the top of the stairs and looked down at her. She saw him struggling to get his reactions under control. "No, I'll find something. Soon."

He entered the house and she watched through the front door as he mounted the first two steps slowly, gingerly. Then he stopped, stared up the long flight of steps rising in front of him. His shoulders sagging once again, he came back downstairs and turned into the living room.

Rose's heart went out to him. She didn't know exactly what his situation was, of course, but she knew the feelings of frustration and loneliness and wanting desperately to control things that were out of her control.

She followed him into the house, poured two tall glasses of iced tea and took them into the living room. He was sitting in Uncle Bump's chair, staring into the empty fireplace and rubbing his knee.

She stood by him for a moment, holding the glass of tea. When he didn't seem to notice, she leaned over and took his free hand, placing the glass in it. He looked at it and smiled. "Thanks, Rose."

Smiling back, she dropped to the floor and leaned against the chair to the left of the one where he sat. "Some days are worse than others, aren't they?"

He nodded, still unconsciously rubbing his knee.

"How about some of Uncle Bump's liniment?"

She saw the automatic refusal in his face, then saw him hesitate. "It always helps him," she added.

"Maybe that would be nice."

When she returned with the tube of liniment, he had already unwrapped the bandage, revealing a knee that was crisscrossed with faded scars. She knelt beside him again. "It was pretty bad, wasn't it?"

He shrugged. "Could have been worse. A lot of them were."

But something in his eyes told her that it was far worse than the random network of scars revealed.

He reached for the liniment, but she had already uncapped the tube and squirted some into her palm.

"I can do that," he protested.

She grinned up at him, teasing him with her eyes. "Better let me. We wouldn't want you leaning over too far and putting your back out, too.''

He chuckled and the sound warmed her.

His knee was hair-roughened. Hard and unyielding and warmer than she had anticipated. She almost flinched away from that first touch before she could stop herself.

It's only his knee, you silly goose, she scolded herself. *It's not like you're messing around where you shouldn't be.*

That thought proved far more disconcerting than the touch of her hand on his leg.

He laid his head back against the chair. She felt him relaxing into her gentle massage.

"Who takes care of you, Rose?" His voice was almost a whisper.

Her hand slowed. "Why, what makes you think I need anybody to take care of me?" She laughed uncertainly.

"We all need it sometime."

She drew her hand away, painfully aware that she didn't want to stop and that was the best reason of all to stop. She recapped the tube and stood. But before she could take a step to circle around him, he reached out and took hold of her wrist.

Wide-eyed, she looked down. His blue eyes were so gentle she wanted to turn away.

"And you deserve someone who'll take good care of you."

She shrugged, thinking of tossing off some flippant retort. But no words came. His eyes captivated her with their intensity and their promise. When he pulled her toward him, she told herself to resist. She reminded herself there were reasons not to give in to this...this tidal wave of sensations. The tingling, electrical, whirling sensations were as alien as they were overwhelming. And against her better judgment, she gave in to them.

She dropped into his lap and his arms wrapped tenderly around her before she had time to question her capitulation.

"Ben..."

He silenced her protest with his finger on her lips. "Don't."

So she didn't. She ignored the war within her, both the side that urged her toward control and the side that would seduce her, daring her to seek deeper, darker, more tumultuous feelings.

He didn't try to kiss her at first. He merely held her. His hands eased along her back, her shoulders, her arms, spreading warmth and lassitude and a kind of comfort Rose was unaccustomed to. All the while his eyes were begging for her trust and promising her things she couldn't quite label.

"This is crazy," she whispered as she brought her smooth cheek against his stubbly one. Their lips edged closer with each movement.

"Maybe. Maybe it's crazy not to. When it feels so..." His lips nuzzled hers, briefly, a test. She nuzzled back. "So right. So necessary."

She knew what he meant. His touch was necessary. His kiss necessary. As necessary as breathing.

They kissed. Soft and seeking, his lips played over hers. Hers answered, soft and giving. Their kiss deepened, joined by tiny sounds rising from deep inside her. She pressed herself more deeply into his embrace. She must find a place to lose herself, here in his arms, in the scent of him, kissed with fresh air and exertion. In the feel of him, hard beneath his T-shirt, stirring beneath his cotton shorts, rough where the hair on his arms brushed against hers.

When his hands worked their way beneath her shirt, she moved in his arms to give him access. Where his fingers explored, along the ridges of her spine and around to the upward slope of her ribs, she was warm and alive in a way that stunned her, drew whimpers of acquiescence from her.

His lips left hers, trailing along her chin, her jaw. All fire and softness inside, she opened the curve of her neck to invite him down. His lips nuzzled into the vee of her shirt, whispering damp heat into the valley between her breasts. In the tiny corner of her brain that still entertained conscious thought, a voice was urging her to loosen her buttons, to let him in.

"Can't," she whispered back to the urging voice.

He stilled. "Rose?"

"No, I..."

She meant for him to understand that her words weren't for him, weren't a protest. But her mind was too lost, too disconnected to command her voice. And then it was too late. His hands slipped away and his lips broke contact with her skin and she sat, aching, on fire, weak with heat.

"Rose, I won't rush you."

His promise was gentle, filled with concern. And she wanted

to cry. She wanted him to rush her. Rush her so fast she could blame something else for her lack of good sense. But Ben wasn't like that.

And now it was too late.

Ben's voice was infuriatingly understanding. "I know you don't...we hardly know each other."

Stiff now in his arms, sensible thoughts rushing back to fill her head, Rose swallowed her disappointment. He was right. But she didn't give a damn about that. She wanted him and he wanted her. Wasn't that all they really needed to know? She didn't want to meet his eyes, but he lifted her chin and forced her to look at him.

"I don't want us to do anything you'll regret."

His words were gentle, solicitous. And they reminded her of Maxine, repeating the same words.

She jumped up, her disappointment now boiling into unreasonable anger. "When I want you to worry about me, I'll let you know, Ben McKenzie. Until then, you can assume I'm capable of taking care of myself."

Then she turned and stalked out of the room and into her bedroom, slamming the door behind her.

CYBIL DIDN'T EVEN LOOK down at the shattered china plate. Ninety-eight dollars' worth of bone-and-gold-colored china made a random pattern of chunks and slivers on the kitchen's marbleized tile floor. It would have to be cleaned up. But right now she wasn't sure she could bend over without falling over.

She was only grateful she had been able to move fast enough to duck when Colin hurled the plate.

She supposed remnants of the plum tomato sauce remained on the wall. The impact might have scarred the quietly tasteful wallpaper. But she didn't dare look up for fear he might interpret her glance as accusing. He still stood in the doorway, glaring, waiting for her response.

She couldn't remember what he had asked. She shouldn't have started on the brandy after Ben called. Damn his stupid Sir Galahad mentality. Damn him for ruining her life.

Colin stalked to her side and grabbed her shoulder. She dared not flinch away, although she knew from the pressure he exerted that the flesh would be bruised by morning.

"Answer me!" The fine Scotch whisky on his breath fueled her fear. "Have you talked to his brother? His family's bound to know where he is. Are you going to find out, or am I going to have to? I've got a good mind to go to the police."

Anger diluted the fear clogging her throat and coating her mouth. "You wouldn't dare. You're too afraid of how it would look to all your fancy friends. And Ben's family certainly won't tell *you*. Don't you know that?"

His grip on her shoulder tightened; his voice lowered to a threatening growl. "They'll tell me."

She tried to struggle out of his grasp. "Not you, they won't. Don't you know that? You're the reason he took her. If it weren't for you..."

The venom in his eyes dared her to continue. She knew he was so inebriated it was unsafe to goad him; but she was too inebriated to use good judgment.

"If I left you, he'd bring her back."

"Well, you're not leaving me. And if you won't do anything to get your own daughter back—" he released her with a shove that slammed her against the edge of the tile countertop "—I'll do it myself."

CHAPTER ELEVEN

IT WAS THE WIDOW CLANCY'S sly comment that brought the whole thing out in the open.

"Well, Rose, I understand you brought in quite an unusual recruit for the church's aerobics class last night."

Ida Clancy was exceptionally pleased with herself. Rose could tell that from the tone of her voice. She wished, for one spiteful moment, that every brittle gray hair on the woman's head would fall right out on the yellow-and-white linoleum floor of the Picture Perfect.

Rose had, of course, known the minute Ben walked into the Fellowship Hall that his presence would not go unremarked. But until Ida Clancy spoke up, she'd hoped no one would remark on it to her.

Five pairs of eyes turned toward her, including the Widow Clancy's arch gaze from the mirror in front of them.

"That's right, Ida." Never mind that she had been as stunned as everyone else in the hall. The worst of it was, he had picked Rose out of the crowd and stuck to her side the rest of the night. Talking to her. Letting his eyes say things to her that weren't appropriate for a roomful of Christian women.

Everyone had noticed Ben's attention to her, but it hadn't stopped the women from turning their own attention to him. The only one who hadn't been thrown into a tizzy by his appearance was Maxine, whose jaw had tightened in disapproval. No one else, however, was disapproving. In fact, after class, a circle of fawning women had trapped Ben. Warring with feelings that were ridiculously like jealousy, Rose had dashed home, praying he wouldn't catch up with her.

He hadn't.

And in a case of perverse pique, she had grown irritated picturing him lapping up the attention of the women.

"You and your new...tenant...seem to have quite a friendly relationship."

Alma's scissors paused over the head she was cutting, which also turned almost imperceptibly in Rose's direction. Bunny cleared her throat loudly. Both her co-workers knew just how much Rose despised the Widow Clancy's presumption that engaging in petty gossip and shameless digging for personal details were her constitutionally guaranteed rights.

"That's right, too, Ida." Well, it might not be, but why deny it? Ida Clancy was going to believe whatever she wanted to believe and Rose knew it. "My goodness, you're really batting a thousand this morning, aren't you?"

Ida smiled with pleased self-assurance. "Well, insight *is* my strong suit, Rose. Your mama always said I seemed to know more about the people in this town than anyone else."

"I expect she was right about that, Ida."

Bunny turned away and doubled over in a cough that didn't quite disguise her laughter and Alma grinned and gave the woman in her chair a jab in the shoulder. But Rose kept her face straight as Ida continued.

"Well, all I've got to say, young lady, is to remember your place. You're not too old to shame your mama's memory."

Rose paused and propped one hand on a hip while she studied the back of Ida's head, where the hair was thinning visibly. She wondered if one was always obliged to count to ten before firing off a sharp retort.

Bunny saved her from making a decision. "Y'all see the big story in the paper yesterday?"

Alma filled the air with a nuclear cloud of hair spray. "Which one was that? The one about Estelle's girl's baby shower being canceled or the one about Leland writing a book? You know, I never did think Estelle's girl was expecting anyway. She just did it so her mama'd let her marry that no-account from over in Walker County. And as far as Leland, shoot, he's been threatening to write the *Peyton Place* of Sweetbranch for twenty years. Everybody knows that. Tell me, Ida, he asked you for your insights yet or what?"

"Hush, Alma," Bunny interrupted. "I'm talking about global concerns here. I'm talking about the railroad shutting down."

Rose almost dropped the plastic gloves she was slipping on in preparation for working the color solution into Ida Clancy's hair. "What?"

"That's right. By the first of the year, they're gonna shut down the spur from Tuscumbia. Some official in Birmingham said we don't have enough business to justify it."

Rose sighed. If the railroad line died, so did any chance of luring any more industry to Sweetbranch. The railroad was the lifeline. And that lifeline, it seemed, was hanging by a thread. Like the whole town.

"We don't need that railroad anyway," Ida assured the others. "It's smelly and noisy. And with the world the way it is today, it won't be long before it brings in a bunch of hoboes from the city, all looking for a handout. We're better off without it."

Rose tuned out Ida Clancy. And she made up her mind, as the discussion swirled around her, that the first job her task force would tackle would be asking the railroad to reverse, or at least delay implementing, its decision.

The future of Sweetbranch would be decided in the next few months, Rose realized. And she had to do something to make sure that future went in the right direction.

A strange feeling welled up in Rose as she contemplated the steps she could take to influence the future. She struggled to identify it. If she didn't know better, she would think it felt like power.

The bell over the door jingled and Rose glanced over to see Uncle Bump walk in, holding Krissy by the hand. Conversation stopped in the room as everyone took in the duo. Ida's bushy eyebrows inched up and Bunny gave a short exclamation.

"Why, Mr. Finley," she said, "I hardly recognized you. You're so slicked up you must have a lady friend."

Ida stiffened in her chair, no doubt because she couldn't bear the thought that something so significant had escaped her attention. And as Rose turned her skeptical look on her uncle, she realized Bunny was right. Her uncle had undergone a real metamorphosis. He shaved every morning now, his soft pink jowls no longer looking drab and unhealthy from the gray stubble on his cheeks and chin. His wild hair was not nearly so wild; she wondered if he'd pulled out a forgotten tube of his old hair cream or if he'd been sneaking a little dab of her styling gel. Even his clothes looked... She stared more closely. Darn if it didn't look as if he might have ironed his shirt and pants.

Uncle Bump laughed, a grizzled sound that was about the only familiar thing about him. "Might know I couldn't keep a thing from you ladies. Yep, I want y'all to meet my lady friend. Krissy, this here is the gossipingest bunch you'll ever want to know. Don't tell 'em no secrets. You hear?"

Krissy giggled and looked shyly around the room before her eyes landed on Rose. Her eyes lit up and she ran to wrap her arms around Rose's knees. "Auntie Wose! You want to make me another haircut?"

"*Aunt* Rose?"

Everyone ignored Ida Clancy. Rose barely heard the pointed inquiry. She was too caught up in Krissy's innocent outpouring of affection. She kept telling herself that one day Krissy would realize that Rose Finley wasn't surrogate mother material.

But whenever she thought that—usually at one of those times when Krissy was giving her a sloppy kiss or a big hug for no discernible reason—Rose also wondered if little girls didn't know more about who was good mothering material than grown-ups with faltering self-esteem.

Holding her hands high overhead to avoid touching Krissy with the color solution on her gloves, Rose leaned over and planted a kiss on the child's nose. Krissy smelled little-girl sweet and Rose wished her hands were free. "No time for haircuts today, sweetie. Looks to me like you and Uncle Bump have other plans for the day."

"Bingo!" Krissy hopped up and down.

"Yeah, me and the kid are going over to Muscle Shoals. Church over there's got a big bingo game tonight. We're going to win us a fortune, right, Kris?"

"And buy ice cream!"

"Well, thanks for letting me know." But it seemed odd to her that he'd come by the shop just to tell her that. The best he'd ever done before was leave a note, when he even remembered to do that.

"Yeah, well." He shrugged and she saw a gleam in his dark eyes. "Just thought you'd want to know that you and...that you'd have to fend for yourself tonight. Oh, and I brung you something.''

He pulled an envelope from his back pocket and held it in her direction. Gingerly grasping one corner with her gloved fingers, she noted the familiar crimson-edged stationery. The University of Alabama.

''Thought you might be waitin' on that.''

Catching sight of his satisfied smile, Rose wondered whether she really had any privacy at all or if all Sweetbranch had been waiting word from the postmistress on Rose's reply from the university.

Rose stuffed the envelope in the pocket of her uniform. It burned there, taunting her, stoking the excitement growing out of that other feeling—that feeling she kept wanting to label power.

THE STRONG FEELING swelling up in Rose didn't diminish as the day went on. She kept the envelope in her pocket, taking it out to look at it whenever she could steal a private moment. But never opening it. Unopened, it held a bright, unlimited future. Once she opened it, the future might dim in an instant.

So she savored the feeling of her power. She called the members of her task force and set up their first meeting for later in the week. She walked to the diner at lunchtime, imagining Sweetbranch's Main Street once again lively with thriving businesses. At the end of the day she walked home, bursting with anticipation.

It was only when she arrived at the big house, eyes and ears searching for evidence of another human being, that Rose realized her anticipation had been twofold. Yes, she had anticipated opening the envelope.

But she had also looked forward to being alone with Ben McKenzie, to finding out if his attention the night before had been mere show. But Ben wasn't home.

He isn't here, Rose corrected herself. *You have no idea where home is for Ben McKenzie, but it isn't here.*

''Don't be cranky,'' she scolded herself, leaning over to pick up Boo as she wandered to her room to change into cotton shorts and a shirt. She rubbed the cat on the head and buried her cheek in soft fur. ''Ben McKenzie isn't the reason you feel the way you do. This—'' she hesitated over the word, as if saying it might spirit away the feelings "—power you feel is inside *you*. It doesn't come from him."

It didn't go away when she said it.

She cinched the drawstring on her shorts and pulled her hair back into the ponytail she hadn't worn in twenty-five years. She tucked the envelope into the roomy pocket of her shorts and heated leftovers in the microwave for dinner. Then she sat on the porch, envelope in hand, watching the darkness fall.

Her confidence did flicker and sputter when she actually began to open the envelope. What if it was all a pipe dream?

She ran her index finger under the flap of the envelope, loosening it. She peered inside. There was a white sheet, a yellow sheet and a pink sheet. She pulled out the white sheet first and unfolded it with fingers that almost trembled.

Dear Ms. Finley,

We are happy to accept you, beginning with the fall term.

Enclosed you will find a form providing instructions on participating in our life experience testing this summer. You will see that...

They accepted her. Rose Finely was a college student. When fall rolled around this year, forty-year-old Rose Finley would be hitting the books and studying for exams. She might not be going out for rush week or crowding into a dormitory. And it might be a tough commute two or three days a week. But she would be going to college.

Rose pressed her lips tightly together to push back the joyful sob that threatened to surface. Through a blur of tears, she opened the yellow sheet to find out more about the testing that might give her credit for some of her life and work experience. She could barely see the page for the tears filling her eyes.

"Holy cow, Boo," she muttered, trying to dash away the moisture with a bare arm. "Can you believe this?"

Boo, curled on the welcome mat, opened one eye, then tightened up and covered her face with one paw. She was not impressed.

But Rose was beside herself. She wanted to whoop. Holler.

Run around the yard screaming like a banshee, which was one of the cardinal sins her mother had always forbidden.

So she did it.

Laughing out loud, she ran around the yard, leaving one sandal on the front step and flipping the other toward the sky as she dashed into the yard. The dew was wet on her bare feet, and cool.

"I'm going to college!" she yelled to the treetops, hardly noticing when Johnsie Wooten peered between her calico curtains from the house next door.

She ran around the house, wishing there were sheets on the clothesline so she could run between them. She felt so young right now that she expected LaFern Finley to stick her scolding head out the back screen door any moment.

"I'm going to be so smart! Nothing can stop me now! Nothing!"

And before she knew what she was doing, she had bounded up the giant backyard tree and into the tree house. In the dark shroud of the leaves that had filled out completely since she'd last climbed into her childhood haven, Rose started to sit, then was hit with a memory. Clambering to the back of the platform, Rose found a wooden box that had served as treasure chest, chair or table, depending on the need. She tugged open the lid and found the plastic tarpaulin they had used on rainy days, still wrapped around the two fuzzy blankets.

She pulled the blankets out, spreading one beneath her on the hard platform and wrapping the other loosely around her shoulders. She was so caught up in her actions that she started at the sound of a voice from below.

"What's all that racket?"

Ben. Rose suddenly felt completely and ridiculously satisfied. Who better to share this news with than Ben? What better way to celebrate this start of her new life?

"Did you bring the champagne?" She peered over the edge. From halfway up the tree, Ben's eyes met hers.

"Damn! Left it below. Shall I go back for it?"

She shook her head. "No need. I think I'm already drunk."

"Sounded like it to me." He hefted himself up onto the tree-house floor. Rose scooted over to offer him room on the blanket. "I thought I'd better come after you before your next-door neighbor strained her bifocals. So, what are we drinking to?"

Uncertainty touched Rose with reticence. Would Ben understand?

She drew a deep breath and plunged in. "I...I'm going back to college. I just got my acceptance letter. And now I can take some tests to see if they'll give me credit for some of my experience—I might not have to take freshman math and things like that. And if I do well on the test, I could graduate in about three years. If I work hard."

She paused for a breath, almost dreading his reaction. This had been such a golden moment, as if someone had breathed life into her again. What if he wasn't excited?

Ben's knuckles brushed hers and she looked up to see him offering an imaginary toast. "To new beginnings."

Smiling shyly, she closed her fingers around the stem of an imaginary glass and tapped knuckles.

"Congratulations, Rose. I really am glad for you."

She heard the warmth of sincerity in his voice. She wrapped her arms around the knees that were bent to press against her chest. "You don't think I'm...too old."

She felt his knuckles again, this time brushing softly against her cheek. "Far from it."

"But maybe I'm just kidding myself." She could barely keep her breath from catching as she spoke. The touch of his skin on hers made her aware of how fast her heart was pounding, how warm her skin felt, how demandingly her breasts ached. "Maybe it's too late."

"It's never too late. For anything."

She turned to look at him and knew from his eyes that he spoke of things besides college degrees. "For anything?"

His fingers fell away from her cheek, dropping to encircle her shoulder. "Anything, Rose."

She turned away from his eyes, which were beckoning her to take one more daring step today, to start in one more new direction. She wanted to. But if anything, what he asked was more frightening than the prospect of registering for calculus or choosing a major. She forced an evenness into her voice. "How can you be sure? By the time I graduate, I'll be forty-three."

"You'll be forty-three one day anyway." Although his voice matched her impersonal tone, he slipped closer, his arm tightened around her shoulders. And without questioning the warmth that stole over her, Rose leaned into him. "Would you rather be forty-three and have a college degree or forty-three and just the way you are today?"

"No!" She turned her head and was surprised to find his face so close. His lips were near. His eyes became her world. She was breathless when she spoke. "Ben, I want to change. I want to do things. I want something else out of life. I want..."

"What do you want, Rose?"

Rose felt dizzy, so many dreams seemed to clamor for her attention right now. She wanted to slow things down. She wanted to speed them up. Especially the dreams in his eyes.

"I want you. Right now that's what I really want."

"And I want you, Rose. More than anything."

He eased her slowly onto the blanket, cushioning her head with his arm and pulling her to face him. She pressed gently against the length of him. His chest was hard and warm. His thighs were hard and warm. His arms, his hands. The pulse just beneath the sharp cut of his jaw, where she rested her lips for one brief moment before they kissed.

Only his lips were soft, pleading with hers to yield. And they did. Their lips met, sought, demanded. Rose felt once again the fluttering deep inside her, as if something were coming alive, as if feelings half-slumbering were awakening to new power. She pressed that gentle uncurling in the pit of her belly to him and felt him, too, coming alive.

Ben's hand trailed down the rise of her hip, cresting and following its slope down to her thigh. Her flesh quivered at his touch. His fingers feathered over her thigh, beneath her shorts and up, roaming her softness until he came to the warmth between her thighs.

She tensed. His exploration stilled. Their lips stilled, his hovering over hers.

"I mean it when I say I want you, Rose," he whispered. "Do you?"

She remembered her feelings from earlier in the day, feelings that had felt almost like power. Her power to twist her life to her will. She wanted that power. Wanted to use it for herself.

Rose backed away. She pulled herself to a sitting position on the blanket, holding Ben's eyes with her own.

"You know," she said, reaching for the top button of her shirt and slowly loosening it, "I never understood what it was about this old tree house that made a fifteen-year-old boy want to kiss a gawky little buck-toothed girl."

"You didn't?"

Her eyes followed Ben's, which followed her fingers as they moved slowly from one button to another. "No. I just thought it was kind of spooky at night, the way it's all hidden up here in all these branches."

She tossed her shirt aside and was grateful for the darkness that kept him from seeing how utilitarian her white cotton bra was. She unfastened it and cast it aside, too.

"Spooky?" His voice was now less than a whisper, threatening to rasp and disappear.

"Sure." Her throat was dry and her pulse was racing, half from fear and half from the melting heat coursing through her loins. "Nothing but a little starlight to keep it from being completely dark. Completely isolated."

She stood now, looking down at him, feeling a certain release in the way her bare breasts swayed in the cool night air. Slipping her shorts and panties down off her hips, she drew a long, deep breath and let the air caress her. Her nipples puckered at the touch of the breeze. Or was it from the touch of his eyes on her?

Before she could lower herself to Ben's side, he rose to his knees. Fingers barely touching the sides of her thighs, his lips brushed her knees. A small cry escaped her lips. She tried to drop to her knees beside him, but he held her still. His lips brushed over her thighs, his tongue slipping out to brand her here and there with damp heat. The trail of his intimate kisses rose, stealing her strength and her will.

By the time he buried a gentle kiss in the dark triangle at the top of her thighs, Rose was dizzy. She grasped his head, threading her fingers through the springy silver curls. And when his tongue darted, a damp, insistent arrow aiming for the point of her pulsing need, her head fell back and a long, low moan spilled from her lips.

Ben now rose higher, his arms reaching up, as well, to grasp her around the hips as he pressed his lips to her belly.

"Sweet," he murmured as he gently lowered her to the blanket. "So sweet."

Rose reached to unbutton his shirt. Still on his knees, Ben

pulled the shirt off and cast it aside. But before she could find the snap of his pants, he had bent over her again, this time trailing his kisses up her rib cage, tracing the half-moon curve of her lower breast, then swirling his tongue over the dark, taut peak of her breast.

She murmured his name and arched into the caress of his mouth. With a trembling hand, she raked her fingers down his back and felt the ridge of muscles along his spine quiver in response.

Ben drew aside to remove his pants. His hard shaft glistened in the moonlight. With a sound from low in her throat, Rose reached out to touch him. The tips of her fingers marveled at the satin-smooth skin. She parted her legs and he knelt before her, hesitating.

She reached for his arms to pull him down onto her, but still he hesitated. "What?"

She saw his struggle on his face. "Rose, I...we have to be careful. We don't want..."

Rose chuckled softly, joyful for his concern and what it said about Ben McKenzie. "You don't have any of those big-city diseases, do you, Ben?"

He looked distinctly uncomfortable with her question. That endeared him to her even more. What had ever made her think she couldn't trust him?

"Of course not, but..."

She smiled, feeling an unfamiliar but worldly confidence in the face of his discomfort. "It's never too late to get knocked up, either. Is that it, Ben?"

He smiled now. "I don't want you thinking I take this lightly, Rose."

She let her hands trail down his arms and settle around his hips, drawing him closer. "You can't stop, Ben. I won't let you."

With a low growl, he lowered himself to her, pausing only to brush his silken tip against her belly. "I'll be careful."

Her insides convulsed at his touch. She laughed again, a breathless sigh of a laugh. "You'd better not be."

And he entered her, slowly, gently, easing inch by inch into her tightness as his eyes captured her with a look that wavered between intensity and abandon. And when he filled her, he lay still, hips against hers, eyes questioning.

"Okay?"

"Perfect," she murmured, savoring the foreign feel of his body inside hers, over hers.

And they moved together, slowly. He drove higher, deeper, and she opened wider, inviting him deeper. Until something inside Rose unfurled in shuddering waves of pleasure.

Lowering himself to his elbows, Ben nuzzled her neck and stilled their movements, allowing Rose time to savor the wash of feelings.

As the blossoming of emotions stilled within her and Ben began to move again, Rose felt the answering response in Ben. Felt him swelling, hardening, felt his muscles tighten. But in that last moment, he slipped out of her, then drove his pulsing hardness against her belly. His seed spurted, hot and urgent, over her belly, her breasts. Rose cried out with Ben, then pulled him down onto her as his shuddering release ended.

She lay back, surprising herself with the sensual feel of his seed on her skin, the proof not only of his desire for her but of the sense of honor that drove him to protect her. She looked up through the silvered light flickering through the leaves, smiling, her eyes heavy with satisfaction. She would never want again, she was certain of that.

Then he slid his body off hers and Rose understood that she would certainly want again—soon and often.

And perhaps always.

She pushed the thought aside.

"I'm sorry for the..."

"No." She interrupted his apology. "Don't you dare be sorry for anything."

"But I've made a bit of a mess, you see."

Rose's laugh tickled deep inside her, in the places Ben had just touched. She ran a hand over the moisture that the night air was quickly drying on her belly and breasts. "Good. Can we make another mess again? Soon?"

Ben joined her laughter. "Not just yet. It's never too late, but at my age a slight delay is sometimes in order."

"Ah, Ben. You could make me want to stay in Sweetbranch." She sighed and stretched, feeling Ben's hair-roughened chest along her side and the briskness of the night air along his chest and legs.

"And is that such a bad thing?"

Rose found it difficult to voice the answer that would have been so automatic a month ago. She reminded herself how fiercely she had yearned to escape during those years when she had let her obligations outweigh her wanderlust.

"Yes!" she said at last, but her declaration had lost some of its urgency. "I want more than Sweetbranch can give me. I want some excitement. I want to feel alive. I want things to happen to me." She laughed. "I sound like a teenager, don't I?"

"That's okay. It's okay to let out a little bit of the kid in you."

"Is it?" She turned solemn eyes to his. He nodded. "And is it okay to wonder how long you'll be here, Ben McKenzie, to keep me content with life in Sweetbranch?"

She felt him tense and knew she had broken the spell between them.

"Rose..."

He hesitated. Because, she knew, he had no answer. With a bittersweet smile, she reached for him and pulled him close to her once again. "I know. I know you don't have an answer for that. Maybe one day you'll trust me enough to tell me why you don't have an answer."

When he pulled away to look at her, she saw the fear that her words had put into his eyes. But she wasn't sorry. No matter what the truth was about Ben, she wasn't sorry. Would never be sorry. At this stage in her life, grabbing for a brief moment of happiness was better than letting it slip away completely.

CHAPTER TWELVE

THE ONLY THING ROSE FELT bad about the next day was her underwear. She threw out every piece of prim white cotton she owned—except for what she had to wear that day—and took off late in the morning to play hooky from the Picture Perfect. She headed straight for the Sweet Boutique.

"I want something sexy," she told Agnes Sauter, fingering a rack of champagne-colored lingerie. "Something with a little lace."

An O of surprise transformed Agnes's mouth, which then settled into a satisfied grin. "I heard you was getting tight with that new feller in town."

"Well then, won't it be good to have a little something of your own to add to the story?" Rose winked at the shopkeeper, whose face wrinkled in consternation.

"Why, Rose Finley, you know I wouldn't gossip about my valued clientele!" After huffing out her offense, Agnes then burst into a wicked cackle. "Okay, young'un, how about some satin? Satin's real big these days. And black. You got to have some black."

"I do?" Rose fingered the shimmery black satin Agnes thrust at her. Her nipples tightened at the thought of Ben caressing her through the fabric, pulling it roughly aside and...

"You bet. Besides, it's gonna make a much better story for me if you get something really hot."

Rose laughed right along with the shopkeeper who had fitted a reluctant thirteen-year-old Rose with her first training bra decades earlier. She had no plans to worry about forever. Or even tomorrow. Her new life started today. And today was going to be fun.

After satisfying herself that no one would ever catch her in white cotton again, Rose worked on the agenda for her task force meeting. Brimming with hope and confidence, she decided to assign everyone a job—contacting the railroad, tracking down other towns that had faced Sweetbranch's problems, stuff like that. Yep, she was going to make today count.

Her other important step toward her new beginning was settling things with Maxine. She knew Maxine, for some reason she couldn't fathom, didn't like Ben. But Maxine was her best friend. And she wanted her best friend to share her happiness.

She knocked on Maxine's door at lunch, shopping bags from the Sweet Boutique dangling from both hands. Maxine stared at the bags as she opened the screen door.

"What're you serving for lunch?" Rose dropped her bags on the high-backed antique sofa handed down from Ragan Hammond's family. "Shopping's hungry work."

Maxine led her into the kitchen, where she made two large salads, topped with cheese and boiled egg and chunks of turkey. When Maxine put the bowl down in front of her, Rose looked up, excitement making her breathless.

"I'm going to college." It was a safer place to start, she felt, given Maxine's disapproval of Ben McKenzie.

Maxine's face brightened. With an uncontrolled yelp that was completely out of character, she stood and pulled Rose from her chair. The two wrapped their arms around each other and danced around the room until they were both laughing and breathless.

When the moment of celebration was spent, Rose supplied Maxine with the details.

"And you did not even tell me you had filled out the application, my sneaky friend," Maxine teased.

Rose raised an eyebrow. "I don't tell you everything, you know."

"Is that so?"

"Yes. That's so."

"And what other news have you not yet shared with me?"

Rose could barely contain her beaming smile, but she felt her face heating with a blush. Her usual outspokenness abandoned her as she pondered how to say what she wanted to say. Suddenly, she jumped up. "I'll show you."

Dashing back into the living room, she brought her shopping bags and proceeded to spill her new cache of sensuous panties, bras and camisoles onto the kitchen table. For a long moment Maxine merely stared, while the implication of the piles of satin and lace sank in.

When Maxine spoke, her voice was more subdued. "So. You have made another decision, as well, I take it?"

Rose picked up one of the camisoles, an apricot-colored silk, and brushed her cheek against it, once again feeling heat rise in her at the image it conjured. "Don't fuss at me, Maxie. Please. Just be happy for me."

Maxine pursed her lips. Rose watched the emotions warring for control of her friend's face. At last, Maxine said, "If you are happy, Rose, I am happy for you. And if ever you are not happy, I will be there for you in that, as well."

The friends embraced again, and Rose told herself there was no reason for Maxine's words to settle so heavily on her heart.

BEN PULLED the dust-covered station wagon off the road and into the red-dirt lot surrounding an old service station and general store. Like many things in this part of north Alabama, the store smacked of hard times and little activity. The old man in faded overalls whose cane-back chair leaned into the wall didn't move as Ben got out of the car and ducked under the wide tin overhang.

"It's a good afternoon to be outdoors," Ben said, having no trouble mustering his most cheerful voice and his friendliest smile.

"Howdy." The old man smiled back, a relaxed smile that Ben now recognized as the mark of rural folks whose lives were seldom disrupted by high-stress hassles. "Actually, most folks think it's raining today."

"So it is." Ben looked out at the drizzle and smiled. It had seemed sunny all day to him.

He dropped quarters into a rusting old soft drink machine and pulled a cold bottle from a slot, releasing another bottle into its place. He used the opener on the front of the machine. "Guess I had my mind on other things."

The man nodded.

Walking to the pay phone at the corner of the unpainted building, Ben realized he couldn't remember the number of his own business. Holding the receiver between ear and shoulder, he forced himself to think. The discovery pleased him in some perverse way.

When he finally dialed and Keith answered, Ben found he was also pleased to note that the harried exasperation in his brother's voice sounded foreign to him now.

"Having a bad day, little brother?"

"Yeah. We're a little shorthanded around here," Keith snapped.

Ben refrained from chuckling. He was too content today to feel guilty, even about abandoning his brother to the headaches that came with their printing company. "I looked over the second site today."

Keith spat out a sharp profanity. "I'm sweating bullets over getting the RJR job off the press on time and you're out tooling around the Tennessee countryside. Dammit, Ben, I'm getting fed up with this. If you don't come to your senses soon and..."

"I need you to do something for me, Keith."

A long silence followed his interruption. When Keith spoke again, his voice was tightly controlled. "You need me to do something. Well, what do you need now, big brother? Besides running the company all by myself and keeping your clients from jumping ship, what *else* can I do for you?"

"I want you to make a call to the Seaboard Coastline Railroad district office in Birmingham. See what you can find out about their decision to shut down some of their routes in north Alabama."

Grumbling the whole time, Keith made notes about Ben's request and promised to call. "Just one thing in return, Ben."

"What's that?"

"Tell me when this game of yours is over."

Ben's smile faded. "It's not a game."

"When?"

"Soon."

"You swear it?"

Ben drew a long breath. He owed it to everyone to settle his personal life. He just didn't know how to go about it. His first obligation was to Krissy. He was the only one between her and...things he didn't even want to think about.

"Don't push, Keith."

"Don't push *me*, Ben." There was a hard edge to Keith's

voice. "I won't let you ruin this business. I'll take it away from you first."

Ben considered the irony of that as he hung up. If he went underground, the business would be Keith's anyway. Even if he didn't, Keith would be perfectly justified in carrying out his threat if something didn't happen soon.

But what? It always came back to that. Should he take the irrevocable step Maxine still offered? Did he really have the right to do that to Krissy's life? Did he have the right not to? So far no one had seemed interested in tracking him down, but that couldn't last.

All the way back to Sweetbranch, Ben struggled with a decision that seemed to offer only one option. The legal system wouldn't protect his daughter, so he had gone outside that system. Technically, he was a criminal.

Morally, he was a father who had been backed into a corner.

But the crime didn't stop there, he reminded himself. If taking Krissy by force was a felony, involving Rose to the extent that he had last night was no misdemeanor.

Guilty. On all counts. Ben pinched the bridge of his nose. There wasn't a jury in the land that wouldn't convict him for seducing Rose Finley under false pretenses.

By the time he turned the corner onto Dixie Belle Lane an hour later, Ben's gut was in knots. The glow of happiness from the night before had been swallowed up by well-deserved guilt. As he neared the Finley home, it was nearly dusk. Ben saw the activity in the front yard. Krissy and Kesha Hammond were haphazardly swinging a jump rope. Attempting to jump the rope was Rose.

Ben slowed the car, wanting to watch before they noticed his approach. He'd sensed that Rose had warmed up to Krissy, felt more comfortable with her these days than she had seemed to feel when they first moved in. But this was the first time he had actually seen them playing together. And it looked so natural, for both of them.

Rose, her coppery hair flying merrily as she jumped, was laughing so hard she could barely stay on her feet. The color was high on her cheeks. Shorts and a T-shirt gave Ben an alluring view of her long, lithe limbs. The two girls were giggling, too, and at last succeeded in tripping Rose up. Feet tangled in the uncooperative rope, Rose stumbled around and finally landed with a thud on her backside, mostly, Ben suspected, for the benefit of the delighted little girls, who dropped the rope and dashed to her rescue. But before they could satisfy themselves that she was safe, Rose grabbed the girls and pulled them onto the ground with her. Ben could hear the squeals of delighted surprise from where he sat.

Gratitude and something else that felt oddly like hope welled up in Ben as he watched the little girl he loved so dearly with the woman he...

Ben almost slammed on the brakes, he moved so quickly to stop the thought that had popped unbidden into his head.

The woman he loved?

Rose perched on her knees, brushed the grass out of Krissy's hair and dropped a light kiss on the little girl's nose. Ben's heart twisted with the tenderness of Rose's actions and the openness with which his daughter accepted the woman who had been a stranger a few weeks earlier. Rose and her uncle had drawn Krissy out of the protective shell the little girl had constructed during the past year. With nothing but love and tenderness, they had diminished the effects of hate and brutality.

Who wouldn't love a woman like that? And what kind of scoundrel would drag her into the mess my life is in?

As the two little girls dashed around the house to the backyard, Rose watched them proprietarily, brushing the grass from the seat of her shorts as she did so. She smiled, a satisfied, giving smile that settled on Ben's heart. She had smiled just that way last night when she had let herself feel young once again in the tree house.

Ben stirred, remembering his shadowy glimpses of fair curves and gentle swells, remembering the way she had tightened and shivered and arched at his touch, remembering his own moment of almost primitive anguish at watching his seed spill onto her.

He had wanted to fill her with himself.

Ben swallowed hard. He hadn't realized until this moment what that instant of anguish had meant. Deep in his soul, Ben had wanted to fill Rose Finley with his child.

He shuddered. Tears welled up again and he fought them back. He had no right to such thoughts. Not as long as the only thing he could offer Rose was lies.

Slamming his palm on the steering wheel, Ben made himself a promise. He would get out of her life. Tomorrow. As soon as he could arrange it. He would end this, because he had nothing to offer Rose Finley. Nothing but this feeling that was growing dangerously close to love. A love he couldn't, in good conscience, offer.

THE NEXT AFTERNOON Ben stood in front of the newspaper rack on Main Street and stared at the Friday *Gazetteer*. He dropped a quarter into the honor-system slot and slipped the latest edition out of the wire rack. Shoving it under his arm, he started back toward the house.

He tried not to look dejected, sensitive to the fact that the eyes of Sweetbranch were upon him. He waved across the street at one of the women he'd met in the aerobics class. And he smiled, as he passed, at the woman who ran the little dress shop in town, although he'd never officially met her. In Sweetbranch, he had come to realize, official introductions weren't always necessary in order to know someone intimately.

As she taped the Sale banner to her front window, the shop-keeper stopped and looked at him as if she knew all the secrets he wanted to keep.

"Well, hello, Mr. McKenzie." She smiled almost shyly. "I trust the world agrees with you these days?"

Taken aback, Ben paused. He looked into her heavily powdered face with its carefully symmetrical circles of raspberry color located just in the sunken hollow below her cheekbones and returned her smile. "Yes. Absolutely."

He wondered, as he noted the humor in her eyes, if she could possibly know he was lying. Yet she must. That look in her eyes said it all. Said she knew all about Mr. Ben McKenzie—she even knew his name, for Pete's sake—and he wasn't getting a thing past her.

You've got to get out of Sweetbranch, Ben admonished himself as he continued down Main Street. *It's making you paranoid.*

Ben picked up his pace. He had to get out of town. That's all there was to it. He would leave Sweetbranch. He would tell Maxine he wanted to go underground. Leave everything behind.

Everything. Even Rose. Especially Rose. Before he hurt her any more than he had to.

Ben reached for the paper tucked under his arm and turned to the classified section, reading it on his way back to Dixie Belle Lane. By the time he arrived at the house, he had found two numbers to call. Places to rent in nearby towns. He could check them out tomorrow. If one of them panned out, he would call Maxine. And be gone. Quickly and quietly.

He dialed the first number. An elderly woman answered. He almost hung up. She sounded just like the kind of person he didn't want to involve in his problems. Like all the people he had taken advantage of here in Sweetbranch.

I'll know better this time, he vowed. *We'll keep to ourselves. Maxine will find something soon, once I tell her, and we'll be gone. Before we muddy up anyone else's life.*

"I'm calling about the garage apartment you have to rent," he said quickly. "My daughter and I are looking for a temporary place to live."

The screen door slammed just as he finished his explanation. Ben darted a guilty look in the direction of the noise. Krissy was staring at him, her hand in Uncle Bump's, an accusatory expression in her eyes.

Ben listened distractedly to the details about the apartment, unable to tear his eyes from Krissy's face. When he had heard all the details, he turned back to the wall. "Good. Why don't we come by tomorrow for a look?"

He arranged a time and took down directions, all the while feeling Krissy's eyes piercing the middle of his back. When he hung up, he turned toward her and Uncle Bump with a smile that he hoped wasn't as bleak as it felt. "Hi, you two. How's it going?"

Krissy huddled close to Uncle Bump's knees. "Daddy, we can't leave."

Ben sighed and glanced at Uncle Bump for reinforcement. The look in the old man's dark eyes was as judgmental as Krissy's. Ben knelt, ignoring the stiffness in his knee, to bring himself to Krissy's eye level.

"Sweetheart, I think it's time we moved along." He put a hand on her shoulder, wincing at the tears that welled up in her eyes. "Uncle Bump and Rose have been awfully nice to share their house with us. But we can't ask them to do that forever, you know."

"Why?"

Ben shifted to take some of the pressure off his knee. "We just can't. This is their house. We have to find our own place."

Krissy jerked away from his touch and glared at him defiantly. "No, I won't go!"

"Now, Krissy..." *Oh Lord. What now?*

She stamped a foot. "No! I want to stay here! Or else I'll go home to Mommy!"

"No, Krissy, you can't do that. Listen, sweetheart..."

"No-o-o-o," she wailed. "I want Mommy. I want Unka Bunk! I want Auntie Wose! I won't go!"

With that vehement pronouncement, she dashed past him and up the stairs.

Ben's shoulders sagged. With a heavy sigh, he struggled to his feet, which brought him face-to-face with Uncle Bump, who looked as implacable as Krissy had been.

"Women's tough customers, ain't they, McKenzie?"

Uncle Bump's hard tone belied the commiseration of his words. Ben didn't even know how to answer him. He wasn't used to filling the role of bad guy in his daughter's life.

"Mind you, I ain't had much experience with women. But you might want to listen to that young lady. If she's got a mama, you might not ought to be messing around here, McKenzie. You might ought to take that little girl—and yourself—back where you belong."

After fixing Ben with a long, hard stare, Uncle Bump turned and marched back to his own room, where he, too, closed the door on Ben McKenzie.

CHAPTER THIRTEEN

ON SATURDAY, Rose sifted the thick soil through her fingers, relishing the rust-colored clay staining her hands and clinging in half-moons under her nails.

In a few months, this patch of red earth in her backyard would yield tomatoes and pole beans and okra for frying. It would be tall with cornstalks and thick with runners from the strawberries.

"And weeds," she remembered, turning to the knee-high companion who sat on the edge of the plot. "We'll have plenty of weeds. You and Uncle Bump will be on permanent weed patrol, okay?"

Krissy's dark head nodded listlessly. Rose had been trying ever since the shop closed that afternoon to interest Krissy in something, with little success. Surely, she had thought, a good dig in the dirt would do the job. But Krissy merely sat there, barely speaking, lower lip hovering dangerously close to a pout.

Rose stopped and rested back on her haunches, unmindful of the dirt that was staining her bare knees, and stared at Krissy. Something was wrong, certainly, but she had no idea what. Little girls pouted, she supposed, and big girls were supposed to know what to do about it. But this big girl had no notion whatsoever how to deal with a gloomy little girl.

She decided to try one more time. "Been fishing lately?"

At least that sparked some interest. But as Krissy looked up to answer, she froze, targeting a sullen look over Rose's shoulder. Rose followed her glance. Ben stood over them, hands in his pockets, his expression as glum as his daughter's.

Rose felt instantly warm and scrambled to sit up, wondering at the impropriety of her feelings with Krissy as a witness. She tried to feel prim, which was difficult with Ben in her line of vision.

"We're planting," she explained, wondering if her smile looked as giddy as it felt. "And assigning weeding chores."

Then she noticed he wasn't looking at her. Not directly at her. More like over her shoulder. Or at her chin. But not into her eyes. Rose's smile faded.

"Hello, Rose."

But it didn't sound much like a hello. It sounded, if anything, like a goodbye.

Don't be paranoid. Just because Ben hadn't been around much since the night in the tree house, just because he'd shown no sign of wanting to be alone with her again, just because the contraceptive foam she'd bought the very next day still hid, unused, in the bottom of her box of sanitary pads...

Quit borrowing trouble.

"Hi, Ben." Despite her anxiety, her voice was soft with the memory of making love with him. "You've been kind of scarce today."

She knew that wasn't the right thing to say. Not at all coy. Or subtle. A big mistake in man-woman etiquette, she was sure. But it was on her mind.

His gaze shifted. He seemed awfully intent on his feet. A little chill nestled, unwelcome, in the middle of Rose's chest.

"I know."

No apology. No attempt at excuse. His voice was far from harsh, but it didn't need to be. The implication was plenty harsh enough for Rose.

And she'd thought...that is, to her, their lovemaking had seemed so...

"Krissy, are you ready to go?"

Now Krissy's little body tightened itself into a rigid, resistent little ball, knees to her chest, cheek to her knees, arms wrapped around her legs. "Not weady."

Ben sighed, impatiently it seemed to Rose. "Come with me, Kristen. Now."

"No. Don't wanna."

Rose gave Krissy's knee a quick pat, then stood. She didn't belong in the middle of a family squabble. She leaned over to gather up her tools when Krissy spoke again, her voice truculent.

"Don't wanna move away. Auntie Wose said I could be a weed twoll. Don't wanna move."

Rose's hand froze on the way to gripping the trowel half-buried in clay. She looked up, straight into the eyes that had been avoiding hers. Small wonder. They looked guilty. And hers, Rose knew, filled with quicksilver anger. She straightened, leveling a glare at him as she squared her shoulders and accused him with her look.

"I guess you're going to be even scarcer."

"Well, I..."

The apology she saw in his eyes made her even angrier. "Don't you do it, Ben McKenzie."

"Do what?"

"Make flimsy, weak-kneed excuses to me. Don't you dare do it. If you made a mistake and want to hightail it out of here, just do it. But don't pretend it's anything else. Do you hear me?"

"It's not...Rose, don't you see..." And he stopped, his eyes begging her to understand that he had nothing else to say. "I'm sorry, Rose."

She whirled and stalked away, not even slowing her steps as she hurled over her shoulder, "You ought to be."

WHEN BEN LOOKED through Krissy's eyes at the garage apartment in the town twenty miles away, he simply couldn't go through with it. Little sunshine came through the cramped windows and the steps were steep, with just enough room beneath the rickety railing for a tiny person to tumble through. And the little old lady seemed anything but pleased at the prospect of a child on her property. She looked around her carefully groomed yard and down at Krissy and back up at Ben and said, "She won't damage my flower beds."

It wasn't a question at all but a statement of immutable fact.

Three-and-a-half-year-old girls don't fit in just anywhere, Ben realized as he and Krissy drove back to Sweetbranch.

Krissy bounced up and down on the front seat as much as her seat belt allowed. "So we won't move, Daddy?"

"Not yet, sweetheart."

"Why can't we stay with Auntie Wose and Unka Bunk, Daddy?"

Why, indeed? "Because they aren't really our family, sweetheart. They're our friends, but not our family. So we can't stay in their house forever.''

Ben wished for some miracle to make life as simple as it was in Krissy's eyes. His heart told him it should be simple. Rose had brought light back into Krissy's world. And he would have loved her for that alone. But there was more. He also loved her for the light she had brought to him. A light that was hope and warmth and passion and a belief in the little everyday things that made life worth living.

And as much as he would have liked to view things simply, he knew it was impossible. Because it would be a miracle if things ever returned to normal. And without that, without being able to fit into the wonderful, quiet life that Rose offered, Ben and Krissy had no place there, no right to disrupt that peace and quiet.

Krissy lapsed into brooding silence. It was only as they crossed the rickety covered bridge leading into Sweetbranch that she spoke again.

"I want my mommy."

Ben's heart ached so badly at the tiny, hurt-filled voice that all he could do was pull off to the side of the road once he'd crossed the bridge, unbuckle their seat belts and take his daughter into his arms. She didn't yield to his embrace at first, holding herself rigid to register her many complaints against him.

"I know you do, sweetheart. I know you do and I'm sorry she isn't here right now."

"Does Mommy love me anymore, Daddy?"

Despite squeezing his eyes tightly shut, one tear escaped and followed a grim trail down Ben's cheek. "Of course she does, sweetheart. She loves you very much. And she doesn't want anyone to hurt you anymore. That's why you can't be with her right now. Until no one there can hurt you again. Do you understand?"

He wasn't surprised when she shook her head against his chest. He felt a sob rising in him behind that movement and did his best to stifle it.

How did someone with only the best intentions, he wondered sadly, *do such a bang-up job of botching everything?*

No one seemed to like Ben much the rest of the weekend. That didn't surprise Ben; he didn't like himself very much, either.

Krissy remained distant, and when she looked up at him her eyes pleaded with him to make things right again. Uncle Bump rolled out his best curmudgeon routine. While he continued to be Krissy's best pal and companion, he took every opportunity to grumble at Ben.

Rose did her best to show Ben how little any of it mattered to her. She didn't hide away in her room, she didn't try to avoid him in any way. She barely acknowledged his presence.

Instead, she lavished plenty of attention on Krissy. It was as if Ben's betrayal had intensified and solidified the closeness that had been blossoming between the two in the past few days. Suddenly, they were inseparable.

Rose taught the little girl three new songs, sitting in the front porch swing while Ben listened from the solitude of the living room. At another time he might have smiled at the sound of Krissy's high, tuneless voice following along behind Rose's throaty contralto.

"And every time you sing those songs," he overheard Rose saying, "I want you to remember me and Uncle Bump and all the good things we did while you were in Sweetbranch. And be happy when you remember them, no matter what. Promise?"

Krissy promised. And Ben knew with a sharp, poignant ache that every time he heard the songs, he, too, would remember.

After supper that night, Rose brought out an old rag doll and refurbished it with new patches of gingham. Ben watched in fascination as Rose and Krissy picked through a canvas bag of scraps for the color that pleased Krissy the most. Watched as Rose carefully stitched a scrap of red onto the blue gingham pinafore, smoothing it carefully and looking pleased with her handiwork.

Then Krissy picked new buttons for the eyes from a metal canister Rose brought down from the shelf—big brown ones to replace the shiny blue button eyes.

"Want bwown ones," Krissy insisted. "Like Auntie Wose."

The rag doll would have been put to shame by any one of the expensive dolls sitting on the shelf in Krissy's room back in Winston-Salem. But Ben had never seen her hug one of those dolls as tightly as she hugged this second-generation ragamuffin whose best adornment was the handiwork Rose had put into it.

"Can I keep her always?" Krissy asked.

"Always."

And Rose hugged the little girl to her chest as possessively as Krissy hugged the doll. As he watched the two people who had touched his life so profoundly, Ben wanted to kneel on the floor with them and add his hug to the one they shared.

Krissy was right. They should stay here. They should be family. The old-fashioned kind of family where children grew up safe and happy, learning songs and making rag dolls and fishing with querulous old uncles.

The old-fashioned kind of family where the daddy and the mommy were in love with each other, and not in love with their position in society or their power at work.

As Ben held the wonder of that kind of love in his heart, Rose opened her eyes and looked at him over Krissy's head. For a fleeting moment he saw what she had been careful to hide all weekend—a longing so powerful, so sweet, that it bruised his already hurting heart.

Then, as if realizing what she had let him see, she lowered her eyes and shut him out again.

Ben made up his mind at that moment. He was tired of being the outcast. He also acknowledged that he was the only one who could correct that. And correct it he would. Right away. He would talk to Maxine. He would talk to his attorney. He would talk to Cybil.

But first, and most important, he would talk to Rose. He would do what he should have done from the very beginning. He would be completely honest with her.

So when Rose dressed Krissy for church the next morning, Ben joined them without waiting for an invitation. And he made a point of catching Maxine Hammond after the service and maneuvering her to a quiet part of the church lawn.

Without preamble, he made his announcement. "I can't go through with it."

She studied him carefully, her dark eyes examining his then delving deeper, as if to make sure she also saw what lurked behind them. "It is good you have decided."

She turned to go, but Ben put a hand on her arm. "Maxine, I'm...thank you for showing me a way out. It gave me time to think. To figure out what to do."

A smile that was half sorrowful acceptance crossed her face. "Is that truly what I have given you time for, Ben?"

Once again, her look was so compelling that he knew no way but to tell her the truth. "Not completely. You led me to Rose."

"And it is for that you thank me." When he nodded, the sadness in her eyes deepened and she looked away. "Then I must only pray that I have not been the instrument of her pain."

The blunt truth of her words hurt. "No. I don't want that, either."

"It is never what we want. It is sometimes what happens."

"I'm going to work this out. I'm going back this week. To straighten things out. You said yourself life underground isn't easy, even for the child. It'll be best for Krissy, too, if I can work things out."

"Yes. *If* you can." She reached out and squeezed his hand. For the first time since he'd met her, he saw a moment of fear in her eyes. "But, Ben, sometimes it cannot be worked out. If the child is in true danger, do not send her back to it." She paused; he saw the struggle in her normally composed face. "I fear I have come to care about Krissy too well myself to be objective. She has been here much longer than most of the children I get to meet through the network. But...there are some risks you will never forgive yourself for taking, Ben. Remember that. If you find there is no help for the situation, I will help. Never feel you cannot turn to me again, Ben."

Then, with the sheen of tears in her eyes, she turned to go, leaving the problem in Ben's hands. Ben felt the weight of that as he watched Maxine walk away, her back straight with a strength he envied.

After following a half block behind Rose, Krissy and Uncle Bump as they walked home from the morning service, Ben cornered Uncle Bump. Rose and Krissy were changing from their Sunday clothes. The old man was shoving biscuits into the oven to go with the chicken casserole he had prepared the night before.

Ben leaned against the kitchen counter, remembering with a vivid tightening in his groin the morning he'd kissed Rose over the sink. "Will you take Krissy fishing this afternoon?"

Uncle Bump cast a narrow-eyed glance in his direction, then busied himself pulling plates from the cabinet. "Why? So you can try more tomfoolery with my niece? I don't think she's much in the mood for any of your tricks, son."

"No tricks. I want to talk to her."

Uncle Bump's gaze was no less suspicious as he dropped the stack of plates on the kitchen table. He grunted.

Ben looked the older man straight in the eye. "I want to clear things up. I know I've left a lot of questions unanswered. Rose doesn't deserve that."

"You're dang right she don't." Uncle Bump waved a fork in Ben's direction. "She's worked hard and sacrificed all her life. And I don't aim to see her led astray by some slick feller who's got a wife out there somewhere."

If he hadn't felt so miserable over everyone's poor opinion of him, Ben would have been amused at the crusty old man's unexpected streak of protectiveness. "No wife, Uncle Bump. Just an ex."

Carelessly dropping napkins into the middle of each plate in a way that always prompted a complaint from Rose, Uncle Bump looked little placated. "Maybe so. Maybe not. Whatever it is you've been so fox-eyed about, I don't like it."

"I'll straighten it out. I promise."

As he watched Uncle Bump and Krissy, fishing poles in hand, heading toward the river after a strained Sunday dinner, Ben wondered if he could live up to that promise.

He wandered slowly through the house, surprised at the dread in his heart as he looked for Rose. He wanted to clear things up. But he didn't want to see the look in her eyes if she condemned him for the way he'd handled everything. What if she didn't understand?

What if she turned him in?

The thought stalled Ben in his tracks just as he was peering from one end of the empty porch to the other.

What if Rose called the police or the FBI and told them he was a kidnapper and they came after him and hauled him to jail and sent Krissy right back to Cybil and everything they'd been through in the past month was wasted?

Even as he let the scenario play itself out in his head, Ben knew it would never happen. Rose would never do that. She might not forgive him for deceiving her. She might not understand what he'd done. But she wouldn't put Krissy at risk. Never. He knew that much about Rose.

Drawing a deep breath, he stopped in front of her closed bedroom door, listened to the silence for a moment, then pounded on it.

The only answer was the creak of a floorboard from within.

He pounded again.

Rose flung the door open. "What?"

"I want to talk."

"Well I don't."

Ben took a step forward and put his hand on the door just as she was shoving it closed. "I'm sorry I hurt you."

She pushed the door more forcefully against his palm. "Apology accepted. Now, if you'll..."

"But we still have to talk."

"No we don't, Ben. Leave me alone."

With gentle force, he eased the door open enough to permit him to lean against the door frame. "I can't do that, Rose."

He saw in her face that her determination to send him away was wavering. A flicker of hurt replaced the hostility that had flashed in her eyes. Her chin trembled and she pursed her lips to regain control.

"Okay." She shoved her bedroom door wide open and turned her back on him. She stood at the window, straight-backed. "Talk."

"I kidnapped Krissy." No time for pussyfooting. Straight-out.

After a moment of silence, a short, brittle laugh came from across the room. "You expect me to believe that? I have eyes. She's your daughter, Ben. Anybody can see that."

"Yes, she is. And she was being abused. So I kidnapped her." He sounded calmer than he felt, he knew that. He wasn't sure his heart had pounded with this much trepidation since the night he'd walked out of Cybil's apartment, praying she couldn't read his intention in his face.

Now Rose wheeled around and looked him in the eye. "What are you talking about, Ben?"

His fists were balled up inside his pant pockets. "Her stepfather was abusing her. Her mother didn't...couldn't...stop him. I went to the courts. To the social workers. They couldn't prove anything. Wouldn't do anything. So I took her."

She took a step in his direction, her hand raised to him. He looked up and saw the concern and indecision in her face. "Ben?"

"I couldn't let him hurt her anymore. No matter what. If you'd seen her, Rose, the way she was...when she was bruised...and burned. Once she was burned. Not seriously, but... And the look in her eyes. Seeing a three-year-old who has distrust in her eyes..." He squeezed his own eyes shut against the memory. "I couldn't let it happen anymore, Rose. I just couldn't."

Her arms were around him. She held him close, one arm tight around his waist, one hand cradling his head into the bend of her neck and shoulder. "Oh my heavens. Oh, Ben. Why didn't you tell me?"

In that moment, hearing the concern in her voice, aware of the need to heal in her touch, Ben had never felt so unburdened, so safe. He smiled at the incongruity of a big, strong man feeling protected in the embrace of a slender, vulnerable woman.

But he did.

"I couldn't tell you," he whispered against her shoulder, breathing in the Sunday perfumed scent of her. He slipped his arms around her waist and clung. "I couldn't let you get involved. I'm breaking the law, Rose. I couldn't let you get messed up in that."

He felt her gentle laughter vibrate against his chest. "I *am* messed up in it, Ben. Have been all along. At least now I know what I'm messed up in."

With a nod, Ben followed Rose as she led him across the room to her bed. They sat, pillows propped against the headboard, wrapped in each other's arms. Ben felt the comfort of Rose's body against his, as well as the comfort of knowing he was no longer hiding behind a wall of lies that was growing taller and wider and more insurmountable with every day that passed, every lie he told.

"Tell me about it, Ben. I want to hear everything."

He told her almost everything—about the minor injuries and the lawyers and the social workers. He told her about his fears. The only thing he didn't tell her about was the underground network. That wasn't his secret to share.

"I had to do better this time, you know," he whispered against the soft hair where he pillowed his cheek. "I couldn't let...I've seen one child die. I couldn't let it happen again."

"What are you talking about, Ben?" He heard the alarm in her voice but held her close to his side when she would have straightened to look him in the eye.

He said a silent prayer that Rose would understand.

"In Vietnam." His mouth went dry. He could feel the pain starting behind the bridge of his nose. He'd never told anyone. Never put it into words. "I saw babies die. I could've stopped it. I tried. But...I didn't."

He was barely aware that Rose went very still in his arms. "Tell me, Ben."

And he told her. He told her about Wahn-Lei and the villagers he had come to know and love, people who were his friends. He told her things he hadn't remembered for a long time, about the songs they sang together and the games they played, the food they'd shared with him. Then he told her about the betrayal, about his futile warnings to his Vietnamese friends that their village would be ravaged by the Vietcong. They should leave, he had told them, urgently at first. Panicked, finally. Save yourselves, he had said. But they had smiled their fatalistic smiles and stayed in the village.

And they had been massacred. All of them. Even the child who had grabbed Ben's knee, seeking safety.

He felt Rose's arms tighten around him. He felt the tears hot on his cheek, and the softness of her fingers as she dried them.

"It wasn't your fault, Ben. You tried. You warned them."

"Trying didn't matter. They were still dead." He drew a long, shuddering breath and looked, at last, into her eyes. "If I'd tried harder..."

"They wouldn't save themselves, Ben. You did all you could."

"Maybe. All I know is...I was never the same after that. As if I didn't trust the whole world. Until Krissy came along. So I wanted to do the right thing. Had to do the right thing. This time."

Rose smiled, a reassuring smile. "And you did."

A frown clouded Ben's face. "I suppose. Except that I broke the law."

"To protect your daughter," Rose said, defending him.

"But it's hurt her, too. She misses her mother, you know. This isn't something you can explain to a three-year-old."

"No, I suppose it isn't." She reached up and caressed his cheek. "Oh, Ben, how awful for you."

"Not so awful. I met you. I met you, Rose Finley, and that balances out a hell of a lot of awful."

With a breathless laugh that was so innocent it almost broke Ben's heart, she turned her face to his. He couldn't help himself. He kissed her.

It was the first kiss they had shared that wasn't clouded by the shadow of his lies. It was the first truly honest kiss, a kiss he could give himself to as completely as he could accept what Rose was giving. He was hungry to give, hungry to accept.

Her lips were soft and gentled the raw desire in Ben. He cradled her face with his hands, coaxing her, loving her with his touch.

Loving her. Right now that was all he could offer her, but he wanted her to have it. Wanted her to feel it. Wanted her never to doubt it.

As he deepened the kiss, he felt the uncertainty in her response. He pulled away and looked into her eyes. "You're not sure? Rose, if you're not sure...?"

The flush of emotion on her face darkened, but she didn't look away. "It's not that. I'm...I don't have a lot of experience. I worried the last time, when you never wanted to...be with me again...maybe I wasn't very..."

Her explanation stumbled to a stop. Her eyes begged him to understand.

"Rose, you were *very*. Trust me on that. I've never been with anyone who was as *very, very* as you were." He shifted against her so she could feel how powerful her effect was on him. "I want you, Rose. But I'm afraid I'm no more prepared to love you...safely...than I was last time."

Her eyes came into sharp focus and widened. "Oh! Oh, you mean——" She slipped out of his arms and sat up on the bed. "But I am. I hoped...that is, after what happened...well..."

A powerful surge of desire hardened his body even more as he watched her shy, awkward explanations. "Then go, woman."

And she was gone in a flash. Gone, it seemed to Ben, forever. He lay there, staring at the pale pink rosebuds on her wallpaper and trying not to think of all the reasons he shouldn't be doing what he was about to do. He tried to think, instead, of the one reason he should do it.

He loved Rose. And this might be the only way he ever had to show her.

When she returned, she smiled stiffly. He pulled her to him and she sank into his embrace again. He felt her against him, slim and soft and filled with the kind of unquestioning giving that he'd never before felt in the arms of a woman. His fingers trembled with the need to be gentle as they moved over the thrust of her breasts, the slope of her ribs, the swell of hips, which urged him on with their movement. He touched her, willing his emotions into every caress.

He undressed her, mindful of the daytime shyness that made her more inhibited than the first Rose who had made love to him, wanton and needy in the evening darkness. He took time to worship each part of her as he uncovered her, from the dark tips of her breasts to the long expanse of creamy white thigh.

And when he was undressed and kneeling before her, looking down into her flushed face and dark eyes that were foggy with the same desire he felt, he paused. "Rose, there is one more thing."

She tugged on his waist. "Not now, Ben."

"Now, Rose." He bent his elbows and lowered his face to hers, brushing a kiss over each eye. "I love you, Rose. That's what this is all about. I want you to know that."

The tears that rushed to her eyes startled him.

"You do?"

He touched his lips to the tears trembling on her lashes. "I do. I may never be able to do anything about it, Rose, but..."

All the timidity seemed to disappear from her face. While a tear trickled out the corner of her eye, she smiled and again tugged him closer, this time more forcefully. "Do something about it, Ben. Now."

He entered her, his breathing growing instantly shallow as her tight, hot flesh accepted him, surrounded him. They moved together, slowly at first, Ben striving to make every thrust and every retreat a caress of infinite clarity and emotion. Slowly, they moved together. Her hands played over his back, softly at first, then more urgently, her nails raking his back gently, then fiercely. He heard the cries rising in her throat, driving him, urging him, filling him to bursting with the knowledge of her satisfaction.

Suddenly, her throaty little cries melded into one long, deep moan. He felt her tighten and release, once and then again, her hips rising higher into his with each movement. With every thrust, he couldn't stop himself from enjoying the fantasy he had denied himself before, the fantasy that he was filling this woman he loved with the seed that would grow into their child.

That thought carried him over the edge.

CHAPTER FOURTEEN

BEN PULLED the Durham Bulls baseball cap lower on his forehead. Again and again, his eyes skimmed the dark, smelly bar.

He felt foolish for getting himself into this charade. Sipping lukewarm beer in a Winston-Salem dive he wouldn't set foot in on a normal day, Ben knew he had overreacted. But after talking to Cybil, all he knew was that he had to act. His indecision was ruining too many lives.

Intent on a rational conversation, he had called Cybil the night before. With Rose standing by, clutching his hand, he had spilled out his thoughts on the breath he'd been holding as the phone rang.

"Cybil, I want to work this out. I don't want to keep you away from your daughter. But I won't put Krissy in danger. Do you think we can talk? Find some kind of solution?"

"Yes, Ben." She sounded breathless, almost frantic. "Yes, I'm ready to do that. If Krissy..."

Her voice ended in a muffled grunt and was quickly replaced by another voice, this one enraged and obviously intoxicated.

"You son of a bitch! I'll kill you! If you don't bring that kid back, I'll break every bone in your body!"

"Colin, calm down." Ben struggled to keep the anger and dislike out of his voice. Rose squeezed his hand and he grasped it as if it were the only life preserver in deep water. "Let's talk about this like..."

Ben flinched as a crash and a shrill squeal sounded in his ear.

"Don't patronize me! You're nothing but a criminal. And when I get my hands on that kid, you'll never see her again. Do you hear me, McKenzie? Never!"

As all hope of a solution had vanished in the wake of Colin's obscene ravings, Ben had hung up, a sick turmoil filling him.

Rose's arms around his waist and her hair soft against his cheek had gradually calmed him.

"There must be some way to fight him," she had said softly.

Still fired with the feeling of invincibility that had followed their lovemaking and Rose's support, Ben had believed the determination in her soft brown eyes. So he had called his attorney and arranged a meeting. But the trek back to Winston-Salem had punctured yet another fairly substantial hole in Ben's sense of euphoria. Being in such familiar surroundings yet still feeling exiled was bad enough. And the phone call to Keith had actually frightened him, more even than Colin's threats.

"Holy mother! You're where?" The ever excitable Keith had exploded when Ben called to ask if they could meet for lunch somewhere quiet and out-of-the-way. "I don't believe you! You stay away from me. You hear? That sweetheart ex of yours has private investigators all over my tail. I'm running into 'em when I brush my teeth. If you even try to leave a note on my car, they'll nail you, big brother."

So Ben had a long, depressing afternoon to kill before his meeting with his attorney. She had almost refused to see him, so when his watch showed forty-five minutes past the time they had agreed on, Ben was stewing. What if she didn't show? What if she changed her mind? Where would he turn then?

Sweaty-palm nervous, Ben had been tempted to leave more than once. He was on the verge of doing just that when she walked in the door.

Backlit by the late afternoon sunshine, she paused at the entrance. Tall, thin and champagne blond, Janis Weiss drew instant attention from the blue-collar workers manning the stools and booths in the Devil's Den. Her gray suit was stylishly short and accented with bloodred blouse, breast pocket square and leather belt. Her challenging dark eyes surveyed the room until they finally landed on the dark corner where Ben sat. She marched across the room and flung her briefcase into the booth.

"Did you have to come looking so much like a lawyer?" Ben asked, not allowing himself to look around the bar to gauge the attention she'd drawn.

"Did you have to come looking so much like Magnum, P.I. in jeans?" She frowned and laid her hands, flat and loose, on the table. She barked at him in the same cold tone she had used to castigate Cybil's attorney in one of those futile meetings. "I'm amazed you have the gall to call me after the stunt you've pulled. You're lucky I even showed up."

"I need help, Janis. I want to straighten this out."

She glared at him as a waitress slouched beside their booth. Ben ordered two beers and the waitress disappeared.

"You want to straighten this out." She stared at him. Ben didn't waver, but he developed an instantaneous sympathy for anyone who faced Janis Weiss on the wrong end of a cross-examination. "I would like that very much, Ben. Do you realize I have private investigators breathing down my neck?"

A jolt of anxiety shot through Ben. If Cybil—or Colin, if last night's conversation meant anything—was so intent on finding him, how long could he reasonably expect to hide?

"Janis, you've got to do something. I can't bring Krissy back to what she went through before." He pushed the bill of his cap back. "You should see her now. She's a different little girl. Isn't there something else, some other tactic..."

Janis's deep laugh cut him off. "You don't get it, do you? Don't you realize you've jeopardized any chance you ever had of winning the courts over to your side?"

For a moment, Ben's veins ran with ice. "What do you mean?"

"You've committed a criminal act, Ben."

His stomach churned. Slumping against the unyielding plywood booth, Ben started to protest. But he had no effective argument to offer. Janis knew the truth. Colin knew the truth. Even he knew the truth.

"How much good do you think you'll do Krissy if you're behind bars?"

Ben pulled off the cap and ran a hand over his head. This wasn't going right. This wasn't happening the way he'd been sure it would when he'd been wrapped in the warm afterglow of Rose's lovemaking. The waitress slid their beers onto the table and he thrust some bills in her direction. His first swallow of the cool liquid was bitter. "Cut me some slack, Weiss."

She pursed her lips and studied the rim of her glass. She wiped the lip of the mug before taking a swallow. "What do you want from me, Ben?"

He told her about his call to Cybil and his hope of working

out an agreement that would give him custody in exchange for supervised visitation with Cybil.

"She's afraid, Janis, and getting desperate. I can hear it in her voice. If you could sit down with her, give her something to cling to, to hope for, I think she'd work with us. I think she'd leave him if she thought it would bring Krissy back."

"You don't know much about battered women, do you?"

Ben collapsed against the rigid plywood of the booth. "Battered? You think he's..."

The idea stunned Ben as much as anything that had happened in the past twenty-four hours. He couldn't envision the proud and dignified Cybil accepting that kind of treatment. But didn't it make everything easier to explain? "She's battered?"

Janis shrugged. "Physically, maybe. Emotionally, certainly. And getting a woman in that situation to take any kind of action isn't going to be easy."

"But if she can see Krissy, surely that will make the difference. She'll see reason. I know she will."

Janis wrapped her hand around her mug and took a long draw. "I'll do what I can. I'll bring her into the office. Alone. I'll have an offer on paper. I'll bring in someone from the women's shelter to talk with her. We'll see if she's ready to take charge of her life again."

Ben shook his head. It was hard for him to imagine his haughty ex-wife throwing her life at the feet of someone who didn't hesitate to walk on her. "She will be. I know she will be."

"I hope so."

Ben reached for a paper napkin and the pen in his shirt pocket. "Here. This is where you can reach me. After you've talked to her, call me."

With one swift motion, Janis snatched the napkin out from under his pen and wadded it up. "I don't want to know, Ben." She stood and collected her briefcase, stopping long enough to finish her beer in one final swallow. "I'm going out on a limb for you. I hope you know that."

"Don't do it for me, Janis. Do it for Krissy."

BY THE TIME Ben's car pulled into the driveway the following evening, Rose felt as if she had been holding her breath the entire two days he'd been gone. Her heart careened, urging her to jump up from the porch swing, cross the yard at an unladylike gallop and throw herself into his arms.

Instead, she kept the swing moving with the toe of her canvas shoe and continued brushing Krissy's cheek with the pad of her thumb. The little girl had insisted on waiting up for her daddy, but the rhythmic swing and Rose's crooning had long since ambushed her determination.

Rose knew the moment she saw Ben's face that things hadn't gone as he had hoped on his trip to Winston-Salem. At last she had been able to attach a name to the place that was home for Ben and Krissy. On her lunch hour yesterday, she had gone to the library and looked it up. One of the largest tobacco manufacturing markets in the world, located about thirty miles from the Blue Ridge Mountains. The home of more than one college. She had latched onto the details and tried to envision the place. Would she ever, she wondered, see it for herself? With Ben and Krissy at her side?

While she'd daydreamed about the town, she had prayed that things would go well there, that Ben could find a solution to a situation that should have been so simple to resolve.

But his broad, square shoulders wore his defeat heavily. Rose would have given anything to see him march confidently across the lawn and up the steps. But he didn't. He was weary. And not just physically. More than the long drive from North Carolina had worn him down, she knew.

Still, he stopped at the top of the steps and smiled at her.

"You know the only thing I felt good about all the way home?" he whispered softly to avoid waking the sleeping child in her lap.

"What?"

"Knowing she was here with you. Knowing I'd be coming back to the two of you."

Gladness swelled her heart despite the solemn expression in his eyes. She smiled and held her hand out to beckon him closer, stilling the swing with her toe. When he drew near, he leaned close and dropped a light kiss on her lips.

"Not enough," he murmured, and covered her lips with his again, coaxing them open, drawing her into one of those moments of mounting need that still stunned her with their intensity.

As she strained into his kiss, a drowsy little voice whined, "Daddy?"

They jerked quickly apart. Rose looked down guiltily, her anxiety easing only slightly when she realized that Krissy was still rubbing her closed eyes.

"I'm here, sweetheart."

In an instant, Krissy was wide-awake and jumping into Ben's arms, calling out to him and wrapping her arms around his neck. As she watched the two talk and cuddle, Rose felt once again the full flower of fulfillment within her. Her lap was still warm where she had cradled Krissy's head; her lips were still warm where Ben's kiss had branded her as his. And Sweetbranch, Alabama, seemed the best place in the world to live out all the daydreams those feelings evoked. Right here, on this front porch, in this house she had chafed to escape for so long.

Her escape, it seemed, had come to her. And she was content to be its captive. Forever.

Or as long as it was possible, she reminded herself as she and Ben linked arms to take Krissy upstairs and tuck her in.

BEN REFUSED to let reality intrude on his life in Sweetbranch in the weeks that followed. He was in touch with Janis Weiss almost every day and tried not to grow discouraged by her lack of encouragement.

When Janis told him Cybil had canceled their appointment, he told her to try again. When she told him Cybil tore up the agreement she had drafted and scattered it all over the dhurrie rug in her office, he told her to try again. And when Janis began to realize that Ben wasn't giving up and recommended that they bring in one of the country's foremost attorneys in difficult and controversial custody cases, Ben wanted to celebrate.

If sheer force of will could resolve this situation, Ben knew, he would have his way before it was over.

Between the phone calls to Janis, Ben concentrated on slowly building a new life in Sweetbranch. His days were busy following up on the possibility of opening a plant in Sweetbranch. He did everything quietly and anonymously—he didn't want to be guilty, along with everything else, of raising Rose's hopes for a normal life together. He commissioned an out-of-town real estate agent to look around for available land. He opened communication with the railroad about keeping their line to Sweetbranch operating. And without letting on what his underlying intentions were, he even helped Rose with the task force that was looking for ways to boost industry in the community.

Bringing Sweetbranch out of its economic depression was only part of the dream he pursued. He also allowed himself the luxury of pretending that he and Rose were taking the first steps toward building a life together. He knew it might never happen. And he was careful to shield Rose from his hopes. But he couldn't deny himself the pleasure of entertaining those hopes deep in his own heart.

He hoped when he and Rose and Krissy and Uncle Bump went to church every Sunday, walking down the wide, tree-lined sidewalks in what Uncle Bump called their "Sunday-go-to-meeting" clothes. He hoped when Rose asked him if he'd like to meet the youth group she worked with at the church, and was amazed to discover yet another facet of Rose's nurturing personality. He hoped when they taught Krissy to help weed the garden, joining Rose's laughter when Krissy pulled up almost as many young shoots and seedlings as she pulled up weeds.

And he hoped when they made love, which they did as often as they could without flaunting it in front of Krissy, who was frankly curious about their relationship as only a child could be. Or in front of Uncle Bump, who hid his proprietary satisfaction behind querulous mistrust of the whole situation.

"Don't worry about Uncle Bump," Rose whispered after they made love one night, her breath warm against his chest, her head tucked into the crook of his shoulder. "He has a reputation to uphold as an old grouch."

Ben closed his eyes and smiled, letting his hand slide down the long, sleek expanse of her back. "I don't. He slips up and calls me son too often for me to worry much."

Rose laughed. "He's nothing but an old softie."

"Runs in the family."

"I guess so."

Ben hesitated. There was another part to the dream life he was working on here in Sweetbranch. And he wanted this part so badly, so deeply, he was almost afraid to bring it up. "Rose, do you ever want family of your own?"

She stiffened so slightly he might not have noticed it if her answer hadn't mattered so much to him.

"No."

"Why not?"

"I'm too old for that, Ben."

"This isn't a woman who's too old for anything," Ben murmured, caressing the firm roundness of a breast and letting his hand come to rest on the smooth expanse of her belly.

"I know what I'm talking about. My mother was too old. She..."

"She what?"

Rose was silent. "I'd never want a child of mine to give up her life just because I was too old to take care of myself."

"You aren't your mother, Rose."

"How do you know?"

"And your daughters won't be you."

"I won't have any daughters, Ben. I tell you, I'm too old for that."

"Krissy doesn't think you're too old."

Her lengthy silence told him he had at least made her think beyond the beliefs she had long held. And when she spoke again, at last, her voice had lost some of its certainty. "She's just a little girl. What does she know?"

"More than you think. Children know these things. Their instincts tell them who has enough love, who will keep them safe."

"Really?"

Her tremulous voice told him not to push her any more right now. So he gathered her to him and gently lowered his face to hers. "Really. Krissy knows. And so do I."

She hesitated only a moment before melting into his arms, all slender and soft and fragrant in the moonlight that peeked between the curtains. He did his best to make her feel as young as she made him feel.

But he didn't press her about children. Until he was free to make his dreams come true, he had no right to tell her that his favorite recurring fantasy involved watching her grow round with his child.

He had never realized until he met Rose how much he had missed sharing parenthood with someone else who enjoyed the wonder of it as much as he did. Cybil had been more concerned with stretch marks and how soon her body would recover its former shape than she had been with the dark fuzz standing straight up on Krissy's little head or the flat little button that was her nose. Cybil had wondered how quickly Krissy could be potty trained. Ben had wanted someone who would get misty-eyed with him each time Krissy added a new word to her vocabulary.

Rose would be that way, he knew.

Equally important, he knew she would always love Krissy as much as she loved a child they made together. Her every action with Krissy told him that. And it made the days of waiting, the days his life was in limbo, a little easier to survive.

One Friday Ben drove with Rose to Tuscaloosa, where she was scheduled to take the battery of tests that would determine just how much college credit her life experiences were worth at the University of Alabama. She was nervous and exhilarated.

"What if I do badly?" She stood on the sidewalk in front of the building where the tests were being given, shifting nervously from one foot to the other.

He put his hands on her shoulders and tried to still her jittery movement. "You'll do as well as you can. That's all you have to do."

"But what if they tell me everything I've done isn't worth anything? What if..."

"Rose." He spoke sternly, capturing her attention with the voice fatherhood had taught him. "Your life has been worth far more than a few college credits. If the college also decides it's worth some credit, that's gravy. If not, you'll have to take chemistry and Western Civ just like the rest of us poor stiffs had to do."

"But what if..."

He took her by the shoulders, turned her to face the building and gave her a gentle push. "Now go. Quit stalling. You don't want to be late."

She looked over her shoulder, some of the consternation going out of her face as she fashioned a wry smile. "I'm already twenty years late. What's another ten minutes?"

She came out hours later, elated that she had finished the tests, a hurdle that seemed almost as important to her as doing well on them. They walked the campus, arm in arm, and decided it was even more exciting than it had been when they were eighteen-year-old freshmen. Then they drove to Birmingham, where they were to meet the youth group from the church to take in a show by a Broadway touring company.

The show was fun. The kids were fun. Being with Rose in the theater, holding her hand in the darkness was fun. Realizing he could barely concentrate on the plot of the show thanks to his consuming desire for the woman at his side, that was fun, too.

As they were leaving the theater, with Ben and Rose and another couple from Sweetbranch commandeering the group of excited teens through the crowded lobby, the fun evaporated from the evening.

"Ben! Ben McKenzie!"

At the sound of his name, Ben started as if he'd been shot. He saw Rose whirl in his direction, her face drained of color. Striving for composure, Ben turned toward the voice and saw a Winston-Salem commercial artist who brought some of her brochures and other projects to Ben's company for printing. She was smiling the careful, curious smile of someone who knows she's on the trail of something good.

"Why, Ben McKenzie, everyone back home has decided you joined the foreign legion."

Cindy Olan held out her hand. Ben took it, knowing his felt cold and clammy from fear. He responded to her quip with the laugh he knew was necessary, but it sounded thin and weak in his ears.

"Just traveling. A little business travel."

Cindy's eyes slid around and landed on Rose and the clump of teens, who had by now been shepherded out of earshot. Rose turned abruptly and hurried after the group.

"I see. Well, Ben, how long before you'll be back in Winston?"

"I'm not sure, Cindy. I'm combining a little business with a...sort of a leave of absence."

"Midlife crisis, Ben?"

Ben attempted a hearty laugh. "You could say that."

"Well, it's so strange I should run into you. I'll be sure and let everyone know I tracked down the elusive McKenzie brother."

Ben wondered as they drove back to Sweetbranch whether his idyll was finally at an end.

CHAPTER FIFTEEN

"GOOD NEWS." Relief washed through Ben at the first words out of his attorney's mouth. "We've caught a big fish."

Ben was ready for some good news. He'd done nothing but worry since running into Cindy Olan in Birmingham. "How's that?"

"Bernard Hartmann has agreed to be cocounsel." Janis repeated the name of one of the country's most notorious attorneys with relish. "Well, actually, I agreed to be cocounsel. Hartmann'll be running the show. A reputation like his certainly can't hurt our cause."

The blood was pounding in Ben's head. Things might actually start to happen now. The end might be in sight. He wanted nothing more than to tell Rose. But he knew that was premature; just as it would be premature to share with her his very real interest in the acreage north of Sweetbranch that a near-bankrupt developer was trying to unload. He wouldn't risk her disappointment, no matter how optimistic he might feel at the moment. "What does he say? What happens now?"

"We meet with Cybil tomorrow. He'll try to intimidate her into an agreement."

Ben cringed at the thought of the frightened, unstable woman he'd heard on the phone facing one of the country's toughest trial lawyers. It was a tactic that wouldn't have bothered him four years ago; right now, his stomach rolled at the thought.

"There's more, Ben. He wants you to go public with your story."

"What do you mean?"

"Take it to the news media."

"Forget it, Janis. I'm not going to drag Krissy *or* Cybil through that."

"Hear me out, Ben. Hartmann says a public outcry over the unresponsive system may be the best way to effect real changes—and your case could be the first to benefit."

"No. I don't care. I can't do that. I won't do that."

"Don't discount it, Ben. I think he's right. You know the system. It's deaf, mute and blind about things like this. We have to do something to force them to listen, to act. Besides..." She paused, a technique he'd seen her use in court to make sure she had the jury's undivided attention. "It may be the only way we can resolve this without going to court."

"Then we'll go to court."

"No court's going to negotiate with a fugitive, Ben. If we go to court, you'll have to come back. And you'll have to send Krissy home—to her mother."

AS THE LAST LONG FLY BALL finished out its wobbly spin into the waiting hands of a pudgy little girl and the first Little League game of the season drew to a close, Rose stood in the bleachers and stretched her back.

"Summer's finally here." She swept a satisfied look over the Edmond Gilchrist Memorial Park, which was little more than a dusty red baseball diamond set off from unsteady wooden bleachers by a sagging chain link fence. The first Little League game at Gilchrist Park was where summer had officially started in Sweetbranch for as long as Rose could remember.

Last year she had enjoyed the enthusiasm and the vibrancy of the children, as always. But there were times, as her restlessness grew, that the very monotony of it had threatened to draw frustrated tears.

This year, something about the continuity, the permanence of it, cozied up to her heart. Right next to Ben and Krissy.

Ben jumped off the edge of the bleachers and reached up to lift her down. "Summer? We've still got three more weeks and at least another fifteen degrees Fahrenheit before you can call it summer. Not to mention another twenty percentage points of humidity."

"Outsider," she accused cheerfully, wishing the moment when his hands had wrapped around her waist to lift her hadn't ended so quickly. "You've got a lot to learn about tradition in Sweetbranch. Now, where's Krissy?"

Ben pointed toward the tailgate of Maxine Hammond's station wagon, where Krissy and three of her new best friends had dangled their stubby legs and giggled their way through the game.

"I'll wait here." Her smile fading, Rose drifted away while Ben retrieved Krissy for their walk home.

Maxine was the only person in Sweetbranch who persisted in disapproving of Rose's relationship with Ben. During the weeks she and Ben had been openly seeing each another, everyone else, from the bawdy-tongued Alma to the stiff-backed gossip queen Ida Clancy, had shown some kind of support for Rose. Alma prodded her to rate Ben's performance—a nearly daily occurrence that Rose had finally learned to ignore without a blush. The Widow Clancy intimated none too subtly that a wedding was the only acceptable route for LaFern Finley's daughter to take. Even Agnes at the Sweet Boutique had ordered a catalog of wedding dresses, which Rose had been sorely tempted to thumb through. And Bunny had taken her aside to make sure Rose was up-to-date on safe sex practices.

Only Maxine maintained a stony lack of acceptance. And right now, exhausted after a week of standing on her feet all day every day, Rose couldn't bear to dwell on it. She'd been too emotional lately—one wrong word from anyone these days seemed enough to bring tears to her eyes. Some days it felt as if she'd had a world-class case of PMS for weeks. She knew it was nothing more than the uncertainty getting to her, but the situation was beginning to exhaust her. And knowing Maxine wasn't on her side just made it worse.

Maxine will come around, she told herself. *I know she will.*

The task force was one more thing that had Rose running herself ragged. In the midst of persistent rumors that a major business was considering Sweetbranch as a location for a new plant, the task force was putting the finishing touches on a step-by-step plan for recruiting industry. Ben had been impressed with the work they'd done when Rose had asked him to look it over.

"We won!" Krissy's feet barely touched the ground as she bounded up and pitched herself at Rose's knees.

Rose laughed and bent to swing the little girl into her arms for a hug. "That we did, Krissy."

When she deposited Krissy back on the ground, the youngster ran ahead, turning back occasionally to beckon them on.

"She's happy," Ben said. And Rose heard the contentment in his voice at the simple observation.

"So am I." They turned the corner onto Dixie Belle Lane. Rose looked ahead longingly at the house, she couldn't wait to put her feet up and her head back. Maybe she would rest all weekend.

Ben looked down and smiled. "I'm glad."

"Are you happy, Ben?"

His obvious hesitation sent her emotions spiraling downward again.

"I will be, when this is all resolved."

She nodded and reached for his hand, giving it a reassuring squeeze. "It will be. Soon, I'm sure of it."

He didn't respond, just kept his eyes trained on Krissy, who had stopped a half block ahead to commune with a neighborhood puppy.

"Ben? When it is resolved... I think Sweetbranch will make a wonderful place to raise Krissy. She's thriving here. Haven't you noticed?" Suddenly her own reservations about her hometown faded as she thought of the child's happiness. She realized that she, too, could have everything she wanted, everything she needed, right here in Sweetbranch.

"Yes, I think you're right." Ben's slight smile pleased her and gave her the courage to go on.

"Then, when everything is resolved, would you like to get married, Ben? To me, I mean?"

There. She had said it. Finleys never had been shy about speaking their mind. Thanks to all the busybodies in town, this had definitely been on her mind. And she kept thinking if *something* was resolved, if she knew the outcome of just *one* thing...

Ben stopped so suddenly she was three steps ahead of him before she realized it. She turned back and saw a mixture of feelings on his face that did nothing to reassure her.

"Is that a no?" She tried a nervous smile to set him at ease. Better that than screaming out the protest that was already taking form in her mind.

But he merely stared. As if he thought she'd lost all her senses. Well, maybe she had. But, hey, wasn't this supposed to be the nineties? Wasn't it okay for women to take the lead? She'd seen it on the cover of one of Bunny's magazines. So it must be okay.

"Well, speak up, Ben. Or should I send for the rescue squad? Are we going to need artificial respiration?"

Ben passed a hand over his forehead, pinching the bridge of his nose in a gesture Rose had come to recognize. His stress indicator.

Well, I guess that answers that.

"Rose, we need to talk."

Her embarrassment and moodiness were mixing to form anger. She tried to forestall it. "No, that's all right, Ben. I understand. I put my big old foot in it, I guess. No need to explain."

She turned to go but he grabbed her by the arm. "I mean it, Rose. We need to talk. Or I need to talk. You need to listen."

Pointedly slipping her arm out of his grasp, she crossed her arms across her chest so tightly her breasts hurt. She didn't let go. "Okay. Talk."

He drew a long breath, his blue eyes unfathomable. "You know how I feel about you. You know that..."

"Do I?"

He drew his lips into a long, tight line. "I'm talking. You're listening. Remember?"

Rose clenched her jaw shut but made certain her eyes did plenty of talking for her. She wanted to make sure Ben McKenzie knew he was not making her happy at this precise moment.

"I love you, Rose. I've told you that and I mean it. And when...*if* the day comes that..." He stopped and stared at the ground. "We have to be realistic, Rose. I may not be able to make this situation go away. And if I can't, there's only one other thing I can do."

The bleak look in his eyes told her she really didn't want to hear what that final step was.

"I'll have to run. With Krissy. We'll have to change our names. Get new identities. New lives. We'll be on the run the rest of our lives, Rose."

At that moment, she didn't like him one bit for dredging up that kind of melodramatic junk just to take her mind off the issue that he obviously didn't want to address: marriage.

"Ben McKenzie, you've been reading the covers of too many women's magazines at the drugstore," she snapped.

"I'm serious."

"Well, so am I, Ben McKenzie. If you don't want to be saddled with an over-the-hill, undereducated hairdresser, say so." Seized by anger and frustration, she jabbed a finger in his chest. "But don't think just because I don't have a college degree and haven't had all the advantages of city living that I'm so gullible I'll fall for that kind of flimsy excuse. Even if you did have to leave, we could start over somewhere else. Why don't you tell me the truth—just say straight out that you don't have it in mind to marry me."

Then she wheeled and stalked the rest of the way to the house, too angry even to think about crying.

How dare he treat me like some country bumpkin that he can tell any old dumb tale to and get away with it? She slammed the front door behind her, startling Uncle Bump, who sat drowsing in his living room chair.

He looked up and favored her with a knowing grin. "Guess we lost?"

"Go back to sleep, Uncle Bump," she ordered, not even slowing down on her way to her room. "I don't want to talk to you, either."

DUSK WAS a long, drawn-out affair in June in north Alabama, lolling in the air until almost 9:00 p.m. After he caught up with an inquisitive Krissy—"Whatsamatta with Wose, Daddy?"—and deposited her in Uncle Bump's capable, gnarled old hands, Ben trudged through the gathering darkness for what seemed like days.

Everything was a muddle. And it was all his fault. He had no trouble admitting that. And everything he tried to do to fix the problem made the mess bigger, it seemed.

He felt backed against the wall. By Cybil and that poor excuse for a husband of hers. By the court system. By the hotshot attorney who wanted him to drag his private life through the newspapers.

And now by Rose.

What would he do without Rose, Ben wondered as he wandered, head lowered, fists in his pockets, down Main Street. At this moment, he could no more imagine living without Rose than he could imagine handing Krissy back over to Cybil and Colin.

"Good game, wouldn't you say, Mr. McKenzie?"

Ben looked up into the friendly face of the editor of the *Sweetbranch Weekly Gazetteer,* who was walking toward his office, a narrow notebook jutting out of his back pocket.

"Yes, it was, Mr. Wilcutt."

Harley Wilcutt dropped into step beside Ben, a casual move that nevertheless raised a cautious prickling along Ben's back. His right hand came out of his pant pocket and began to open and close as if with a will of its own.

"You're fitting in right nicely here in Sweetbranch."

"It's a nice little town. I like it here."

"Well, I like it. Has its problems, though, you know. Unless you believe the rumors."

"Rumors."

"Oh, you've heard the rumors, haven't you? About some big company sniffing around. Maybe opening a plant here." He cut a sideways glance at Ben. "You're a businessman. Think there's anything to the rumors?"

Ben didn't want to ask about Harley's assumption that he was a businessman. In fact, what he wanted was to get out of this conversation. Quickly. He hadn't forgotten Maxine's warning about the newsman's probing instincts.

"Hard to say."

Harley nodded. "Yeah. My gut tells me there'd be no reason for a legitimate business to snoop around so quietly if they were interested in Sweetbranch. Know what I mean? Seems they'd just come out and make it known. Unless there was some reason they had to hide it. Don't you suppose, Mr. McKenzie?"

Ben's blood pumped fiercely. He recognized the edge to Harley's questions. "I really couldn't say."

"Well, I've got a story to write," Harley said, stopping in front of the newspaper office. "About the game, I mean. Hope we'll have a chance to talk about this again sometime."

Ben nodded, barely waiting for Harley Wilcutt to unlock the door to the *Sweetbranch Weekly Gazetteer* and disappear inside before he sauntered off, as casually as he could manage given the apprehension pounding through him.

Newspeople. Always digging for dirt. Always ready to stir up something. Ben's jaw worked angrily. He didn't feel safe anywhere.

And might never again. Unless...

Ben stopped in the middle of the deserted sidewalk and looked back in the direction he'd just come from. There, about a block away, was the pay telephone. He stared at it, as if gauging it for evil intent, for a long while. Then, with a muttered oath, Ben headed back to the phone.

He'd tried everything else. How much worse could it get? Maybe it was time to follow some of that legal advice he was paying so much money to ignore.

He called his attorney first. But when she wasn't in, he decided he would tell her after the fact. Because if he didn't do this now, before he had time to think about it, he might never do it.

Ben dialed long-distance directory assistance and asked for the number of the *Winston-Salem Journal.* He stared at the number for a long time before he finally dialed it and asked to speak to someone who would be interested in a story on child abuse.

When the woman's rushed, bored voice came on the line, Ben almost hung up. He forced himself to think of Krissy. Of Rose.

"My daughter is being abused and no one cares," he said. "Do you?"

She hesitated, but when she spoke again she no longer sounded rushed or bored. "Yes, I do. You want to tell me about it?"

KEITH CLOSED HIS DOOR to shut out the noise from the outer office and fingered the dog-eared edges of the report on his desk. Sweetbranch, Alabama. Just thinking about it made him uneasy. Ben had been right; he'd been better off not knowing.

Not that he officially, beyond a shadow of a doubt *knew.* But he trusted his gut on this one. Ben and Krissy had to be holed up in this town of 3,593 (down from 4,211 in the official 1990 census, according to Ben's report), approximately 37.9 miles from the northeastern border of Alabama. He knew what timber was native to the region. He knew the climate. He knew the demographics of the population—aging, up to a median age of 37.2—and he knew the soil analysis.

And he knew that his brother—his starry-eyed, idealistic brother, who after all had once upon a time been as hard-nosed as anybody—had fallen in with the people in this dying little town and appointed himself its Sir Galahad. Ben was like that.

"Damn!" Keith flung the report to the edge of his desk. He was ticked off at Ben. Even after reading the big story in Sunday's paper about the inadequacies of the system that was supposed to protect kids like Krissy, Keith was still ticked off. Because he missed Ben. Ben was his brother and his partner and his best friend, and Keith wanted him back.

A loud noise that was different from all the other loud noises a print shop generated cut through his preoccupation. Before Keith could get up to investigate, his office door came crashing open.

The man looked overdressed in the six-hundred-dollar suit. The silk tie was slightly askew and the suit coat sat just a bit off center, as if someone had grabbed the man by the shoulder. His short, dark hair was carefully razor cut, but a lock flopped out of place over one eye. But his eyes, ah, it was his eyes that were truly out of place. They were the wild, unfocused, bloodshot eyes of one of those homeless people Ben had dragged him to the shelter to visit last Thanksgiving.

Keith shuddered.

"Who the hell are…"

"I'm asking. You answer." The voice was loud with anger. Keith sensed just enough lack of control in the voice that he knew he had reason to be afraid. "Where is that son of a bitch?"

Keith's tongue stuck to the roof of his suddenly bone-dry mouth. This was Colin. No question about it. And right now, he was living down to everything Ben had ever said about him. Bile rose in Keith's throat as he thought of his tiny little niece in this maniac's hands.

The thought of himself in this maniac's hands also had distressingly little appeal.

Don't let 'em see you sweat, Ben had always said in his wheeling-and-dealing days. He hadn't said anything about not letting 'em see you shake, but Keith knew that went with the territory.

Damn you, Ben, for getting me into this. He drew a deep breath and used the calming voice you'd use while backing away from a mad dog. "Listen, pal, just calm down and let's see if we can't…"

Colin's right arm shot out, sending a halogen lamp careening against the bookcase, which shuddered and spit out a half-dozen volumes. "Tell me. Now! I want that kid and I want to break that bastard in half. He's through spreading lies about me all over the paper."

In two swift moves, Colin hurled the lightweight side chair in front of Keith's desk against a wall and knocked aside the desk lamp that obscured his view of Keith. Keith didn't even look toward the sound of splintering wood. He didn't open his mouth, either.

"Where is he?"

"I don't have any idea. You ought to know he's too smart to tell me where he is."

Keith was pleased that his voice sounded so strong and undaunted; at least this orangutan wouldn't know he was jelly inside. Big brother could hardly have done it better himself.

Colin grabbed the front of Keith's shirt, knotting it under his chin and gouging Keith's Adam's apple with his knuckles. Keith prayed he wouldn't flinch, but he felt all the color drain from his face.

"It's here somewhere. Got to be. And if you don't tell me, you're gonna wish you had."

ROSE FLOPPED DOWN in the canvas chair on Maxine's front porch, grabbed a fistful of beans from the bag at her feet and started stringing and snapping.

"You were right."

Maxine chuckled. "This must be a first. Rose Finley admitting that I am right about something. And stringing beans at the same time. A momentous occasion, indeed."

"This isn't funny, Maxie. You were right about Ben McKenzie."

The steady rhythm of Maxine's rocker slowed, but Rose didn't dare look up at her friend.

"Tell me, Rose."

Stringing and snapping the beans furiously, Rose swallowed her bitterness and the lump in her throat.

"He's hiding out, Maxie. He said Krissy was being abused by her stepfather and the courts weren't doing anything about it." She looked up, dropping a green bean into her lap. "He says he may have to disappear to keep Krissy safe. The more I think about it, the harder it is to believe. Nobody's going to make a little girl like Krissy stay with somebody who's hurting her. I think he just wants to avoid making a commitment. I guess he thinks a man can tell anything to a woman if she feels like she's facing her last chance. You were right, Maxie, I was... Maxie? You all right?''

The bean Maxine was snapping into bite-size pieces had slipped out of her hand. Her eyes seemed to focus on one of the freshly painted boards of the porch. And both her hands were trembling—the one that had frozen in midair and the one that covered her mouth.

Rose grabbed her friend's hand. "Maxie? What's wrong? Tell me what's wrong.''

With a shudder, Maxine drew her eyes from the board where she had fixed them and pressed the back of her hand against her lips. "Forgive me, Rose. I believe I am fine now.''

"Uh-huh. You're going to have to tell me what this is all about or I'm going in there right now to call Ragan and tell him his wife is having some kind of attack.'' Rose tossed the beans in her lap back into the sack and dusted her hands. "Now, tell Auntie Rose what's going on here.''

Maxine drew a deep breath and smiled, the serene smile that Rose knew so well, with one difference—Maxine's eyes were still clouded with trouble.

"Sometimes, Rose, a parent can play by all the rules. And sometimes a child is the loser.''

The ache in Maxine's voice chilled Rose. "You know about Ben, don't you?''

"Yes, Rose, I do. And what he has told you is not some clever cover-up designed to deceive you. What he has told you is the truth. An ugly truth, but a truth nevertheless.''

"But the courts...a judge...how could...nobody would...'' Rose shook her head. "I just find that hard to believe, Maxie.''

"Believe it, Rose. It happens.'' The ache had now robbed Maxine's voice of all its serenity, all the honeyed smoothness that was at the core of her personality. "And if you love Ben, if you truly love Ben, you may be called upon to make a greater sacrifice than any you have made yet.''

Rose's anger was growing into fear. "What are you talking about?''

"Ben and Krissy *may* have to disappear, Rose. They may find it necessary to become other people, to give up the lives they've had until now. And if they go underground, if that is the only way Ben can keep his daughter safe, you may have to decide whether or not you are willing to give up your life and go with them."

Rose's head whirled. This was the same silly story Ben had been trying to peddle. Now it was coming from her sane, ultrarational friend Maxine. Her heart raced wildly. "But that's... You mean it, don't you?"

"Yes, I do, Rose."

Unbidden, Rose saw herself walking out the front door of her home, the home she'd lived in all her life. Saw herself turning away from Uncle Bump. Locking up the Picture Perfect. Driving out of Sweetbranch. Away from all the people who were her life. And she couldn't complete the picture. In spite of the way she'd railed against fate for holding her hostage in Sweetbranch all her life, and in spite of what she'd said to Ben, she couldn't really imagine walking away and leaving it, irrevocably, forever.

But if Ben were driving away? And Krissy? Could she watch them drive away without her?

Panic rose in her chest.

"But why? Surely something could be..." She saw understanding in Maxine's eyes. "Maxie, how do you...? If you knew about Ben, why didn't you tell me? Why didn't you warn me?"

"I tried to warn you, Rose."

"But if you'd told me the whole story. If..."

"Would it have mattered? Would you have been able to stop yourself?"

Rose slumped against her chair. "No. No, I don't suppose so. But, Maxie, how did you know? Why you?"

"You know too much already, Rose. Forget what you know and don't ask any more."

Rose swallowed back the fear and panic in her throat. "You're...you're all mixed up in this, aren't you, Maxie?"

Maxine was silent for a long time, but Rose waited her out.

"I am the contact." Maxine spoke slowly, her voice lowered. "I am the first stop in the underground network. I help people like Ben find safe places to live. I help them build new identities. Usually they go into the network immediately so there is no chance of being discovered. Your friend Ben, however, had a difficult time making that decision. He has put us all at risk. Even you, Rose, although that was not his intention. I know he would never want to involve you further by asking you to share this with him.''

A hysterical laugh bubbled up in Rose's throat. "Oh Lord, and I'm the one who wanted a little excitement in Sweetbranch.'' She laughed until she realized how close she was to sobbing instead. "Why, Maxie? Isn't this dangerous? You could go to jail. Ragan would be ruined. And your kids... Why, Maxie?''

"Because once I did nothing,'' Maxine said, so softly Rose could barely hear her. "Once I played by the rules when the courts sent a child back to his father. I was unfit, you see. Consorting with a man of a different race. Hoping to raise my son with a man of a different race. So I did what the courts told me, even though I knew my first husband's rage. I didn't know what else to do.''

Maxine's eyes closed. Her face crumpled, but no tears squeezed out of her eyes, no sobs shook her body. "My son died, Rose.'' She leaned forward, her eyes filled with fire, her fists clenched in a strength she normally kept in check. "And I will not let that happen again, Rose, as long as I have breath to fight. No other child will die because I lack courage. Never again!''

ROSE FELT that someone had emptied her of emotion by the time she left Maxine. For almost two hours, rage, bitterness and despair had spilled out of Maxine and Rose had responded the only way she knew—by pouring out all the compassion and tenderness in her heart.

Yes, she was drained as she walked down the quiet streets of Sweetbranch toward home. But the intimacy she had shared with her normally self-contained friend was feeding a new strength into her.

So was her new appreciation for the sheltered life Sweetbranch had given her for four decades.

But the closer she got to home, the farther she felt herself moving from that serenity. Each step seemed to take her farther along the road to a world that was not only unknown but studded with danger and fear. Each step that took her closer to Ben, closer to the reality of what he faced, made Sweetbranch's placidity seem more like an unattainable fairy tale.

But the closer she came to that daunting reality, the faster she moved.

Because she knew, somehow, that the only future she was interested in was to be found in Ben's arms.

She was almost running by the time she turned the corner onto Dixie Belle Lane. She had to find Ben. Had to know, from the feel of his arms around her, that life could be stripped of its ugliness, if only for a moment.

He wasn't in the house.

"He headed out back a bit ago," Uncle Bump responded from the kitchen as she dashed breathlessly through the house calling Ben's name. Then her uncle shouted in the querulous tone he always used to disguise his concern. "What're you in such a hissy over, girl?"

Rose dashed into the kitchen, where Uncle Bump and Krissy were spooning mayonnaise into the big blue bowl Uncle Bump always used for potato salad. Thinking how wonderful it always tasted, thinking how glad she was to see his perpetual frown, Rose planted a big kiss on his crinkled forehead, then leaned over and picked up Krissy for a long, squeezing hug. "I love you both."

"What the..."

Then she was out the back door. Looking around. No Ben. She was headed for the path to the fishing pond, calling his name, when a voice beckoned her from the trees.

"It's quiet up here now that it's all leafed out. They'll never find us."

She looked up. Ben was peering down at her from the platform of the tree house, where he was lying on his stomach, chin propped on his elbows. "Ben! Oh, Ben!"

She scurried up the precarious footholds until she stood face-to-face with him, her hands holding on to the edge of the platform. "I love you, Ben." She kissed him, wishing her hands were free so they could roam over his lean, hard face. She kissed his eyes and his nose and his forehead and his lips and the square stubbornness of his jaw. "I love you and I love Krissy and I'll go with you."

He laughed and pulled her up beside him, wrapping her in his arms. It felt as secure, as solid, as unassailable as she had known it would. "I love you, too, Rose. Lord, I love you."

"I mean it, Ben," she insisted as he began to cover her face with light but fervent kisses of his own. "I'll go with you. No matter what happens." She pulled away just enough to signal him that something important was being said. "Are you listening to me, Ben?"

"Okay. I'm listening. Now, what are you talking about? I'm not going anywhere."

"If you have to, I mean. Because of Krissy. If you have to...start a new life...I'll start it with you."

His hands dropped and his voice grew hard with determination. "You can't do that. I won't let you."

"You can't stop me."

"I'm serious, Rose. You don't know what you're saying. You have no idea what you're saying."

"I most certainly do. I talked to Maxine. I know exactly what I'm saying."

He pushed her down, sitting beside her on the old blanket. "It might sound glamorous now, Rose, but..."

She jabbed a finger into his chest. "Don't patronize me, Ben McKenzie. I'm a grown woman and I know it won't be any picnic."

"No!" His voice was stern, adamant. "I won't have you sacrificing everything you have for me."

"Sacrificing is what I do best," she quipped, then instantly realized that flippancy wasn't going to move Ben when he was in this mood. "Listen, it's not like I have that much to sacrifice. A job that kills my feet—I've been so worn-out lately, I've wondered sometimes if I was going to make it. Do you know how many hairdressers have varicose veins? Ben, listen, I've wanted to get out of Sweetbranch all my life."

"That doesn't mean it'll be easy," he protested.

"No. I know that. In all seriousness, I know that." She looked around at the tree house and the days of her childhood flooded over her. Then she looked up at Ben and the days they had spent together filled her, too. "But I love you, Ben. And I'll tell you right here and now, I'm not going to sacrifice you just to keep things easy and simple."

CHAPTER SIXTEEN

AS HE WATCHED ROSE PACK, Ben couldn't rid himself of the guilt nagging him quietly but insidiously.

He'd meant for their weekend in this antebellum bed and breakfast to be a romantic sealing of their commitment. Instead, every time they'd made love, every time Rose had draped herself in the silk robe she'd bought for the occasion, every time she turned her trusting brown eyes on him, Ben had wanted to groan under the weight of his guilt. The whole weekend had felt too much like a poor substitute for the romantic honeymoon Rose actually deserved.

But you couldn't have a honeymoon without a wedding. And that was something Ben wasn't yet in a position to offer. Ben wanted to turn away, but he forced himself to pay penance by watching Rose. Carefully, precisely, she prepared to leave the bedroom where they had spent all but four of the last forty-eight hours. Each article of clothing folded neatly. Each toiletry item tucked into a special nook. Everything smoothed by the slender, long-fingered hand that had explored and loved his body so thoroughly.

"I'm just stalling," she admitted, looking over at him wistfully. "I'm not sure I want to go back to Sweetbranch, after this."

"I know." He smiled, hoping she wouldn't read his thoughts in his eyes. She was half-teasing; he wasn't.

She gave the room a final look for the few belongings they had brought with them while he acknowledged that reality beckoned. It had been days since he'd talked to his brother, and as much as he dreaded it, he picked up the phone and punched out Keith's number. When Keith's answering machine kicked in, he hesitated. He really didn't want to leave a message, wouldn't want the wrong person hearing it. But he hadn't talked to his brother since the story ran in last weekend's paper. The machine beeped.

"Hey, Keith, sorry I missed you. I'll try to catch you at the..."

Keith's voice broke in. "Ben? Is that you?"

"Hey, little brother." He smiled despite himself at the sound of his brother's voice. He missed Keith. He missed armchair quarterbacking with him on Monday nights and fighting over major company purchases on Wednesday mornings. "Have you driven us into bankruptcy yet?"

"Dammit, Ben, I'm not in the mood for you to horse around. What the hell did you have in mind, stirring things up by talking to the paper last week?"

"What happened?" He tried to keep the tightness out of his voice, but he saw Rose turn away from the window to look in his direction.

"Let's just say Cybil's husband took it as a personal offense."

"What happened?" He ground his teeth tightly together in impatience and anxiety.

"He trashed the office, big brother, that's what happened."

"What?" Impotent rage flared up in Ben. "That son of a... Did he hurt anybody?"

"No, thank God. Let's just say our insurance agent is rubbing his hands together just thinking about how much they'll be able to jack up our premiums. And the big press was out most of the week. I've been up to my ass in alligators all week, trying to hold clients off and keep them from yanking their jobs."

Ben heard the growing frustration in Keith's voice and let it boil over for a while. He knew his brother well enough to know that he hadn't shared this tirade with anyone else—he tried too hard to appear invincible to everyone else at the company. So he listened to Keith's war stories from the week past, only trying to soothe him once he sensed that the bottled-up anger was diminishing.

"I'm sorry, pal. It'll be over soon. I know it will." But he didn't know it. And now, without the soft haze of passion to cloud her vision, Rose would know it, too. He saw her look at him sharply, then glanced away to the view out the window.

"Well, it had better be. Where was Cybil's head, marrying a maniac like that in the first place?"

Ben didn't want to talk about Colin and Cybil. Didn't even

want to think about it. "What about the proposal I sent? Had a chance to look at it?"

"Hell, I can't even find it. We've spent the whole week crawling around on the floor scooping up paper and reinventing the filing system. Besides, I have no intention of trying to close a deal like that until you've got your life together again. Got it?"

"Keith, there's no reason to..."

"Don't bother, Ben. I'm hanging tough on that one."

Ben sighed. "Okay, okay. Anything else?"

"No, I guess not. Oh, except that..."

"What?"

"Well, after our visit from Cybil's better half, I decided, well, you know, to make sure she was all right. You know." Keith sounded uncomfortable explaining his protective urges. "Anyway, I couldn't get in touch with her. Couldn't find her. Anywhere."

"Anywhere?"

"I tried her folks. I tried that friend of hers, the one with the art gallery over in Raleigh. Nobody's heard from her, Ben. Just thought you'd want to know."

BEN CARRIED THE SICKNESS in the pit of his stomach all the way back to Winston-Salem the next day. If anything was wrong with Cybil, if she was hurt, if...

She was his daughter's mother. He had loved her once. And still loved her for the part she had played in giving him Krissy. And if he had been the cause of anything bad happening to her, he knew it would haunt him forever.

He had to remind himself every ten miles or so that driving like a wild man wouldn't solve anything. Seventy miles an hour wouldn't make Cybil all right if she was hurt.

So he slowed down, forcing himself to concentrate on the rolling green of north Alabama as it metamorphosed into the craggier, hazy mountains of Tennessee and North Carolina. And forcing himself, each time his concentration strayed to things internal, back to his surroundings. Back to the highway. Back to the See Rock City billboards and the roadside Cherokee Indian tourist shops.

Back to the winding strip of road leading to whatever wrath he had brought down on his ex-wife.

Although his body nudged him with reminders of his physical exhaustion, once he drove into Winston-Salem and checked into a cheap motel right off the freeway, Ben's mind was too wired to rest. He pulled out the dog-eared motel phone book and started calling.

He called Cybil's parents and endured their hostility. "You're driving Cybil to the brink, man!" her father said. "Not to mention what you're doing to my wife. Bring Krissy home before you cause any more grief."

Cybil's mother sobbed in his ear. "I can't believe you're doing this to us, Ben. I thought you'd changed. I told Cybil how good, how kind you were. But now..."

And in the end they knew nothing, except that now their granddaughter wasn't the only one missing.

He called every acquaintance of his and Cybil's that he could think of. Some were cold. Some were friendly but surprised. Some were downright nosy and Ben knew it wouldn't be long before his circle of friends and colleagues in Winston-Salem would know that something funny was, indeed, going on with Ben McKenzie and his ex-wife.

And, finally, he called Cybil's best friend in Raleigh, the gallery owner who had already told Keith that she knew nothing about Cybil. The prickling on the back of his neck when she spoke told Ben that she wasn't speaking the truth.

"Tell me the truth, Terri. I'm worried about her. That's all."

"You poor dear. I'll bet you're absolutely gnawing your gut out with worry, aren't you?"

"Just tell me she's okay."

"What the hell do you care? Dragging her little girl away like that? Driving her to drink? And now you've got the nerve to come around asking if she's okay. If she's not, it's on your conscience. I hope you know that, McKenzie. Whatever happens to Cybil, it's on your head."

"I want to talk to her about Krissy. I want to work this out."

"I know how you work things out. Running to the paper like that, do you know how that made her feel?"

"You've seen her. She's there, isn't she?"

He endured her sniping for another half hour, certain that Terri knew where to find Cybil. Finally his persistence wore her down. She promised to call Cybil, then call him back if she agreed to see him.

Ben paced for the next forty-five minutes, staring at the mottled, mustard-colored carpet at his feet, starting with every sound.

He was in his car and back on the freeway ten minutes after Terri called back with reluctant directions to her cousin's apartment. He made two wrong turns. The twenty-minute drive took thirty-five. He was shaking when he knocked on the door.

It took several seconds for Ben to recognize the woman who peered out the door as his ex-wife. Her shining platinum hair was dull, dark at the roots and pulled severely back in a ponytail. Her skin, always fashionably taut over her perfect cheekbones, was now merely tight and sallow, except under her eyes, where it looked puffy and shadowed.

Ben felt his heart break a little more. No matter what had happened between Cybil and him, he would never forget that they had shared a life for almost a decade. And because he cared, he tried to keep the pity out of his eyes.

"I should slam this door in your face." But there was no force, no anger, no bitterness in her voice as she opened the door wider to admit him.

"I'm sorry, Cybil." He stopped just inside the door of the apartment and turned to her, his voice softened by his need for her forgiveness and understanding. "I wouldn't hurt you for the world. I did it for Krissy. I did what I thought was right."

She stared at him for a long time, as if searching his eyes for the Ben McKenzie she had married. Ben knew that man no longer existed, just as he knew that the suave, confident woman he had married no longer existed, either. Gradually, as she studied him, he saw her fragile protective wall crumble. She closed her eyes. Her face sagged.

"I know. I know. Still..."

Her shoulders drooped. She leaned against the door for support. Ben reached for her and pulled her into his arms, against his chest. She huddled into him as he comforted her for a few moments before leading her to the couch.

"Are you all right, Cybil?" He eased her down onto the couch. "What can I do to help you?"

She smiled vaguely and Ben remembered how stunning her cool smile had been in the old days.

"Still the knight errant, Ben?"

He grinned. "You know me, Cybil."

Her smile faded. "I do now," she conceded. "Krissy? How is Krissy? Does she...does she ask about her mommy? Does she miss me?"

Ben recognized the fear in her eyes. He patted her thin hand, which fluttered over the paisley throw pillow she had pulled into her lap and now clutched to her chest. No amount of torture could have driven him to tell Cybil how happy Krissy was in Sweetbranch and how at home she seemed sitting in another woman's lap.

"Of course she misses you. She wants to see you. She asks about you all the time."

Cybil drew her lips in and nodded. Ben realized that in all the time he'd known her, he'd never seen her so close to tears. "I'm not with Colin anymore, Ben. I've left him. So you could bring her home now. Everything is fine now. Krissy will be fine. There won't be any more trouble, Ben."

Ben stared at the floor. "I'm not sure, Cybil. I understand Colin is pretty out of control right now."

"But I've left him, Ben. Don't you see? He won't hurt Krissy now. He's out of my life now."

The frantic note in her voice told Ben all he needed to know. No, he didn't want to hurt Cybil. But he hadn't put all of them through the pain of the last few months just to bring Krissy back to a situation fraught with jeopardy.

"Why are you hiding from him?"

The flash of anger in her silver blue eyes was a split-second reminder of the old Cybil. Then it died and her face twisted with her effort to maintain control. "Don't, Ben. Don't do this to me. I need her, Ben."

Ben pinched the bridge of his nose, where a quiet throbbing was turning more insistent. Then he reached out and took one of Cybil's frail hands in his. "I know you need her. But this isn't about what you need. It's about what she needs."

"She needs me. I'm her mommy. You said so yourself, that she misses me. Ben, I won't let you do this. It's not right. If you don't bring her back, I don't know what will happen to me, Ben.

I can't..." She stopped abruptly, as if she suddenly recognized the hysteria in her voice.

"What will happen if Colin finds you, Cybil?"

She tossed the comfort of his hand back at him and jumped up from the couch. She stalked across the room, stopping in front of a cabinet, then turning to pace in front of it. "Okay. You're right. He's angry. He's out of control sometimes."

"He ransacked the print shop."

She jammed her hands into the pockets of her lounging pajamas. "He's crazy. More every day. I...I wanted to file for divorce. But...I'm afraid of him, Ben."

"Do you really want to expose Krissy to that again, Cybil?"

She whirled and opened the cabinet, revealing shelves of liquor and glasses. She pulled out the Scotch and filled a shot glass. Then, giving him a defiant glare, she tossed it back and filled the glass again.

"How much are you drinking now, Cybil?"

"Too much," she snapped. "I drink too much and I picked a lousy second husband and my life is in the toilet. Is that what you want to hear?"

"No, Cybil. All I want to hear is that you want what's best for Krissy. That's all I really want."

She sipped at the amber liquid in the tiny glass, staring at him intently. She crossed to the window and finished off the rest of the Scotch, then returned to set the glass on the liquor cabinet. When she faced Ben, he saw once again a hint of the chin-in-the-air woman she had once been. He was only sorry the change in her had come out of a bottle.

"She truly is fine?"

He nodded.

"Good. You keep her safe until I get this business with Colin behind me."

"If my attorney calls, will you sign the papers she has? Temporary custody, that's all I want right now."

She looked hesitant.

"I'm tired of being on the wrong side of the law, Cybil."

Her laugh was a trifle brittle, but he saw the grudging affection in her eyes.

"Always Mr. Do-gooder, aren't you, Ben?" She smoothed

back the already sleek hair over her ear. "Temporary custody, Ben. Just until I work this out with Colin. Then I want her back."

Ben knew he should simply agree. Anything for her signature, his better sense told him. "And the drinking, Cybil. You have to work on the drinking."

"You bastard." Her smile was weary and weak. "But I want to see her, Ben. First. Before I sign anything. I want to see her."

Ben weighed Cybil's actions over the past year against the paternal urges in his heart. Parenthood won out. "I promise."

THE SMART THING TO DO, Ben knew, would be to climb between the thin, scratchy sheets in his cheap motel room. Eight hours' sleep behind him would be a much better way to head back to Sweetbranch.

But he also knew he wouldn't sleep. Wouldn't rest until he was back home.

Back in Sweetwater, he corrected himself as he pointed the station wagon west on I-40.

He had to see Krissy. Had to touch the dimples on her pudgy little hands and brush her dark silky hair off her round pink cheek. Had to feel her arms around his neck. Had to see the delight in her eyes when he walked in the door.

She is happy now, he reassured himself. *She misses her mother, but she's happy with me.*

She was happy in Sweetbranch with Rose and Uncle Bump and all the friends she had made. She was happy walking to church on Sundays and playing in the park and trekking through the woods to Uncle Bump's fishing hole. She loved darting around Rose's big yard, blowing dandelion seeds and weeding the garden and learning to hold a big cat like Boo quietly on her lap.

And if Ben opened a plant in Sweetbranch, they could stay there. They could live the kind of slow-paced, easygoing life that too many people had forgotten existed. Rose and Krissy and Ben.

And one day, Krissy's little brother or sister.

Ben's heart lightened. The life, the family he wanted, was right there in Sweetbranch, his for the asking. And best of all, he could have it without exacting a sacrifice from Rose. Rose, who had sacrificed all she'd ever wanted out of life for everyone else.

Rose, who had even offered to sacrifice her freedom and her future for him, if it had come to that. But now he could have her without that sacrifice. They could both have the life they wanted, right there in Sweetbranch.

Until Cybil squares herself away.

And what would the courts do then? Ben wondered. Wouldn't they send Krissy back to her mother? Wasn't that the way those cards were stacked?

And if that's what was in the cards, Ben knew in his heart that he couldn't ask Rose to give up Sweetbranch, not when she was just realizing how much she loved her hometown. He couldn't expect her to follow him back to Winston-Salem. He couldn't live with himself if she had to give up her college plans, her friends, her family. No, Ben wouldn't allow Rose to sacrifice her life for him as she had been doing for others for the past twenty years.

But the alternative would be to live hundreds of miles away and see his daughter only on holidays and two weeks in the summer, and that he could never do. If Krissy was in Winston-Salem with Cybil, wasn't that where he would have to be, also?

"I'm a father. I can't just walk away from that."

Even for Rose, he admitted, forcing himself to finish out the thought despite the pain that seared his soul. What the hell was he going to do?

COLIN NUDGED UP the volume control on the CD player. Too damn quiet. The whole place was too damn quiet. First the kid left. Then Cybil. And now there was nothing in the whole damn place except silence.

He walked back to the black-and-chrome dining table, which was surrounded by scattered papers. There was more paper on the cream-colored carpet now than was left on the table. He grunted and dropped into the chair.

"Has to be here somewhere."

He took a long swallow from the old-fashioned glass and pulled a stack of papers in front of him. A moment's satisfaction rolled over him as he remembered the terror and the helplessness in the eyes of the people at that son of a bitch's company. They'd been afraid of him, scurrying off to call security while he stuffed papers in his briefcase and turned the whole place upside down. They'd been terrified. And for the moment, that had fed the need in him.

Now he needed more. Now he needed to find what he was looking for in the documents and files he'd brought from the office.

So far it had all been a waste of time, invoices and purchase orders and bids on jobs.

The only thing that looked different was this report in the blue folder. Site Analysis: Sweetbranch, Ala, it read. All about this dead little town in north Alabama where the McKenzie brothers might build a paper manufacturing plant. Big deal. Another dirty little manufacturing operation. Paper plants smelled bad, he knew that. Like printing companies were dirty. How Cybil had gotten herself tied up with somebody like McKenzie was beyond him.

So they were expanding their little company. Into Alabama. Colin grunted again and tossed the report onto the floor.

But as the folder slapped against another folder at his feet, it struck him.

Would the McKenzie brothers open up a plant somewhere that neither of them had ever been? Somewhere nobody had even heard of?

He leaned over and picked up the file, hastily thumbing through it for a signature, a clue to who had filed the report.

There was no name.

And that seemed significant enough to Colin to justify a little more checking around.

Standing and shoving the chair out of his way, he walked into his study. Sitting snugly against the edge of the desk was his over-size, leather-covered atlas. He opened it to the map of Alabama.

It took some careful looking. Sweetbranch didn't pop off the map at you. No, you'd have to be darned lucky to stumble onto a place like Sweetbranch, hidden away as it was in the northwest corner of the state.

He flipped back to the mileage chart and started calculating just how long it would take to stumble into Sweetbranch, Alabama.

CHAPTER SEVENTEEN

"Now, Uncle Bump, if you fall and break your leg, I swear I'll break the other one for you," Rose fussed in the direction of the ladder that disappeared into the treetop.

Wide-eyed, Krissy clutched her paintbrush in her fist.

"Keep your shirt on, girl," came the grumpy reply. "I said I'd get this board up here replaced for you and I'm not so blamed feeble I can't do what I say I'll do."

"Yes, Uncle Bump." Rose winked at Krissy, who didn't even try to hide her giggle. "So, are you ready to get the tree house back in tip-top shape?"

"I can paint," Krissy declared, holding up her toddler-sized brush for inspection.

"Soon," Rose promised, squatting to give the little girl a hug, a gesture she hoped she hadn't overdone in the day and a half Ben had been gone. Whenever she held Krissy in her arms, she felt linked to Ben. She had needed that link often, to keep her worries at bay. "As soon as Uncle Bump puts a new board in the floor, I'll take this hammer up and tighten everything that's loose. Then you and I will go to the general store for some paint. Okay?"

"I want pink." Krissy leaned against Rose's chest, tugging a bristle out of her brush.

"Pink paint?" Rose tried not to sound as doubtful as the vision of a pink tree house made her feel.

Krissy nodded. "You said."

"You're right. I said you could paint it any color you wanted. And if you want pink, pink it is."

If they were lucky, it would need repainting by the time the leaves fell in October. And maybe by next summer, Krissy would have graduated into another color stage.

When Krissy flopped onto the ground to wait, Rose eased down beside her with another concerned look up at Uncle Bump's clattering and grunting.

Some women look after two children at the same time, she thought wryly. *Why can't I?*

It might be easier, she excused herself, if she'd felt better lately. But she felt so rundown and overwrought—by Wednesday, she would've bet a jar full of tips that she would never make it to the end of the workweek. And this unsettling business over Krissy had left her feeling queasy and uncertain half the time.

Telling herself her uncle would have to take care of himself for the moment, Rose lay back on the grass beside Krissy, trying to think of anything except when Ben would return.

"Krissy, look." Krissy's gaze followed the finger Rose pointed at one of the fluffy white clouds overhead. "That cloud looks like a cat."

"Not like Boo," Krissy observed dubiously, following Rose's lead and lying on her back for a better view of the sky. "Boo has spots. More like Puff."

Rose looked over at her young companion, remembering the first day they had met, the day Krissy had talked about her kitten named Puff. The solemn expression on the little girl's face tugged at her heart.

"Do you miss Puff?" she asked, wanting more than anything to believe that Krissy didn't miss the life she had left. And knowing that wasn't likely.

Krissy nodded. "And Mommy."

Not knowing what else to do, Rose simply eased closer and wrapped her arm around Krissy. The contact didn't quite fill the empty spot Krissy's words had opened up in Rose's heart, but it helped. She hoped it would help Krissy, too.

"I know you do, sweetheart." Then she was silent, letting the hug do whatever healing it could while they watched the clouds float across Sweetbranch.

"Look! A train!" Krissy's chubby finger shot skyward at a big, lumpy mass of cumulus that bore no resemblance Rose could see to a train. "Whoo-whoo!"

Rose stopped in the middle of her laugh at Krissy's imitation of a train whistle when she realized hers wasn't the only voice raised in laughter. She and Krissy looked around to see Ben standing at the edge of the vegetable garden, leaning on the shovel Uncle Bump had left standing upright in the earth.

"Daddy!"

"Ben!"

They were both off the ground and throwing themselves into Ben's arms in an instant. He swept Krissy up into one arm and grabbed Rose with the other. "I missed my two best girls."

And he gave them both a kiss on the cheek. But his eyes promised Rose that another kiss, a more thorough kiss, awaited her once they were alone.

"What are you two ladies up to, lying out here in the grass?"

"Painting!" Krissy wiggled out of his grasp to go in search of her paintbrush.

"We're remodeling the tree house," Rose explained. Still pressed comfortably to Ben's side, she watched as Krissy toddled across the yard looking for the brush she had abandoned. "How did it go?"

"Pretty good." The pleasure on his face faded perceptibly. "Remodeling, huh? What, a room addition? Wall-to-wall carpet?"

"And new kitchen appliances," Rose said, giving him a gentle jab to the midsection. "It needed some work, that's all. I've never seen much point in keeping it repaired, when there were no children to use it. But now I thought...well, it just seemed like a good idea."

She turned her head to look at him, but he avoided her gaze. "Just in case. That's all."

He nodded but didn't reply. Rose told herself he was preoccupied. And with good reason.

"Did you find Krissy's mother?"

"Yes." His voice tightened with tension. "She's...okay. She's left her husband."

"That's good, isn't it?" She ignored a surfacing anxiety. How much simpler would Ben's life be if his ex-wife was free again? Free to...what?

"She said she would sign the temporary custody papers. But she wants to see Krissy first."

"Well, of course she does." Rose didn't feel as understanding as her mild response sounded; she felt an irrationally protective urge toward Krissy. Almost as if Krissy had become hers in the past two months. And she was afraid of being usurped. Not just in Ben's life but in Krissy's, as well.

The feeling helped her realize just how fearful the little girl's mother must be right now; how fearful Ben had been to take the drastic steps he had taken. Parenthood was a vulnerable place to be.

Her arm tightened around Ben's waist. "That's good news, Ben. No more hiding."

And as she said the words, their full implication hit her. *No more hiding.*

They could go home. They didn't need the isolation of Sweetbranch anymore. They didn't need her any more.

She fought to keep from stiffening in his arms. If she pretended she didn't understand, if she ignored it, maybe it wouldn't happen. Maybe Ben wouldn't realize, either, that he could now pack up and drive back to North Carolina and resume his life as if the last two months had never happened.

Or maybe this was the perfect solution to a sticky situation. A clinging woman. Promises made and love declared more because it was the easy thing to do than from any real sense of commitment. After all, she had offered to go with him even if it meant going into hiding.

But had he ever agreed?

The answer hit her right in the pit of her stomach, right at the back of each already shaky knee. As vehemently as everything in her refused to believe that what Ben had given her wasn't really love after all, Rose forced herself to be realistic.

"So, I suppose you'll be going home soon." She pulled away from Ben, keeping her eyes carefully trained on the little girl running through the grass and calling up the ladder to Uncle Bump.

"Not...right away." He looked so uncomfortable, Rose knew she had to do whatever she could to make this easier on him. Krissy came first. Maybe he had loved her, a little. But Krissy came first. She had to keep reminding herself of that.

"But soon?"

"If things go right."

"Well, that's the best thing, of course. For Krissy, I mean. And you, too, I suppose. Your business and everything."

"Rose, I..."

"Don't worry about it, Ben. I know how these things are." *Wimp!* screamed the demanding voice in her head. "You have to do the right thing. That's what life is all about. I know that. I..."

A familiar bellow rescued her. "I'd come down before I fall down if I could get a little help holding this goldurned ladder!"

And Rose scurried off to hold the ladder for Uncle Bump, grateful that some kind of duty called. Grateful she had something to do besides break down and cry.

"Now, Auntie Wose!" Krissy tugged on Rose's shorts once Uncle Bump was on the ground again. "Now can we paint?"

Rose had lost her heart for the project. But as she looked down into Krissy's blue eyes, then over into the matching set that was Ben's, she decided she wasn't going to give in to self-pity.

We'll finish the tree house, she decided, *and it'll always remind me that I'm not the old Rose anymore.*

Hah! taunted the more belligerent voice in her head.

She tried to sound as enthusiastic as possible as she took Krissy by the hand and led her toward Dixie Belle Lane. "We're off to the general store for paint. Now, you're sure you want pink?"

Krissy nodded emphatically. "Neon."

"Ah, neon pink. Nice. Very nice." *And a very vivid reminder,* Rose told herself with a wry smile. "Well, we'll see just how close old Mr. Whitley can come to neon pink. I'm not sure he has much call for it, but we'll do the best we can. Okay?"

They chattered all the way to the store. Actually, Krissy did most of the chattering and Rose tried to lose herself in it, tried not to think how overwhelming the silence would be in the old farmhouse once Ben and Krissy left.

Tried not to think how overwhelming the silence in her heart would be.

You'll deserve it, she castigated herself, *if you let them walk out of your life without a battle.*

All the way down Main Street, Rose tried to convince herself that it didn't matter whether Ben had really loved her or not. Because knowing him had changed her. And life in Sweetbranch wouldn't revert to its pre-Ben monotony because she had changed. She was strong now. A doer. Her task force was going great guns. She might even offer to help Maxine with this crazy underground she was involved in. Because she was different now.

Which is a good thing, she thought as she spotted an unfamiliar car parked along Main Street, *because Sweetbranch still hasn't changed.* She could still spot a new car in town without even trying—that's how dead things were.

She tried not to let the thought drag her down as she and Krissy walked into the old general store, which had also changed only imperceptibly since her own childhood.

Picking out the paint was a welcome distraction. Krissy was so fascinated by everything—from the bins of nails and bags of peat moss—that the little girl barely had time to look at the paint samples. So Rose gave the order for a mixture that was as close as old Mr. Whitley could come to neon pink.

When they finally left the store, Rose had a paint can in her hand and Krissy had an all-day sucker in hers. As they passed the unfamiliar silver car, its engine purred to life.

It was only when they turned the corner from Main Street onto Dixie Belle Lane that Rose realized the big car had turned the corner right behind them. She couldn't think of any reason why that should seem odd to her, but nevertheless it made her feel uneasy in a way she couldn't remember ever having felt before.

She tightened her hold on Krissy's hand and quickened her pace slightly.

Then the car stopped, just ahead of them. The engine was still running when the driver stepped onto the sidewalk directly in their path. Rose was so taken aback by the tall, dark-haired man's action that she almost didn't hear Krissy's whimper.

But she instinctively pulled Krissy to her other side, away from the street, away from the man in the charcoal suit. "It's all right, sweetheart."

She braced herself to walk around the man, armed with determination and a smile that strained to be small-town friendly, the way she would be to any stranger in town. But as she tried to continue walking in his direction, Krissy refused to move forward. Rose turned to her. And realized, as she turned back to the man, who he was. She saw it in Krissy's face; and she saw it in the embittered eyes he trained on the little girl.

Dropping the paint can, she scooped Krissy up in her arms. But before she had even completed the action, he was at their side. He grabbed Krissy, tugging her from Rose's grasp. Krissy wailed. With a cry of outrage, Rose refused to relinquish her hold on Krissy. Then she felt the blow across her face, a stinging strike with the back of his arm.

"No!" She staggered against the attack, fighting to stay on her feet, and went back at him again, reaching for Krissy. His fist came at her, harder this time. Not a sting but a solid thud.

Her vision went black. Falling, she fought the darkness. She tried to find the light. Tried...

HER EYELIDS FLICKERED. The sunshine hurt. So bright. She closed her eyes again, embraced the darkness. Then she remembered...something. She had to open her eyes.

She tried again. Still too bright, but blurry, too. Through a fog—a bright, sunny fog—she strained to focus.

Abigail Warner, her rounded form still blurred, leaned over Rose, cooing hysterically and waving a blue gingham apron under Rose's nose.

"Oh, my dear, you lie still now," Abigail said shrilly as Rose struggled to prop herself on one elbow. "The rescue squad is on its way. You just lie still and let them make sure you're all right."

"No, can't stay here." Rose's head spun out of control as she sat up on the sidewalk. She closed her eyes against the kaleidoscope of pain and light in her head. She couldn't remember why, but she knew she had to get up. Had to...do something.

"But you must, my dear. Oh my goodness, imagine my surprise when sister and I looked out the door and saw you lying here. Did you faint, my dear? You don't suppose it was anything more serious, do you?"

"Got to go," Rose protested, opening her eyes slowly.

The first thing she saw clearly was the red all-day sucker lying on the edge of the sidewalk, already attracting a troop of ants. Beside an overturned bucket of paint.

With an anguished cry, she jumped to her feet. Krissy. She staggered, then held on to Abigail Warner long enough for the spinning in her head to stop. Krissy was in trouble. As soon as the world stopped whirling, she directed her unsteady gait toward her house. Ben. She needed Ben.

CHAPTER EIGHTEEN

THE MOMENT BEN HEARD the edge of panic in Rose's voice, he knew something had happened to Krissy.

Dropping the tool chest he was carrying back to the house for Uncle Bump, he ran toward her voice. Running, he had to push aside scraps and flashes of running toward other sounds of fear. Even as he rounded the corner to Rose's familiar front porch, he felt the jungle tugging at his shoulders, wrapping itself around his legs, splintering his thoughts, multiplying his fears.

The faraway sound of gunfire and grenades whirred in his ears when he reached Rose. She was leaning weakly against the porch rails and he grabbed her shoulders when he reached her. He recognized the dazed expression in her eyes.

"He took her, Ben. He took her. He knocked me down and she's gone."

A frightened toddler screamed in his head, one moment dark-eyed and the next blue-eyed, both tugging at his pant leg, both afraid, both in danger. One dead. One...

Ben shook himself. Cleared his eyes. Focused on Rose. Focused on the porch. Focused on right now.

Right now didn't have to end that way. Not if he could keep his grip on reality. Mouth dry, coated with the sour taste of fear, Ben fought the dizziness in his head.

"I'm sorry, Ben. I tried to..."

"It's not your fault, Rose. Call the sheriff."

And he cupped her face with his hands, realizing only dimly that his hands were ice-cold against her cheek, which was already swelling, darkening. He kissed her quickly, fiercely, felt the fierceness in her response and knew her fear was as great as his own.

Knew her guilt would be as great as his own if...

He turned, hurriedly reaching into his pocket for the keys to his car. He heard the front door slam behind her as he started the engine and wondered how long it took to marshal law enforcement in a place like Sweetbranch, where law enforcement was seldom needed.

He sped through town, driven by fear and fury, taking only enough care to make sure he didn't crash. He had to follow Catch up before Colin made it back to the highway.

He plowed through intersections, bringing pickup trucks and station wagons to a screeching halt in his wake. And occasionally, a split second of steaming jungle and acrid smoke touched his skin, filled his lungs.

No time for that.

Years seemed to pass before he was outside the town limits, where he could punch the gas pedal further to the floor.

Please, God. Please, God.

Even though he couldn't allow himself to articulate what he feared, Ben prayed.

A clear head, God. Keep me sane, God. Get me there in time. Please, God.

Then he careened around the deep bend in the road and saw the ramshackle covered bridge that was the joke of the town. It sagged precariously to one side. Worse than before. The hood of a sleek, shiny car jutted through a gaping hole in the rotted wood and rested in the shallow creek bed, its back tires still hanging on to the rickety edge of the bridge.

With a roar of denial and fear, Ben shoved his car into Park and jumped out. He splashed into the creek, stumbling over slippery rocks, his eye trained on the car, willing it to stay put.

If she's hurt...

Just as he reached the car, Colin staggered out on the driver's side, blood trickling from a gash over his forehead. The moment Ben saw him, his fear dissipated and in its place was the cold-blooded rage he had felt on more than one occasion. His hands twitched. He felt the murder in them. Watching the dazed man, Ben knew with frightening clarity just how easily he could overpower Colin and bury his face in the rocky creek bed, holding him there until his lungs filled with water. Even if Colin struggled, Ben knew his own rage was too strong to be overcome.

Or he could snap his neck. Quickly. Cleanly. And it would be over.

Then he heard a whimper from the car. The rage flooded out of him, through his fingertips. In its place was the instinct to protect.

In two long strides, Ben reached Colin and grabbed him by the front of his shirt. With a knuckle-crunching punch, he landed Colin flat on his back in the creek. He restrained his urge to go to Krissy just long enough to make sure the almost unconscious man had no weapons on him, then dashed around the front of the car and carefully opened the door.

Krissy looked up warily, her pale, round face brightening instantly when she saw him.

"Daddy!" She held her arms up to him, a trembling smile on her face. "See, Daddy. I did my seat belt. Just like you told me."

Ben gave in to his tears as he unstrapped his little girl and lifted her out of the car. She felt warm and tiny in his arms and he had to remind himself not to squeeze her too tightly.

"I love you, sweetheart," he whispered into her ear as he accepted a candy-sticky kiss from her. "I love you so much."

"I love you, Daddy. Is Auntie Wose okay? He hit her, Daddy. So I hit him back. I'm sorry I hit him back, Daddy."

"That's okay, baby. You did the right thing."

Ben wondered if he would ever stop crying.

ROSE LISTENED to the sounds overhead. Excited laughter and hurried footsteps assailed her ears as she capped the fresh strawberries from the garden.

They were packing. To go back to Winston-Salem. So Krissy could see her mother, Ben had said.

But Rose thought that was most unlikely. To get on with their lives, that was the more likely reason. She just wished he'd had the courage to say so instead of pretending otherwise.

You didn't show much courage yourself, her inner voice chided as the fragrance of the berries brought on another wave of nausea. *Did you confront him? Did you make him tell you the truth?*

She made excuses for herself. This morning, Rose had felt bad again, too weak and queasy to invite more trouble. And the afternoon before had been too hectic and too traumatic for Rose to add to it. The sheriff had arrived at the bridge and arrested Colin; he would be charged with kidnapping and, if Rose wanted to press charges, assault. Ben's attorney warned them that as a first offender he might not win much real prison time. But the mitigating circumstances of Krissy's abuse—which both Krissy and Cybil now seemed ready to testify to—might sway a judge who was leaning toward leniency.

All that was good. And Krissy hadn't been hurt. In fact, she seemed to have been traumatized less by the whole ugly episode than any of the rest of them. She had chattered about it all night, showing everyone how she had tried to defend Rose with a swift left to her stepfather's forearm and a right jab to the jaw.

And she had chattered about seeing her mother. She was so excited it had been after midnight before she had calmed herself enough to go to bed.

"How soon, Daddy?" she had asked time after time. "We'll see Mommy soon?"

"That's right, Krissy. Tomorrow afternoon you'll see your mommy."

And Krissy had clapped her little hands, oblivious to the fact that no one else in the Finley household was even remotely pleased at the prospect.

So they were going. Soon, Rose supposed. By lunchtime, certainly. Rose felt more exhausted and emotionally fragile than she had in her entire life.

The front screen door slammed. Uncle Bump eased himself into a rocker, a scowl on his face. "You just going to let 'em march out of here without doing a dang thing about it?"

Rose dropped her paring knife into the bowl of fresh strawberries. "And what am I supposed to do about it? They can go home now. That's the way it should be."

"The hell it is!" he growled. "Girl, it's one thing to get a late start in life. But it's another thing to keep lettin' life pass you by without even trying to join the party. Do that long enough and you'll end up like me, a cross old goat with nothing to show for it."

Rose shot a swift glance at her uncle. She'd never heard him come close to admitting that he was less than happy with his solitary existence or that his perpetual cussedness might not be all act, as she had always assumed.

"So what do you suggest, Uncle Bump?" She turned back to her task of snipping the stems off the plump red berries. "Maybe I should follow them. Throw myself in their path and refuse to move until they invite me to join them."

"Might work. A little melodramatic, I'd say, but it might work." Uncle Bump chuckled. "Although women did it simpler in my day. Being in the family way seemed to nudge things along right smart in those days."

"Uncle Bump!" She looked up, glad at least to see the gleam in his eye once again, even though his words jarred a distinctly uncomfortable feeling in her. Tender breasts and an overwhelming weariness and wild mood swings. She had forbidden the thought to enter her head, but...

She smiled, an unexpected satisfaction sneaking up on her, filling her with urges so strong, so protective... She placed her flattened palm against her belly and felt something she'd felt only once before—the same thing she'd felt the previous day when Krissy was in danger.

She looked down into the bowl of berries in her lap. They were blurred. Her eyes stung.

Well, even if it was so, it was actually one more reason to let Ben and Krissy drive away without an argument. She wasn't interested in trapping any man.

But if she was...there was something almost delicious about the thought. Even at her age. She caught sight of Uncle Bump's smug expression and wiped the grin off her face. "I'm too old for that kind of thing. And who'd want to get a man that way, anyway?"

He laughed, the grizzled, gravelly laugh that she suddenly realized she hadn't appreciated nearly enough. If she did what he said, if she tossed caution to the wind and went flying after Ben, who knew when she would hear that laugh and see those wicked old eyes again?

But he was right, wasn't he? How many more chances would she have? And what would she turn into without Ben? A bitter old woman? A gossipy, spite-filled, shrivel-hearted old woman, the kind who made it her business to keep Sweetbranch in line? Or one of the bossy, strong-willed women who ran the town because there was little else in her life that mattered?

Old Miz Finley, they would call her.

Old Miz Finley, who got her heart broken by that slick fellow from the city, the one that punched the lights out on that other fellow from the city who kidnapped his daughter and ran off the bridge. Why, look, you can still see where they patched the bridge.

But if Ben had left a little part of himself behind, that might help. Maybe. She'd changed enough to handle that, hadn't she? It was not, she suddenly realized, too late at all.

It had simply taken her forty years to get ready for this.

She smiled again. She might have changed. But she hadn't changed so much that she would let herself act like a gullible ninny.

Krissy wasn't the only one with instincts about people. Rose had instincts, too. And her instincts had told her, long before, that Ben loved her. Why had she let herself doubt it?

Uncle Bump grunted and pushed himself heavily out of the rocker. "Well, reckon I'd better run that paint back down to the general store."

"What?" *Ben loves me.* And she knew it with as much certainty as she knew his love now grew inside her.

"The paint you and the little 'un bought yesterday. One of the Warner sisters brought it by. Don't reckon we'll be needing it after all."

"You leave that paint right where it is." The conviction of Ben's love settled over her and gave renewed strength to her command.

Uncle Bump raised his bushy white eyebrows. "You planning to do a lot of tree house sittin'?"

"Just leave the paint, Bump. It's my tree house. If I want to paint it neon pink and do nothing but stare at it out my bedroom window, that's what I'll darn well do." *Because Ben loves me. And that makes me strong enough for anything.*

He shook his head and turned back toward the house. "That's your problem, girl. You get pigheaded about all the wrong things."

Rose heard the door squeak shut behind him and thought she was alone again until she heard footsteps on the wooden porch.

"What are you getting pigheaded about now?" Ben's voice was soft, almost apologetic, she thought as he pulled up the rocker Uncle Bump had just abandoned.

She shook her head and lowered her eyes to the berries. "All done packing?"

"Just about."

She sensed his discomfort. Her first instinct was to do something to soothe his unease. But she didn't. It wouldn't hurt him to squirm a little before he rode off and forgot her.

The thought boiled through her.

What the heck was she thinking! If she loved Ben and he loved her—and he did—how in the heck could she let things happen this way? Not without a fight. Not if she had really changed. Not if the old self-sacrificing Rose was really gone.

She dropped her paring knife into the bowl, leaned over to set the bowl on the porch and wiped her hands on the terry dish towel she had tucked into her jeans.

"I'm going, too." She stood up and stared down at him, hands on her hips. *Take that, Ben McKenzie.*

"You're what?"

"I'm going with you. Back to North Carolina."

"But you can't. You have to..."

"I most certainly can, Ben McKenzie." *So he was going to make it tough, was he?* "I'm no kid and I can do anything I darn well please."

"Rose, I just don't think you need to come back to North Carolina right now. If you'll just wait here..."

"Wait here? I've been waiting here all my life, Ben Mc-Kenzie!" Now she was furious. She wanted to kick him in the shin. A nice, sharp jab. But it might hurt his bad knee. And she didn't want to do that. And realizing she shied away from hurting him, even when he was hurting her, made her even angrier. She could show him what hurt was. "And here I thought you'd want to be around when your baby's born."

Rose instantly regretted the words. She saw the shock in his face. Worse, she saw the shock quickly transform itself into pure pleasure. What if it turned out she'd jumped the gun? The shotgun, so to speak. Oh Lord, she'd have to get out of this in a hurry.

Ben stood slowly and put his hands on her shoulders. "My baby? Rose, my baby? *Our* baby?"

"Don't dither," she said crossly. "Oh, I'm sorry, Ben, I don't even know for sure. And even if I am, you know I wouldn't use that to push you into anything. Me and my big mouth. I just wanted to say something to get your attention, because I didn't want you going off without me, but I wouldn't have you tied to me by..."

"Shut up."

"What?"

"Shut up. And kiss me."

"But it might not be true. I don't really know for sure and..."

His lips on hers muffled her anxious words. It was a deep, satisfying kiss that promised things she wasn't sure she wanted him promising. But she couldn't help melting into him, accepting the promises and telling herself it didn't matter what had prompted them.

Then he held her close, tucking her head under his chin. She listened to his heart and wrapped her arms around his waist. At that moment, even if he drove off and never came back, she hoped she was right, hoped there was a life growing inside her.

"I want you to stay here, Rose. I'll be back by the end of the week. I've got work to do here."

"What work?" she asked absently, allowing herself only to enjoy this moment. His voice hummed in her ear and she smiled at the vibration.

"We're building a new plant, a paper plant. Right outside of town. I'll need to be here to oversee the project. And I definitely want to be around when my baby's born."

She pulled away from him. "A new plant? Here?"

"How far along are you?"

"You're kidding, right?"

"Have you been to the doctor yet?"

"A paper plant? With jobs? Right here in Sweetbranch?"

"We'll get married as soon as I get back. You're not going to want a big deal with lots of flowers and stuff, are you?"

"I might. I've never done this before, you know." She wondered how quickly they could plan a formal wedding, and if they could iron out all the details before the baby started to show. "How many jobs, Ben? Will the people need special training to do the work?"

"Wait till I tell Krissy she's going to have a baby brother. I think it'll be a boy. Don't you?"

"Ben, you're not listening to me."

"And you're not listening to me. I think our new baby is a lot more important than a new paper plant."

"But I don't even know if there is a baby, for sure."

"If there isn't, we'll make one. We'll just get married first instead of after, that's all."

"You mean you want to get married even if there isn't a baby?"

"Of course I do. You haven't been listening to me. I'll be back in about a week and..."

"But you can't come back to Sweetbranch. What about Krissy? You can't go off and leave Krissy. I know that, Ben. I wouldn't ask you to do that."

"You wouldn't?"

"No, I wouldn't."

"Then you'll understand, Rose, that I can't leave this baby, either. When there is a baby. And I think there is one. Right now. Already. I knew it the last time we went sneaking off to the tree house."

"Did you really? So did I, Ben. I just felt it, like something came alive inside me and I knew, except I wouldn't let myself admit it. But, Ben, what about Krissy?"

"She'll want to be here when her baby brother's born, too. You don't mind starting out with a ready-made family, do you?"

"But her mother?"

"Has still agreed to temporary custody while she works on her drinking and the courts take care of Colin. Krissy will be coming back with me, Rose. My attorney said that's a positive step toward getting permanent custody."

"But if you don't get custody, Ben? What then?"

For the first time Ben seemed to lose some of his confidence. He looked pained as he said, "I won't have you giving up your life for me, Rose. I don't want you to sacrifice the things..."

"Ben McKenzie, it's time I started making things happen in my life. I'm not talking about sacrifice. I'm talking about taking what I want in life."

"You are?"

"I am. We'll worry about who lives where when and if we have to, Ben."

"You're sure?"

"Right now, all we have to be sure about is that Sweetbranch is going to make the perfect hometown for you and Krissy and me.''

"And little Ben Junior."

She wrinkled her nose at him. "We're not going to have to name him Junior, are we?"

"Why not?"

"I thought we might name him after Uncle Bump."

"I don't think so."

"Well, maybe the next one."

And Ben laughed out loud, filling her heart, filling the whole town of Sweetbranch with the sounds of his happiness.

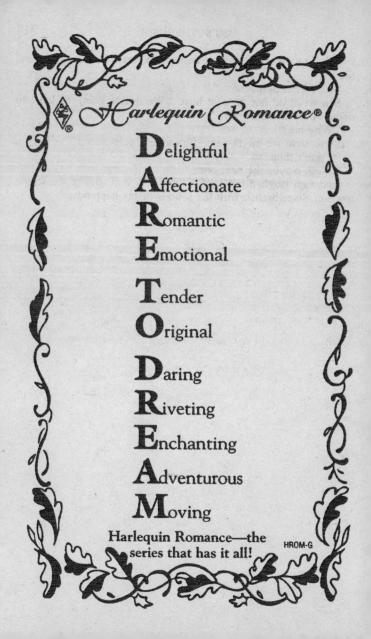

Harlequin Romance®

Delightful

Affectionate

Romantic

Emotional

Tender

Original

Daring

Riveting

Enchanting

Adventurous

Moving

Harlequin Romance—the
series that has it all!

HROM-G

HARLEQUIN ✦ PRESENTS®

HARLEQUIN PRESENTS

men you won't be able to resist falling in love with...

HARLEQUIN PRESENTS

women who have feelings just like your own...

HARLEQUIN PRESENTS

powerful passion in exotic international settings...

HARLEQUIN PRESENTS

intense, dramatic stories that will keep you turning
to the very last page...

HARLEQUIN PRESENTS

The world's bestselling romance series!

Harlequin® Historical

If you're a serious fan of historical romance,
then you're in luck!

Harlequin Historicals brings you
stories by bestselling authors, rising new stars
and talented first-timers.

Ruth Langan & Theresa Michaels
Mary McBride & Cheryl St.John
Margaret Moore & Merline Lovelace
Julie Tetel & Nina Beaumont
Susan Amarillas & Ana Seymour
Deborah Simmons & Linda Castle
Cassandra Austin & Emily French
Miranda Jarrett & Suzanne Barclay
DeLoras Scott & Laurie Grant...

You'll never run out of favorites.

Harlequin Historicals...they're too good to miss!

HH-GEN

HARLEQUIN®

I N T R I G U E®

THAT'S INTRIGUE—DYNAMIC ROMANCE AT ITS BEST!

Harlequin Intrigue is now bringing you more—more men and mystery, more desire and danger. If you've been looking for thrilling tales of contemporary passion and sensuous love stories with taut, edge-of-the-seat suspense—then you'll *love* Harlequin Intrigue!

Every month, you'll meet four new heroes who are guaranteed to make your spine tingle and your pulse pound. With them you'll enter into the exciting world of Harlequin Intrigue—where your life is on the line and so is your heart!

Harlequin Intrigue—we'll leave you breathless!

INT-GEN

LOOK FOR OUR FOUR FABULOUS MEN!

Each month some of today's bestselling authors bring four new fabulous men to Harlequin American Romance. Whether they're rebel ranchers, millionaire power brokers or sexy single dads, they're all gallant princes—and they're all ready to sweep you into lighthearted fantasies and contemporary fairy tales where anything is possible and where all your dreams come true!

You don't even have to make a wish...Harlequin American Romance will grant your every desire!

Look for Harlequin American Romance wherever Harlequin books are sold!

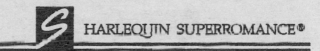

HARLEQUIN SUPERROMANCE®

...there's more to the story!

Superromance. A *big* satisfying read about unforgettable
characters. Each month we offer *four* very different
stories that range from family drama to adventure and
mystery, from highly emotional stories to romantic
comedies—and much more! Stories about people
you'll believe in and care about. Stories too
compelling to put down....

Our authors are among today's *best* romance writers.
You'll find familiar names and talented newcomers.
Many of them are award winners—and you'll see why!

If you want the biggest and best in romance fiction,
you'll get it from Superromance!
Available wherever Harlequin books are sold.

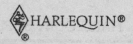
HARLEQUIN®

Not The Same Old Story!

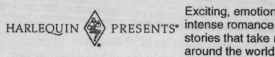 Exciting, emotionally intense romance stories that take readers around the world.

 Vibrant stories of captivating women and irresistible men experiencing the magic of falling in love!

 Bold and adventurous—Temptation is strong women, bad boys, great sex!

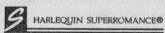 Provocative, passionate, contemporary stories that celebrate life and love.

 Romantic adventure where anything is possible and where dreams come true.

 Heart-stopping, suspenseful adventures that combine the best of romance and mystery.

LOVE & LAUGHTER™ Entertaining and fun, humorous and romantic—stories that capture the lighter side of love.

Look us up on-line at: http://www.romance.net   HGENERIC